OPERATION RED TIDINGS

Lt. Col. JP Cross is a retired Brit........................ ....Gurkha units for nearly forty years. He h............ ......Indian frontier soldier, jungle fighter, policeman, military attaché, Gurkha recruitment officer and a linguist researcher, and he is the author of twenty books. He has fought in Burma, Indo-China, Malaya and Borneo and served in India, Pakistan, Hong Kong, Laos and Nepal where he now lives. Well into his nineties, he still walks four hours daily.

Operation Red Tidings is the sixth in a series of historical military novels set in Southeast Asia comprising *Operation Black Rose*, *Operation Janus*, *Operation Red Tidings*, *Operation Blind Spot*, *Operation Stealth* and *Operation Four Rings*. The first four books may be read in any order; the final two are sequential. The series features Gurkha military units, and the author draws on real events he witnessed and real people he fought alongside in various theatres of war in Southeast Asia and India.

'Nobody in the world is better qualified to tell the story
of the Gurkhas' deadly jungle battles against Communist
insurgency in Malaya in the 1950s. Cross spins his tale
with the eye of incomparable experience.'

John le Carré

'... a gripping adventure story ...
learn the ins and outs of jungle warfare from a true expert'

The Oldie (on *Operation Janus*)

Also by JP Cross

FICTION
The Throne of Stone
The Restless Quest
The Crown of Renown
The Fame of the Name
The Age of Rage
Operation Black Rose
Operation Janus
Operation Blind Spot
Operation Stealth
Operation Four Rings

NONFICTION
English For Gurkha Soldiers
Gurkha – The Legendary Soldier
Gurkhas
Gurkha Tales: From Peace and War
In Gurkha Company
It Happens with Gurkhas
Jungle Warfare: Experiences And Encounters
Whatabouts And Whereabouts In Asia

MEMOIRS
First In, Last Out:
An Unconventional British Officer In Indo-China

The Call Of Nepal:
A Personal Nepalese Odyssey In A Different Dimension

'A Face Like A Chicken's Backside':
An Unconventional Soldier In South-East Asia, 1948-1971

ORAL HISTORY
Gurkhas at War

OPERATION RED TIDINGS

JP Cross

monsoon

monsoonbooks

First published in 2021
by Monsoon Books Ltd
www.monsoonbooks.co.uk

No.1 The Lodge, Burrough Court,
Burrough on the Hill, Leicestershire LE14 2QS, UK

ISBN (paperback): 9781912049943
ISBN (ebook): 9781912049950

Cover design by Cover Kitchen.

A Cataloguing-in-Publication data record is available from the British
Library.

Printed and bound in Great Britain by Clays Ltd, Elcograf S.p.A.
23 22 21   1 2 3

I dedicate this book to the thousands of British and Commonwealth soldiers, and British and indigenous policemen who fought in the 10-year war known as the Malayan Emergency which, had it not been for the tenacity, fortitude and reliability, to say nothing of skill at improvisation, ingenuity and adaptability of the Gurkha Rifleman, could well have lasted half as long again. When it is realised that during the time this book covers, it took about one million man hours of Security Force work for twenty seconds of enemy in the rifleman's foresight, patience, self-discipline and superb jungle lore must be added to a Gurkha's military attributes; nor do I forget to thank the Special Angel who looks after wild animals and soldiers in the jungle.

List of Characters

[Note: except for those with a * in front of their name, the others were either born in the author's imagination or their names have been changed to avoid family embarrassment.]

*Ah Chong, guerilla courier

Ah Fat, police 'mole' and non-voting Central Committee member, Malayan Communist Party, a.k.a. P'ing Yee, Flat Ears

Ah Hong, bar owner in Kuala Lumpur

Bickers, James Stuart, Brigadier, in whose brigade were 1/12 GR and 2/12 GR

*Briggs, Lieutenant General Sir Harold, Director of Operations, Malaya, 1950-1951

Chakrabahadur Rai, Rifleman, 1/12 Gurkha Rifles

Chan Man Yee, Malayan Communist Party 'mole' in Police HQ, Kuala Lumpur

Chen Yok Lan, wife of Tang Fook Loong (q.v.)

*Chien Tiang, chief confidant of Chin Peng (q.v.) and propaganda expert

*Chin Peng, alias of Ong Boon Hwa, Secretary General of the Malayan Communist Party

Cox, Peter, manager Rompin Estate

Fremin, Geoffrey, assistant manager, Rompin Estate

Gibson, Henry, Major, later Lieutenant Colonel, Commanding Officer, 1/12 Gurkha Rifles

Goh Ah Wah, senior surrendered guerilla, 2 Regiment, Malayan Races Liberation Army

*Ismail Mubarak, a.k.a. Moby, Head of Special Branch, Seremban

Jasbahadur Gurung, Rifleman, 1/12 Gurkha Rifles

Kwek Leng Ming, surrendered guerilla, 2 Regiment, Malayan Races Liberation Army

Kulbahadur Limbu, Corporal, 1/12 Gurkha Rifles, expert tracker

*Lee An Tung, Head of the Central Propaganda Department, Malayan Communist Party

*MacGillivray, Sir Donald, High Commissioner for Malaya, 1954-57

Mason, James, Colonel, Director of Intelligence, HQ Malaya Command

Minbahadur Gurung, Lance Corporal, 1/12 Gurkha Rifles, radio operator

Rance, Jason Percival Vere, Captain, 1/12 Gurkha Rifles, a.k.a. Shandung P'aau, Shandong Cannon

Ridings, Edward (Ted), Lieutenant Colonel, Commanding Officer, 1/12 Gurkha Rifles

Ridings, Edwina, daughter of Lieutenant Colonel Ridings (q.v.)

Ridings, Fiona, Mrs, wife of Lieutenant Colonel Ridings (q.v.)

Ridings, Theodore (Ted), son of Lieutenant Colonel Ridings (q.v.)

Sim Ting Hok, captured guerilla 'gardener', 2 Regiment, Malayan Races Liberation Army

*Tan Fook Leong, Commander 2 Regiment, Malayan Races Liberation Army

Tan Wing Bun, son of Tan Fook Leong (q.v.)

*Ten Foot Long, British nickname for Tan Fook Leong, (q.v.)

*Too Chee Chew, a.k.a. C C Too, brilliant propagandist, Special Branch, Malayan Police

Vaughan, Eustace, Lieutenant Colonel, Commanding Officer, 1/12 Gurkha Rifles

Vinod Vellu, infiltrator of Malayan Communist Party

Wang Liang, son of Wang Ming, (q.v.)

Wang Ming, a.k.a. Hung Lo, the Bear, close friend of Ah Fat (q.v.)

*Wong, Miss, girlfriend of Too Chee Chew (q.v.)

Yap Kheng, demoted guerilla 'gardener', 2 Regiment, Malayan Races Liberation Army

*Yeong Kwoh, senior military member of the Malayan Communist Party

Xi Zhan Yang, Malayan Communist Party courier

Abbreviations

2ic	Second-in-Command
AOC	Air Officer Commanding
AVM	Air Vice Marshal
casevac	casualty evacuation, where possible by air
CEP	Captured Enemy Personnel
CO	Commanding Officer, commander of major unit
Comcen	Communications Centre
Compo	rations, already packed, ready to heat and eat
CQMS	Company Quartermaster Sergeant
CSM	Company Sergeant Major
CT	Communist Terrorist/s, official name for guerilla/s
DCM	Distinguished Conduct Medal
DSO	Distinguished Service Order
DZ	dropping zone
ETA	estimated time of arrival
FARELF	Far East Land Forces
GHQ	General Headquarters
GM	Gurkha Major, the senior Gurkha officer in any Gurkha unit
GR	Gurkha Rifles
HQ	headquarters

ID	identity
Int	intelligence
JCLO	Junior Civil Liaison Officer
KL	Kuala Lumpur
LMG	Light Machine Gun
IO	Intelligence Officer
LP	landing point
MA	Military Adviser
MC	Military Cross
MCP	Malayan Communist Party
m.i.d.	mention-in-despatches
MI Room	Medical Inspection Room
MM	Military Medal
MRLA	Malayan Races Liberation Army
MTO	Mechanical Transport Officer
NCO	non-commissioned officer
NTR	nothing to report
OC	Officer Commanding, commander of sub-unit
'O' Group	'Orders Group': sub-commanders for whom any orders are relevant
ops	operations
PA	Personal Assistant
Psyops	Psychological Warfare Operations
QM	Quartermaster
RAAF	Royal Australian Air Force
recce	reconnaissance
resup	resupply
RMO	Regimental Medical Officer

RV	rendezvous, the appointed place for assembly
sitrep	situation report
SEP	Surrendered Enemy Personnel

Glossary

Chinese

I sincerely thank Mr Bernard C C Chan, MBE, AMN, for his unstinting help in matters Chinese.

feng shui	'wind and water': a system of good and bad influences in the environment and correct alignment with nature
gwai lo	foreigner, literally 'devil chap', 'old devil
Sinsaang	Mr, sir
t'o yan	'soil man', aborigine
wei	hello (telephone calls)
yanshu	mole

Malay

ladang	aboriginal settlement
lalang	Imperate arundinacea, a coarse, weedy grass
ringgit	Malay dollar

Nepali (Gurkhali)

Ayo Gurkhali	(loosely) Here come the Gurkhas
ba	'father,' a suffix often used when talking to a CSM, 'Major Ba'
bahaduri	bravery award
chhatiwan	Alstonia neriifolia, 'Devil Tree' in Nepal
daku	'dacoit', used by the Gurkhas for the Communist guerillas
gora	fair-skinned, Gurkhas' word for British troops
hajur	term of respect, inert conversational response (literally 'presence')
hunchha	is, okay
sarkar	government, officialdom
syañ	dead man's spirit
ustad	'teacher', word used in some Gurkha units to an NCO

Note: the '-bahadur' at the end of names is often shorted to '-é' when talking, so, instead of Kulbahadur, it is Kulé etc

Signals jargon

96 Foxtrot	Auster aircraft pilot
Acorn	Intelligence Officer
Big Sunray	Brigade Commander (unofficial)
blower	radio
Roger	'understood'
Sunray	commander of unit or sub-unit concerned
Sunray Minor	deputy commander of unit or sub-unit concerned
Wilco	'will comply with your message'

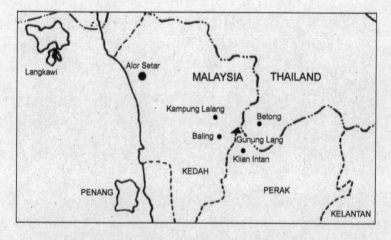

ABOVE Detail of Baling and the intersecton of Kedah, Perak and Thailand.
FACING Peninsular Malaysia.
BELOW Detail of Negri Sembilan.

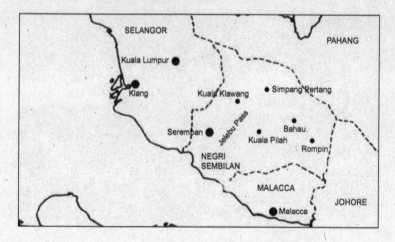

1

Friday, 13 August 1954, Jelebu pass and Seremban, central Malaya: For three days the guerrillas had been lying in ambush, overlooking the steep, winding road leading to the narrow Jelebu pass. Their special target was the vehicle carrying the Commanding Officer of the 1/12 Gurkha Rifles, travelling south from Kuala Klawang to Seremban, the battalion's headquarters.

In charge of the ambush was Tan Fook Leong, commander of the 2nd Regiment of the Malayan Races Liberation Army, MRLA, a bright, experienced, well-educated man with considerable jungle experience in operations against the Japanese during the late war.

'Comrade commander, no military traffic has moved along this normally busy road while we've been in ambush. Why are we still here?' a comrade asked, absent-mindedly scratching a leech bite on his leg.

To grumble openly meant a demerit and a self-criticism session when conditions were back to normal so not to show any disquiet only innocent questions were asked. Ambushes were not easy to stay in for long periods; movement was restricted, it was difficult to relieve oneself, there were midges, mosquitoes, leeches, poisonous centipedes, there was nowhere to go when it rained. In the Jelebu pass area it rained so regularly in the afternoons that one could set the time by it: twenty past four. Also the ambush area was high enough to be cold at nights, so the innocent question, 'why are we still here?' really meant 'we have been long enough, uncomfortable enough and bored enough with nothing happening so why not get up and go, *now*?'

The answer, likewise, had to be firmly explicit to quell any misgivings. 'Comrade, I happen to know that there is a new CO of the Gurkha battalion in Seremban, Lieutenant Colonel Ridings. My spies have told me that he had planned to visit his "out companies" around now. He has to return to his HQ along this road and I think he'll be along soon as today could be his unlucky day,' Commander Tang explained patiently.

'Comrade, why should you think that?' *That was, surely, only a wild guess.*

From long habit he spoke in a low voice and only the men near him could hear what he said. 'I'll tell you why. When I was in England in 1946 for the Victory Parade I learnt that the *gwai lo* have a strange fear; whenever the 13th of the month is a Friday it is unlucky. Today is Friday the 13th. Have any of you ever heard such nonsense?'

No, no one in earshot had.

'Comrade,' called out the man at the lower edge of the ambush, 'I hear transport coming.'

'Get ready for action. Open fire on my order. Only the Snatch Group move out after I order stop firing.' Tan Fook Leong's order loudly reverberated.

The Communist-inspired war in Malaya against the colonial power, Britain, known as the Emergency, had been a feature of everyone's life for six years, since mid-1948. Sometimes flaring, sometimes subsiding, it rumbled on, waxing and waning, until 1959. By 1954 it was simmering, taking advantage of 'opportunity' targets, 'as and how'. And one was about to be presented to the waiting ambush.

Lieutenant Colonel Edward Ridings had only recently taken over command of 1/12 Gurkha Rifles (1/12 GR). He was an able and likeable man, with a good war record. Just over forty years of age, medium-sized and barrel-chested, he had black curly hair, an open face and, what he was secretly proud of, an extremely trim and athletic figure. He had been posted in from another Gurkha regiment so was eager to 'get to know' his company commanders and the men. His family had come with him: Fiona his wife, Theodore his son, who said he, too, wanted to serve in the Gurkhas, and Edwina his daughter, both children going to King George V School in Seremban.

1/12 GR had been on jungle operations since mid-1948 and every three years underwent six weeks of re-training which included modern warfare tactics, range classification, administration, a drill competition and games, especially the inter-company football tournament. After a battalion parade to celebrate the new Champion Company's triumph, three of the four rifle companies moved out to tactical bases near villages between fifty and seventy miles away, with the fourth in Seremban. The CO had spent a night with each 'out' company, travelling in an open Land Rover.

A champion rifle shot, he carried a rifle. With him was an armed bodyguard, sitting in the back seat. Behind came an armoured scout car with a Bren gun mounted on a cradle. This the gunner, sitting in a chair with his head showing, could fire with aimed shots – if he had to lower his seat and the cradle to close the roof, he fired it using the cradle's handle-bars, aiming through an open slit in the bodywork.

Glancing at his watch the CO saw it was later than planned so told the driver to speed up. The scout car driver saw the Land Rover surge forward and tried to catch up. Negotiating a steep hairpin bend, he missed his gears and stalled the engine. The Land Rover, unescorted, drove on alone.

To the guerrillas' amazement they saw an unescorted and open-sided Land Rover approaching, a little faster than normal, with an elderly British officer in the front passenger seat – *so our leader was correct!* – and an escort in the back.

When the vehicle was in the centre of the ambush, Tan Fook Leong gave the order to fire. The vehicle slew into the ditch with no movement from the three men inside.

'Cease fire! Snatch Group out, get their weapons and ammunition. Quickly! Kill anyone still alive.'

The guerrillas spilled onto the road and saw all three men were dead. As they grabbed their three weapons and started to search for ammunition, they saw that the CO had been hit in the nose by a single bullet as well as his body being riddled and bleeding. The Gurkhas' bodies were also heavily hit and bleeding profusely.

It was then that they heard a heavy vehicle coming towards them.

As the scout car came into the straight, the driver and gunner saw the Land Rover in the ditch and guerrillas round it. The gunner fired bursts of rapid fire at them.

'Back fastest,' shouted Tan Fook Leong as bullets sprayed the road, luckily, for the guerrillas, not causing any casualties. They fled back into the jungle not minding how much noise they made and quickly moved off. It would be several hours before any soldiers could start tracking them.

With heightened vigilance, the driver, horrified to see what his bad gear change had resulted in, halted near the Land Rover, full of bullets and three dead men. The gunner saw tracks and broken foliage so he fired several more bursts in their general direction.

'Our Commanding saheb is dead[1] and so are the other two,' said the driver to the gunner. 'One was my close friend. I must tell Battalion HQ about this now' and he made his call.

The guerrillas, excited at their success, stopped half an hour later for a breather before being ordered to return to their jungle base, a day's stealthy journey away, in small groups by different routes, so confusing an inevitable follow-up by the Gurkhas.

The guerrilla jungle 'garden' where two disgraced guerrillas were

---

1 The most senior officer to be killed in the Emergency was a lieutenant colonel near the Jelebu pass. A brigadier died in a plane crash.

working lay to the southwest. Yap Kheng, a big, strong man once a forest ranger, had an axe and Sim Ting Hok, a non-descript with the limpid gaze of an entirely stupid man, a mattock. They also had seeds to sow, beans, eggplant, sweet potatoes, pumpkins and spring onions. Yap Kheng stopped working as he heard distant firing, wiped his forehead and said to his companion, 'that's firing we can hear, isn't it?'

Sim Ting Hok stopped digging and listened. 'Yes, in the distance to the northwest. It'll be from the Jelebu pass ambush. Quite a noise'

'I would so much have liked to have taken part in the ambush rather than work here. Why were we kept out, do you think?'

'As a punishment. Demotion. At our last self-criticism you admitted to having written an unauthorised love poem and I was not paying enough attention to what was being said so could not answer the questions.'

'What will our comrades do now, do you think? There's bound to be a big follow-up operation by the *gwai lo* military.'

'They'll get out of the area now. We were not told but a move east is my guess.' Instinctively he lowered his voice. 'Between us two, you know, I'm fed up. So far we have seen nothing really worthwhile for our pains. I've had enough. There's too much bad *feng shui* here for my liking. What do you think?'

Automatically he looked around although he knew there was no one else there. 'That's sedition. They'd kill you for that.' He hesitated. Softly he added, 'But I agree with you.' Then louder he asked, 'if the others go east, what will happen to us here?'

'We were told to stay till fetched. We have only one rifle

between us, your punishment included going empty-handed.'

'I know. But what can I do about it, except trust to luck. We've still got a lot of work to do so let's get on with it.' He shook his head wearily and bent down to scratch his ankles. 'These leech bites never stop itching. If we had the same jungle boots as the *gwai lo* have our feet'd be better off.'

They resumed their tasks.

Back in the Battalion's Communications Centre, the Comcen, the duty operator heard the call 'Hullo 9, hullo 9, urgent message, over.'

'9, send, over.'

'9...' the driver gave details of what and where had happened.

'9, I'll send for Acorn. Wait out.'

Acorn quickly came and told the driver to wait until rescue arrived.

'9, wilco, out.'

The IO immediately told the 2ic who ordered the Duty Bugler to blow that hardly-ever-heard call, the assembly call that ends in five 'Gs', 'Officers Report at the Double'.

By the time the British officers, including the Gurkha Major, had assembled the 2ic, Major Henry Gibson, had made his plans. He told them of the tragedy of the three dead people was why he had ordered them at such short notice. 'It'll be that bloody man, Ten Foot Long, I have no doubt. He's been a thorn in our flesh since 1948. He's had the luck of the Devil so many times. It's now up to us to turn the tables on him. Right, listen to me.'

He pointed to the map. 'The incident seems to have happened

just short of the Jelebu pass. Exactly where will only be known when the Land Rover and the scout car are found. One platoon of A Company, with one day's Compo rations, will be ready to move in half an hour. It's now 1415 hours and it's dark by 1800.' He looked at the OC, Captain Jason Rance. 'One section will secure the area, one will help with the recovery of the bodies and both vehicles and one will track the guerrillas' movements. You, plus your other two platoons, will draw five-days' rations and ammunition for your whole company and move out tomorrow morning, having eaten early, at 0930 hours. This new order from Brigade about not surrounding and attacking a guerrilla camp yourself but using a marker balloon to show the RAF where the enemy camp is so it can be bombed means that you will take one with you.' He glanced at Rance, with a meaningful look, 'and no bloody heroics of "not understanding" and trying to do it with your men,' said with a veiled hint of expected insubordination in his tone of voice.

Major Gibson was a pre-war officer. Sad-faced, balding and wrinkled, he was considered as 'burnt out' by his subordinates. From the earliest days of his service he had tried hard to get to know his men, speaking their language 'well enough' although not as fluently as some of the wartime, emergency-commissioned officers spoke it. He referred to the soldiers as 'the little men' and had been accepted by them because he was an English saheb in the same mould as they, their fathers and their forefathers had known British officers for more than a century. He had a kind heart, was apt to be forgetful and was 'carried' by the other officers.

He inwardly felt that Captain Jason Percival Vere Rance

– *ouch, quite a mouthful* – was only commissioned because of the war as his background was not sufficiently 'sahib-like' although he was a 'good enough type' for this post-war army. Rance was six feet tall, with a taut, lean body and the indefinable air of a natural commander. With fair hair, penetrating, clear blue eyes, his features were almost hawk-like and stern. He showed his pleasure with a wonderful open smile. He was a brilliant linguist and had proved to be an outstanding company commander, an exceptionally talented jungle operator, good with the men, dedicated and hard-working who, if he could get his administrative and staff training as good as his tactics, could go far, but his background was unusual – 'broken the mould' some grumbled. He had been born in Kuala Lumpur, his father had been 'something', never asked what, tax official it was hinted, so probably not really a gentleman, and, from what he had guessed, had married 'beneath him'. Mrs Rance's background was most certainly unusual, although Jason never spoke about either parent: as a young woman she had been a ventriloquist who helped her father run a Punch-and-Judy show. She made sure that her son could master that unusual art and make different voices. Quite why, other than party tricks, she never told him: possibly it was vanity and possibly so that her own gifts need not be lost after her death.

Senior battalion officers were, in fact, jealous of Rance's linguistic ability. Apart from faultless Nepali and good Malay, having had a Chinese playmate, Ah Fat by name, he also spoke fluent Chinese and could read and write many characters. He kept quiet about it, not because he was, well, not exactly ashamed of it – why should he be? – but more likely to keep it as a 'secret weapon'. He made company parties a roaring success as a ventriloquist: he had a dummy which he sat on his knee and the absurd conversations in Nepali and English 'brought the house down'. One of his acts involved a highly coloured model krait which produced some absurdly funny situations. He was a superb mimic and another of his party tricks was getting his dummy to bell like a deer.

Not only his peers, but his seniors seemed almost resentful of his prowess in the jungle. On operations his men were always prepared to go that little bit farther, not worry quite so much if faced with short commons, show maybe a bit more confidence in difficult situations than might be expected and always ready 'to go those last few yards'. He had shown courage worthy of being recognised officially but nothing had 'come through'. *Luck of the draw* he told himself; 'battalion politics' muttered others. What also seemed to upset his seniors was, when off parade, he was greeted with smiles more than were they. *Bad for discipline* they muttered but discipline never faltered.

There was another, unspoken, reason for the 2ic's underlying resentment: during the war, instead of being sent overseas, he had been posted to the 5th battalion stationed on the North-West Frontier where the only activity was being sniped at by Pathans when roads were opened for convoys coming from the plains. Then he was posted to south India to be an instructor teaching camouflage and had been there till the end of the war. He did not have any campaign medals while Jason had the Burma Star and the General Service Medal with bar 'South-east Asia 1945-46'.

At Major Gibson's implied rebuke, Jason merely said, 'I understand, sir' in an abstract tone of voice – just now he was not his usual self for two reasons. One was that at the very end of his recent three-yearly leave of six months in England, he had become engaged to a girl who he felt was to be his and only his. She had said her father worked in the Air Attaché's office in the British Embassy in Washington and that she'd tell them all about it. In her first skimpy letter she had written '...and I'm in such a rush I'll write fully once I get to Malaya where Jason has arranged for the wedding as there's not enough time to marry before his leave finishes.' The wedding was due at the end of the following week and he was radiantly happy. The CO, in his kindness, had let her stay in his bungalow. Jason had arranged for somewhere else to live after the wedding. *Wonderful!* She had written a long explanatory letter to her parents and put it is a blouse pocket ready to take for posting. However, the person who collected her clothes to launder mistakenly took the blouse with the letter in the pocket so it never got sent. Sea mail to the USA, in any case, took quite a time so her parents were not worried in any delay in hearing from her.

The other reason was that he had, unusually, a secret worry. He had been disturbed by a recurrent dream, the meaning he could not fathom. Each time there was black left and right, white above and a grinning daku (a communist guerrilla) who aimed his weapon at him. Whenever Jason had tried to fire his weapon, a carbine, nothing happened, the daku shot at him and when he awoke, it was into another dream. *Where oh where am I? Hospital, prison or lunatic asylum?* Of course he told no one about it and behaved normally. Yet, worry him it did. *I'll take my krait with me, if only as a lucky mascot. It might even come in useful.*

During his reverie other orders were given. The RMO was to get ready with body bags and whatever else was needed and the MTO to detail the ambulance, the Recovery Vehicle with the fitter, a 3-Tonner and another Scout Car for the platoon. The Signals Officer was to ensure communications were to stay open until night-time interference made contact impossible. 'Open at first light tomorrow,' were his orders.

'I will have the sad duty of going and telling Mrs Ridings about her husband; something I'll find particularly difficult, I fear,' the 2ic added. He looked round and asked if there were any questions.

The IO asked if he or the 2ic who would inform Brigade HQ. 'You'd better do it and tell their Duty Officer that I'm closeted with Mrs. Ridings. Any more?' He looked round. 'No. Right. Move.'

The buzz of the CO's death had gone around the lines and men wanted to know why, how and what was to be done about it. Jason Rance wanted to brief his men collectively before any of them moved out so he ran down to his company lines and called to the CSM: 'Major Ba, everybody fallen in immediately for orders,' before going into his Company 2ic's office where the Gurkha Captain, a pre-war warrior, was and told him the same thing. The CSM came in, saluted and told Jason the company had fallen in and was ready for orders.

Jason stood his men at ease and said, 'The Commanding saheb, escort and driver have been killed by the daku. The battalion will mount a large operation to look for the killers but first, as soon as I have dismissed you, 3 Platoon will draw compo rations for one day, weapons and ammo and escort the recovery vehicle and the ambulance to bring back the corpses and damaged Land Rover. I will bring the rest of the company out to the same area early tomorrow morning with five days' rations for 3 Platoon.

'I will remind you of my standing orders for jungle movement: never cut what you can break naturally; never break naturally what you can bend; never bend what you can move; never move that which you can get through without moving; never tread on what you can step over; never step on soft ground when you can tread on something hard. Don't forget that a footprint with the toes the same length is a bear's, not a man's; that cigarette smoke by water can be smelt for up to three hours afterwards and ours are different from theirs, and a dab of wet salt, never a lighted cigarette, is best for leeches. Why are we the best company in the battalion?' He answered his own question, 'because we never forget those points.'

His men accepted him and what he said because he never took any of them for granted.

Before Major Henry Gibson left the office he phoned his wife. 'Jane, darling, drop everything and be ready to go to Ted's bungalow and meet me there. He's been killed in an ambush and we must tell Fiona. Also tell Jason's fiancée. It will be a great shock for her, too.'

'Oh, how terrible! I'll wait until I see you and join you then,' and rang off. With heavy heart, Henry Gibson joined his wife outside the CO's bungalow, which was next door to his. 'Darling, this is just too terrible,' she said, with a sob in her voice. 'Yes, I know,' he answered with a choke in his.

He knocked on the door and called out, 'Fiona, it's Henry and Jane. May we come in?'

Fiona Ridings, a tall woman in her late thirties, had a determined, somewhat militant air with her almost masculine figure and bobbed hair, at once came to the door, saw the grave look on their faces and guessed why they had come to see her. 'Henry,' she burst out. 'I just know why you've both come. It can't be true, can it?'

'Oh, I'm afraid to have to tell you it is. On his way back, Ted was ambushed just short of the Jelebu pass. The scout car driver says he was killed outright so that means he felt no pain.'

'Wi...will you be bringing his body back?' she asked, her voice quavering.

'Yes, Jason Rance's men are escorting the doctor to recover it at this very moment. The doctor will look after him and we'll tell you when he has done all that needs doing.'

'I'm superstitious, you know, my husband wasn't. I just knew that Friday the 13th would be unlucky for him, I just knew...' and she burst into floods of tears.

'Let me get you a drink.' He called the Malay house boy and told him to prepare a stiff brandy for the Mem. It was quickly brought and he gave it to the 2ic.

'Drink this. Jane will stay with you for a while and help you tell the children when they come back from school. I must go back to the office and help sort things out. After you've had your drink, go and lie down on your bed and Jane will sit with you. I think you had all better spend tonight in our bungalow. It'll be no trouble and we'd rather like you to be with us.'

Fiona made a great effort to calm down. 'That would be a great help. Yes, please,' she gulped.

As Henry tuned to go, she said, 'You know I was in the Auxiliary Territorial Service during the war, even got to the rank of sergeant. My job was in Operational Planning in the War Office. Every operation the army mounted was given a code name. To feel I can get my own back on Ted's loss, can the code word for the operation I know you will be planning to capture those terrible men who killed him somehow be related to him? Please, please,' and she started crying once more. Jason's fiancée, overhearing everything said, kept to herself in her bedroom, scared stiff.

Henry called out, 'I'll see what I can do. Please excuse me but I am very busy ...' and went back to the office to call the Brigade Commander, Brigadier James Stuart Bickers, who had a large, square face, red-veined by too much alcohol, a walrus moustache, bloodshot eyes, a strained marriage and a short temper. He mistrusted anyone he thought knew better than he and reacted badly to it: this made for unhappy relations with his company commanders, especially those serving with Gurkhas.

'Yes, your Acorn has told me what you've put into motion. Good. I like it. How's Fiona taking it?'

'Badly, I fear, but how else could she? As you may know she was in the army during the war and has asked me to see if her husband's name can somehow be associated with the code name for the impending operation against the guerrillas?'

'Now that is a strange one, to be sure. I can't authorise it myself but I can certainly put it to the Director of Operations. Have you any ideas? My mind's a blank.'

In his quiet way, the 2ic was a wordsmith. 'I can offer a suggestion, Brigadier, which may make even the opposition not associate it with us.'

'Well, out with it.'

'The man's name is Ted Ridings. Do a spoonerism on him and call the operation *Red Tidings*. No one in the MCP would ever guess we'd use the word "red" in any of our code words.'

'Um. Er. Something tells me that the army...yes, I was once in Staff Duties and the order was that no colour could be used in a code word, certainly not when naming an individual. For instance "Black Prince" was not allowed but "Brave Prince" was. I'll see if I can't swing it.' He chuckled. 'Sorry, not the time for levity but just suppose the opposition were to think it was one of their plans if they come to hear of it so take no notice. Now that could be a big bonus point.'

'Thank you, Brigadier. In due course I'll tell Fiona what we're trying to do.'

'What is your operational plan?'

'Phase 1 is Jason Rance's company to follow up, with my other three rifle companies in reserve. If anyone can track them it'll be him and his men. As you will have seen from the map, the CO was killed on the western road of a large square of jungle that has roads on all the other three flanks. My guess is that the guerrillas will either go north or east into more remote country. They may even think they can hide in the area of the unsurveyed country farther north that shows white on the map sheet. I'll find out if the RAF have managed to take any photos of the area. If so, they'll be a great help though awkward to carry. I hope Rance can pinpoint them in the first five days. If he finds nothing during that time, I'll call him to the road for re-rationing. I'd rather not use airdrops for security reasons. And, yes, I've told him to take a marker balloon and not to try and take out any camp he finds by surrounding it and attacking it.'

'A wise move. The Director of Operations and the RAF are insistent on that. They say the kill-to-contact ratio in such operations couldn't be worse. Their code name for bombing is Smash-Hit' [2] and with that he rang off.

The CO and the other two bodies were recovered and brought back by the RMO himself and taken to his MI Room. The doctor was a phlegmatic and level-headed man, ideal for a Gurkha unit.

---

2 Senior airmen regarded the infantry's kill-to-contact ratio when surrounding a guerrilla camp as extremely poor. The policy of 'Smash-Hit' was their attempt to improve upon it. The one major success was when a notorious guerrilla was located, with Special Branch help, Lincolns of the Royal Australian Air Force and Canberras of the RAF dropped a hundred bombs which killed most of the guerrilla force. In fact it was a fluke because the guerrillas had moved before the bombing but, as the bombers fortuitously dropped their bombs on where the guerrillas had gone and not where they were briefed to, the end result was the same! Because of that, the use of 'Smash-Hit' became mandatory whenever an occupied camp was located.

He called the Gurkha Major and told him that the CO's memsaheb would want to see her husband's body so he would work on that first. Afterwards he would prepare the other two bodies.

'Saheb, let me and the Pandit look after them. Neither has their wife with them. I know that there are two close relatives of the driver's in Battalion HQ and they can help me. I'll get firewood and fuel from the QM and we will burn the corpses before dawn.'

'GM Saheb, that sounds fine. Just tell the Medical Sergeant what you need from here.'

The GM saluted and marched off.

3 Platoon escorted the recovery convoy. One section took up all-round defensive positions at the jungle edge, facing the foliage, and another section helped on the recovery site. Rain slowed the work.

The Platoon Commander ordered the third section to track the daku: 'Leave your big packs here and be back before last light.' The section commander, Corporal Kulbahadur Limbu, a tall, paler than normal Gurkha, was an ace tracker. Initially the tracks were easy to follow as the daku had moved quickly to put distance between themselves and any follow-up party and the ground was damp. Stealthy movement would come later.

They moved down a steep slope, across a small stream and to where they saw from the footprints that the daku had stood still. 'Being given orders,' the corporal said. 'Look around.'

'Ustad,' called one rifleman softly, 'there are some tracks moving off aslant the slope,' he looked at the sun, 'northwards'.

'And here are some more tracks moving eastwards,' called another rifleman.

Corporal Kulbahadur had already seen tracks moving northeast. 'They have split, the crafty fellows, maybe in more than three groups. Pointless our doing anything more now.' He looked at his map and noted the grid reference. 'We must go back fast before the light fails. At least it's stopped raining.'

They got back at dusk and, by the light of a fire, arranged their poncho capes for the night while the signaller, having been given the grid reference of where the tracks split, tried to contact Battalion HQ. He was unsuccessful as the normal nightly interference made transmission impossible.

'Leave it to tomorrow morning and let's eat,' said the Platoon Commander.

After their meal, he detailed the sentry roster and the others went to sleep.

The RMO had a delicate task with the CO's face. Washing off the caked blood from the body was easy but making the face look peaceful enough for his widow's sake was a problem as most of the nose had been shot away. Mending it would be an all-night job. He ordered one of his staff to get a clean jungle green shirt, with medal ribbons, badges of rank, parachute wings and 12 GR shoulder titles already fixed, from the CO's batman, to be brought discreetly from his bungalow– that turned out easy as Fiona and the children had gone to Jane and Henry's place for the night – but the nose was a problem as it had to be rebuilt to look normal. *Almost impossible, I fear*, the doctor fretted. As he shaved the dead man's face he saw how he could minimize the shock the wife would have.

14 August 1954, central Malaya: During the night the doctor laboriously re-built the nose with a solution of plaster of Paris and gauze then covered his handwork with homely sticking plaster. The body, dressed and patched, was put inside a coffin with the shroud draped over it. The lid was temporarily put on it and shortly before dawn the medical staff wearily stumbled off to bed, hoping their efforts would be appreciated.

Gathered in their jungle base, Tan Fook Leong congratulated his men on their ambush tactics and, as a reward for good soldiering, allotted the three captured rifles accordingly. They held a group meeting to discuss what tactics should be adopted now that a hornets' nest had been so violently stirred. Politburo orders were that operations against civilian targets should cease and that guerrillas should move to deep jungle and make 'gardens' for self-sufficiency. 'We will move east then northeast by platoons.' He took a map out of a notecase. 'Look, the imperialists are so behind the times that much of this map sheet,' he held it up for the others to see, 'has yet to be surveyed. It is only coloured white. What I propose is that two platoons move to north of the Bahau area and the third, the smallest, moves to a location suitable for making a garden in the blank map sheet. On our way around Bahau, where people are friendly to us, we will acquire as many mattocks and axes as are available, otherwise we won't be able to manage.'

He took his small portable radio out of his pack and turned it on. Even with a new battery it only hissed. He looked at it in dismay. 'I know it's old but I thought it would last longer than this,' he muttered, forgetting he had had it in his possession for eight years since his visit to London and it was an old model then. He looked around and saw Goh Ah Wah and Kwek Leng Ming, two comrades whom he fully trusted. He called them over. 'Comrades, I want you two to do a couple of things for me. One is to go to the garden where those two disgraced comrades, Yap Kheng and Sim Ting Hok, are working and tell them to come here. The other is to take this radio,' he handed it over, 'and get it repaired or buy a new one. Use your civilian ID cards, wear plain clothes and pretend to be innocent civilians. I'm sure you can manage.' He tore a page from his notebook and wrote something. 'Try and make contact with my wife, Chen Yok Lan, and son, Tan Wing Bun, in Penang. I've written the phone number down.'

'Comrade Tang, that will be our pleasure. It may take a bit of time but I'm sure you'll understand if it does.'

'Yes. After you have collected it, rather than look for me to hand it over, take it to my cave hideaway and stay there till I come.'

14 August 1954, Betong, south Thailand: The Central Committee of the MCP, with the ridiculously young Secretary General, universally known as Chin Peng, a placid-looking person without any stamp of leadership on his face, was carefully hidden in thick jungle in south Thailand, north Malaya having become too unhealthy for it. It had its strict routine, one aspect of which was listening to the early morning news broadcast of Radio Malaya on its Chinese-language channel. All were taken aback by the announcement of the death by a guerrilla ambush of the CO and two Gurkha soldiers of 1/12 GR in the hilly country north of Seremban as they were returning to camp. It sent a frisson of excitement through them as they listened. It was not often these days that such noble and daring deeds were so successfully accomplished.

At the end of the bulletin the Head of Central Propaganda Department, Lee An Tung, a man with a worried look on his face and a perpetual frown, said to his Deputy, Chien Tiang, a squat man who looked at everyone suspiciously, 'That'll be Comrade Tan Fook Leong. He's a canny operator, one of our best. I was with him in London in 1946 for the Victory Parade and I know him well.'

'Yes, so do I,' said Chin Peng. 'He's done us proud. The High Commissioner killed in a similar ambush last year and now a CO. Despite our having to change our tactics from an aggressive mode to being less hard on the civil population, acts such as this happily, for us at least, keep us in the headlines and our morale high.'

Heads nodded but no one offered any riposte. The truth was that a General Briggs had devised a plan to re-settle in 'new villages' the Chinese 'squatter' population that lived on the fringe of the jungle without any land title deeds and who were instrumental in supplying the guerrillas with food, shelter and information about the Security Forces. It had been a painful but necessary decision to uproot so many people and painful, too, for the guerrillas to be deprived of such basic necessities so essential for survival. It had resulted in their having to operate from bases deeper in the jungle than before and grow their own crops in 'gardens'. This was a time-consuming task and originally many were spotted from the air: this, in turn, led to the guerrillas planting their various crops haphazardly under the jungle canopy. The Central Committee had been on short commons until their move over the Malay-Thai border. Once there, local authority's 'blind eye' and the MCP's taking no part other than self defence – and growing their over vegetables – kept life quiet for them.

One of the listeners to the radio was a man named Ah Fat, a non-voting Politburo member. He was well built and solid but his movements were fluid. His eyes were always alert, never missing a trick, even though his peripheral gaze was not easy to follow. He looked a tad glum, was round of face, with high cheek bones. He stood about five and a half feet high. He had a habit of rubbing the palms of his hands together when thinking. His ears, close to his head, had, in some circles, given him the nickname of *P'ing Yee*, Flat Ears. Normally taciturn, he could turn on the charm when needed. He was well educated and spoke excellent English. However, for safety's sake, he kept that skill a closely guarded secret lest his 'other' role be jeopardised. Whenever he did speak English in front of other Chinese it was only of middle-school standard. When asked how he managed to separate his two lives he answered 'my life is grasped in my hand, not by heaven,' which he said was claimed by the 4th-century alchemist, Ko Hung, 'but I keep that to myself as "they" wouldn't accept it as Marx didn't write it.'

He was an only child, born and bred in Kuala Lumpur where his father had worked with the British intelligence representative, Jason Rance's father, and from an early age the two boys became as close as brothers. Ah Fat knew Jason as *Shandung P'aau*, the

Shandong Cannon, the Shandong people being known for their sturdiness and Jason being a sturdy lad. The two boys always playing together was the main reason for Jason's Chinese being word perfect. During the Japanese occupation Ah Fat had become a guerrilla but, with his intelligence roots, he was, in fact, now a 'mole' working for the British. In 1952 he and Jason had become intimately involved in the elimination of a British officer of 1/12 GR who had wanted to join the MCP. Although the two men had become involved separately, their joint venture was still an unknown in the Politburo. The operation had been christened *Operation Janus*.

Ah Fat knew that his friend Jason was an exceptional jungle operator. Pre-war they had played in the jungle, tracking each other, playing hide-and-seek, until they were almost animal-like in their ability. How had Jason described the jungle? He thought back: 'it was a close-horizoned, all-pervading, never-ending green of trees, vines, creepers and undergrowth. Trees grew, trunk by trunk and stem by stem, each one crowding upon and striving to overtop the other, and tied and netted together with the snake arms of creepers into a closely woven web. Aerial roots and liana-nooses hung from high above. Leaves laid themselves out in vast terraces, fantastic umbels descended in cascades and creepers united in stout, tightly-wound, spiral columns. Vegetation teemed in the steamy twilight; great fronds broken under their own weight, ropes which had neither end nor beginning, plants with fat, sticky leaves or with hairy or scaly stems, or stems that opened out like buttresses and some with large, luxuriant flowers, exuding a strange and deathly scent.' It was a good description, the Chinese mole thought. *We practised enough, didn't we!* And he grinned as he recalled 'those days'. They knew that animals were not normally a hazard but the Malayan buffalo, a pink brute, was aggressive towards Europeans – something to do with their body odour which has a different smell from normal rice-eating Malays – and the wild bison hostile towards everybody. Animals are normally more afraid of men than men are of them, yet they have to be treated with respect. Malayan tigers will only become savage when their cubs are threatened.

He remembered the animals they had come across. One time they were startled when they heard a noise neither of them recognised. They crept forward and saw it was a pig scratching its back on a log. It squealed in fright when it saw them and ran away; and once the noise of sticks hitting the upper branches of a tree to their front when they had thought they were alone. They crept ahead and, to their surprise, they saw it was made by a monkey. They had laughed at it but it had taken no notice. *...and that time when we were sitting on the bank of a river some fifty yards wide, flowing in a wide curve. We suddenly heard a mewing noise and, borne towards us by the current from the far bank, we saw a long, thin, black snake with curious little lumps equidistant along its entire length, each bump mewing. We could not fathom what kind of snake it was, but it did seem as if had swallowed a number of piglets whole and the wretched things, still alive, were vainly trying to escape. The current carried this creature past us towards the near bank where it hit a rock. It split in two, the tail end gaily swimming on but the front part disintegrated, each bump growing four legs and moving independently. We were spellbound* and it was only when each moribund 'piglet' scampered away did we realise that we had seen a family of monkeys crossing the river, too wide to jump across from tree to tree, holding on to one another's tail being carried over by the current. We could not decide whether the mewing was from the fear or the fun of it... I must stop day-dreaming!

At the end of *Janus* some guerrillas had surrendered and become a 'Q' Team, whose leader was Wang Ming, a short, squat man, known as *Hung Lo*, the Bear. He had been so impressed by Rance's methods that he said he always wanted to work with Jason where possible. He was in charge of Ah Fat's bodyguard, living near the central camp.

On hearing the news of the death of the CO of 1/12 GR, Ah Fat sat on one side, saying nothing, rubbing the palms of his hands together as he thought: *I wonder how heavily* Shandung P'aau *is involved in this. I must try and find a way of making contact with him.* He brooded. *I wonder if he has heard that the Politburo is making secret arrangements for peace talks now that the British have said that Malaya can have self rule and that, surely, can give him and me an opportunity to meet. There is talk in the Politburo about asking for an amnesty and being recognised as an official political party. It is all desperately secret. I must try and alert my English friend, but how?*

Same day, Seremban: After a stressful night, Fiona Ridings, hardly able to bear the thought of a future without her husband, asked Henry Gibson if she could see her husband's body and where he would be buried. 'Can I take his corpse to England and bury him

42

in our village graveyard?' she asked.

'The complications are many and varied for that to happen,' he answered carefully. 'There are proper military cemeteries here in Malaya. The nearest one is not far down the road from here and official policy is for fatalities to be buried in them. It is therefore incumbent to bury him here with an official regimental funeral and after the Emergency is over consider if disinterring him and taking him back to England is still what you want.' The RAF only took corpses from Singapore; he did not dare tell her that Singapore Customs would only allow a corpse to enter Singapore from across the Johor Causeway if it were declared as 'dead meat'. *Unacceptable!* 'I'll give the doctor a bell and see how matters stand.'

When the widow saw her dead husband's plastered nose she nearly burst into tears with anger. She, not knowing that the nose had been shattered, fought them back and petulantly scolded the doctor for making a mess of her husband's face.

The doctor, bleary-eyed, fought back the answer that immediately came to him and merely said, placatingly, 'Forgive me, Mrs Ridings, my hand slipped when I was shaving him. Please accept my apologies.'

She upbraided him with vigour for his careless ineptitude. 'What do you mean by damaging his nose? That's terrible. I object most strongly. You should be ashamed of yourself,' and, biting her lower lip to stop herself from crying, was quietly led away by Jane Gibson before she could say anything more, in no way appreciating the amount of work and care needed for her husband's renovated appearance.

After she had gone the doctor sighed heavily, shook his head and told his staff to put the lid on the coffin and nail it down. It was later taken to the civilian hospital for refrigeration until arrangements could be made for the funeral.

Jason's fiancée knew that her husband-to-be was heavily involved in chasing the guerrillas and she did not want to become a widow before getting married so, in a state of panic, she left a note for Jason in her bedroom, called a taxi and, unseen by anyone, took the night train to Singapore. Her absence was not noticed for more than a day.

14-16 August 1954, Jelebu pass area: Captain Rance brought his other two platoons to the ambush site by 0900 hours as ordered. He had a look around while his CQMS distributed the five days' rations then asked 3 Platoon Commander to brief him on what had been found. The Platoon Commander told Corporal Kulbahadur Limbu to give the details.

Rance listened intently then gave his orders. 'We will go to where the daku split and one platoon each will follow one of those three lots of tracks. If we find a fourth I'll take the CSM and Chakrabahadur Rai, my batman, leaving the remainder of Company HQ behind. Sections will leave their LMGs behind as this is only a recce.'

Led by Corporal Kulbahadur Limbu the company went off to where the tracks split. 'Take your big packs with you and try to follow any tracks you find. If they are more than your platoon can manage, call me and I'll make a plan,' Jason briefed his platoon commanders. 'Any questions?'

'Where will you be, Saheb?' one of them asked.

'I'll look around with my small group and if we see any other track we'll follow it. Whatever else, we'll be back before last light.'

The platoon commanders saluted and went away to get on with their job.

'Saheb,' said the 2-inch Mortarman, Jasbahadur Gurung. 'Let me take the Signaller's pistol and come with you if you find another track to follow.'

'Jasé, just this once,' said Jason, smiling.

Casting around, a fourth track was found, faintly etched in the damp ground heading southeast. 'Major Ba,' Jason addressed his CSM, 'we four will follow this.'

About midday Jason's small group stopped for a breather. Chakrabahadur Rai said, 'Saheb, I hear an axe on wood. Do you?'

Yes, they all did. Then voices were heard. 'Daku, not far in front of us,' said the CSM.

The jungle in front of them was lighter than normal and they realised they had come up to a daku 'garden' and that men were working in it.

'Let's take them by surprise,' said Rance, in a quiet voice. 'Make sure your weapons are ready to fire.'

Stealthily they moved forward, all senses alert and tingling, adrenalin pumping. This was the first contact for four months so now was their chance for a kill or capture. They crept to the edge of the clearing, fenced to prevent wild pig and deer from entering, and saw two men at the far end, dressed in khaki, bent over, one digging and the other with an axe in his hand. After carefully climbing over the fence – the bars were too close together to squeeze through – feeling most exposed, they crawled between the raised ridges of dug soil to a large felled tree in the middle of the 'garden' for cover, only some twenty yards from the daku. It struck Jason that this was the first time he had crawled as taught when undergoing training in the Indian Military Academy in 1941, thirteen years before.

Hiding behind the felled tree Jason gave out his orders softly, 'Major Ba and Chakré aim at the right hand man, Jasé and I will fire at the one on the left.' Rance's target's body was bent over as he was digging so, not seeing his head, he aimed at his back. '*Fire!*' he said quietly. His bullet struck the middle of the guerrilla's bent back. He sharply turned and faced the unknown firer, with his mattock in his hand as though aiming at him with a short-barrelled weapon before he toppled forward. Jason had again squeezed his trigger as the daku had turned on him but his carbine jammed. *No, no*, his mind shrieked, *my dream! – bright in the middle, dark both sides, a guerrilla hit and turning round, looking at me.* He instantly put his weapon down and pinched himself to see if he was awake, so pent up were his emotions. He had fired his first round and the other three men, thinking Jason had somehow been hit, turned to look as they fired so missing their target.

Jason was instantly apologetic and ashamed of his behaviour at seeing what he had been haunted by in his dreams. Here and now it was for real.

The CSM and Chakré, seeing that Captain Rance was not wounded, opened fire again, but just too late to be effective.

The guerrillas were already climbing over the far fence. Rance scrambled to his feet and shouted the Gurkhas' battle cry, *Ayo Gurkhali, Charge!* ... but in vain. The two guerrillas had disappeared and their tracks were soon lost in a maze of others. Time and few numbers were against a more detailed search.

The daku had left a rifle behind them so Jason turned to Chakré and told him to stay back with him and ordered the other two to return to camp. 'Tell the Company 2ic what has happened and that we two will hide in the jungle near the rifle and kill anyone who may come to recover it. Do not mention the contact to Battalion HQ until I return. And don't tell them I'll be out all night, otherwise they'll think I'm lost or wounded.'

The CSM, looking worried, said he understood and went back to Company HQ. Jason looked at his carbine to find out why it had jammed. He forced the working parts open and found that the case had swollen so making it useless; 'hard extraction' in the jargon.

It was a long night for them as they sat, backs to a large ant hill, facing where the rifle had been dropped. It rained most of the time. Once a tiger's growl throbbed nearby – they found its pugmarks next morning – which Jason wrongly thought was the death rattle of the man he had hit, and a mouse deer whickered in fright by their feet. No one came to recover the rifle so, once it was light enough to move, they returned to where the other platoons were awaiting them, Jason bringing the rifle with him. Before he changed into his spare dry clothes, he gave his carbine to the 2-inch Mortarman and kept the rifle. From then on he never used any other type of weapon.

By being bent over and not standing up straight, the bullet had ripped the skin of Sim Ting Hok's back, just scouring the flesh, so, although it hurt him abominably, he could still run. He followed his unwounded companion blindly until his strength ran out, spurred on by stories that the Security Forces would torture him if he were captured.

Both men were exhausted and hungry but, when night fell, there was nothing else they could do but take shelter under a tree. Where else in thick jungle? Soon after dawn they heard the belling of a deer, one of the guerrillas' recognition signs. They didn't answer the first time they heard it but did so when it got nearer.

Their two rescuers, Goh Ah Wah and Kwek Leng Ming, were shocked to see the state their comrades were in, especially the wounded man. 'Tell us what happened,' one said.

Sim Ting Hok sat on the ground, mind on his throbbing wound. He did not see the poisonous centipede crawling towards him. As it crawled up his bare arm, he automatically made to brush it off, so causing the insect to dig its claws into the man's skin. It was most painful.

'Comrade, help me,' he begged.

Goh Ah Wah knew what to do. Taking his knife out of his pocket, he cut the centipede off, leaving its legs dug in the skin. Sim Ting Hok looked dolefully at his arm and the legs in it and asked 'now what?'

'Now nothing. I'll tie something round the legs and you'll just have to wait until the flesh rots. Only then can the legs be pulled out. Now tell me what happened.'

Out came the explanation. 'That means that the enemy are

looking for us and you are wounded so cannot go back and join the others,' said Kwek Leng Ming, wondering what his boss would say. 'Our best bet is to go back towards Seremban for succour. The enemy certainly won't expect us to return that way. I know a sympathiser's house where we can get food and you can be treated.' The guerrillas had operated in that stretch of jungle since 1942 and knew the place like the proverbial back of their hands.

About midday Jason said to Chakré, 'let's make a brief area patrol. I'm tired of sitting down and we both have had a zizz and a meal.' After about a quarter of a mile they heard footsteps, sounding hollow in the hush, so they hid behind a large tree on their right hand side and peered through the hanging tendrils.

Coming their way were four guerrillas, one, face down on a make-shift stretcher borne by two others, a third with a rifle over his shoulder, the fourth, their escort, also armed with a rifle. As they passed in front of the tree Jason softly called out in Chinese, '*Ch'uan Jia Chan*', May your entire family be wiped out.

This ancient curse is one all Chinese take heed of. Although Communist philosophy recognised no traditional beliefs or folklore, deep, deep in every comrade's soul, there they lay, dormant. Taken completely unawares at such an unusual and unexpected threat from a disembodied voice, the three men came to a sudden halt, astonished at seeing nobody. Came the curse again. Inured not to believe anything 'non-Communist', they could not cover their inborn fear, heightened by seeing no speaker. What they were about to witness was so astonishing any aggressive reaction never entered their shocked heads.

'Follow me at the ready,' whispered Jason to Chakré. From round the other side of the tree, rifles in their outstretched arms, the daku were mentally overwhelmed when Jason said, 'Move and you'll be shot, not killed but wounded so you can never be a father again.' *Brave words. I could never or would ever do it.* 'Give us your weapons or we'll shoot.'

Unable to do anything else, the guerrillas surrendered them and Jason, with Chakré, escorted them back to their temporary base. There, bound by the toggle ropes the soldiers carried, Jason looked at the wounded man's back, took the medical pack and did what he could to relieve the pain. 'That will have to do till we get you to hospital,' he told him. 'You will be properly treated there.'

As the signaller 'got on the blower' to tell Battalion HQ about the captures, a mess-tin full of tea was brewed for each of the guerrillas and they were each given a packet of biscuits, which they wolfed down. 'You'll have to stay here a while', Jason told them, 'but if you say you surrendered to us and were not captured, you', to the two men who had been armed, 'won't have to face a judge and death for carrying a weapon.'

Jason was called to the set and was asked to elucidate, finishing up with, '...as soon as any of my platoons return, I'll be able to send an escort with the prisoners to be picked up on the Jelebu pass.'

This was countered with, 'No, Sunray Minor will get a section of the Brigade Defence Platoon to the Jelebu pass by 1530 hours. Even if the other platoons have not come back you will have enough men with you to take them to the main road. Roger so far, over.'

'1, Roger, over.'

'1. You must return with the prisoners. I can't tell you why but you are urgently needed here. Out.'

Jason looked at his 'dead' handset, seriously unsettled. *How come no reason given?*. He looked at the prisoners and his mind changed gear back to his present task. 'Don't believe, for one moment, that you will be tortured by the British. It does not happen, especially in a Gurkha battalion. The police will interrogate you, of course, but treat you fairly. Have no fear. I know where you'll go the *feng shui* is good so there really is no worry.'

The four men, mightily impressed with what they had heard, how they had been treated and with Jason's fluency, were only too willing to comply.

'I'd like to ask you some questions before we go back to Seremban together,' he said. 'Are you willing to tell me the truth?'

It was obvious that the four of them were still not convinced about Jason's integrity. 'You don't believe I am powerful, is that it?' he queried insouciantly.

They started to prevaricate so Jason looked up and asked, 'what do you see over there?'

As they turned their faces away he threw the model krait on the ground between them, making its almost throaty hissing noise as he did. On facing forward again, they winced with fear as they saw it lying so near them. Jason made as though he was going to defang a real krait – he had done this so often in his 'shows' –

that, once the 'dead' snake was in his pocket and so out of harm's way, the four men were totally convinced.

Jason noticed Sim Ting Hok's bad arm had started to smell. He guessed what had happened. 'It hurts, doesn't it?'

'Yes, and aches.'

'You will get it properly seen to when your wound is dressed but I will give you something to help.' He called over the nearest NCO and said, 'Ustad, bring me your bottle of rum. I'll buy you another one when we get back to camp. I want to put it on the centipede's legs that are stuck in this daku's arm.'

It was brought over and, the legs uncovered, Jason poured some rum over them. Sim Ting Hok jerked his arm away, muttering. The other three daku looked on apprehensively.

'Care for a swig?'

Looking at each other with sideways glances, first one then the other held out their hands for the bottle. This was something never expected. *Surely there can't be any trickery?* The arm ceased its throbbing.

By now there was no point in holding anything back. 'I will tell you all I know,' said the senior man, 'I am Goh Ah Wah and my armed comrade is Kwek Leng Ming.' He then gave Jason the names of the two 'gardeners'.

'Good. What will your commander's plan be now that he is being chased?'

'Oh, he will lead his men over to the east, to the other side of Bahau up to the area of the white map and prepare new gardens till this blows over. You will find nothing in this area now.'

'Thank you,' said Jason. He looked at his watch. 'I and

one man will take you to the Jelebu pass. There I will tell the commander who comes to fetch you how well you have behaved. But first, I need your signatures.'

He took a sheet from the signal pad and, in the Chinese script, wrote that 'We', then four names, 'have surrendered to Captain Rance.' Rifle numbers, date and time were penned and the men were told to sign. This they did.

Jason called his 2ic over. 'Saheb, I have been ordered back to base with the prisoners. I will tell the 2ic that, according to the surrendered men, there is no point in keeping us out any longer.' He called Chakré over: 'You and I will go back with the captured daku.'

He noticed the guerrillas' packs and told Chakré to search them. 'Saheb, here is a portable radio.' He switched it on. 'It doesn't work.'

'What are you doing with that radio with you if it doesn't work?' Jason asked.

Guilelessly Goh Ah Wah told Jason that it belonged to the guerrilla leader Tan Fook Leong and he had been given it for repair or get a new one in Seremban 'but not until matters had quietened down.' He even gave Jason the guerrilla commander's family and phone details, saying he'd been told to phone them.

Jason took the note he had written out of his pocket and added a sentence, 'I recommend that the portable radio be given to Head of Special Branch and not be thrown away.'

It took longer than normal to reach the road although there was no need for any stealth but because the four prisoners were bound and Sim Ting Hok's back made him move slowly. At the

53

Jelebu pass, Jason personally undid their toggle ropes and gave the escort commander the written 'surrender' note and explained what he should say when he took the four men to the police and that one man needed medical attention. 'You can drop me and Chakré off at 1/12 GR on the way.'

Before the vehicle drove off from the battalion, Jason handed the radio over. 'See that gets to the Head of Special Branch in the Police Station, ustad, as it is important.'

'Hunchha, Hajur,' was the answer, with a smile.

The escort took the four guerrillas to Brigade HQ and the section commander handed them over, along with Jason's two notes and the Brigade Major telephoned for Special Branch to come and collect the captives. A doctor looked at the wounded man's back and arm and put him, under guard, in the local hospital. Jason's two notes caused great excitement.

The Head of Special Branch was one Ismail Mubarak, known to all as 'Moby', an exceptional man, actually a Pakistani and a Chinese speaker to boot. Middle-aged and 'comfortable' he had a ready smile which hid an iron personality. He bred crocodiles as a hobby, which showed as he only had three fingers on his left hand. He and Jason had met a couple of years before when Operation *Janus* was taking place and had a high opinion of each other.

If I can't get these four on my side without Jason's help, I'll have to work something drastic out. As for the radio... and an idea came into his mind. *I'll keep it for later.*

The 2ic was due to go and meet the Brigadier but first he sent for

Jason. 'I have called you back to give you this,' and gave him the letter that had been found in his fiancée's bedroom. 'She left here the night of the ambush but so busy were we all we only found out the next day.' He glanced at Jason to see how he took the news as he read the letter. To his amazement, all Jason said was 'Better wedding minus than wedding plus.' Inside him his heart emptied: he felt bitter, angry, resentful as he recalled what H H Munro, 'Saki', had written; 'When love is over, what of love does even the lover understand?'

At Brigade HQ it was decided to recall Jason's company and launch a large-scale battalion operation, code named *Red Tidings*, in the Bahau area, within the next few days.

18 August 1954: Jason was relaxing in the Mess when he was called to the phone. 'Moby here. Can you spare me half an hour straightaway? Down at the police station?'

'Yes, of course. Why?'

'I'll tell you when you get here. Walk down the road, in uniform, and a police vehicle will pick you up at the bridge below your camp. Say nothing,' and he rang off.

Jason walked out of the Mess and down the road to where the police vehicle had parked by the bridge. A Malay driver smiled at him and Jason got in. In fluent Malay he cracked a joke as they drove off. They were at the police station within ten minutes. He went to Moby's office and saw a serious expression on the usually smiling face. 'Jason, Goh Ah Wah and Kwek Leng Mong have renounced their promise to help us. I *must* get them on our side to use against Ten Foot Long. Very briefly, what I have done is to arrange a mock shooting of them and a third, can't do all four as Sim Ting Hok is still in hospital. They are now in the courtyard at the back, tied to stakes. I have three Malay policemen, armed, who will be in a firing position, as if ready to shoot them dead. I want you to break in, remonstrate with me and I'll let them free if they promise to you to come over.'

'Moby, that is strictly against all the rules, isn't it? If anyone finds out we'll be lynched and out of a job,' Jason fretted.

'I know, I know, but to get these men working for us is crucial. I'm ready to risk it. Won't you help me, Jason, please, just this once? I know of no other method. Fear of imminent death cripples peoples' will fast. You'll be away into the bushes soon and now is the only time I can see to do it. Look out of the window.'

Jason did and there three of his four captives were, bound to stakes but not blindfolded. Jason, hating himself, told Moby he'd help 'but let's get it over quickly.'

'Thank you, Jason, you're a pal. I will go and give the orders for them to be shot. The three policemen will come up into the aim and you will break in asking me not to shoot. I will order my men to lower their rifles and you will tell me about their surrender signature, go forward and tell them you just happen to have seen what was about to occur and felt you had to stop it.'

'Wilco, Moby, as we military buffs have it.'

Moby went into the courtyard and, in a loud voice, ordered his men to take up the standing aim position in front of each man. 'You will be shot dead for carrying arms and wearing enemy uniform.'

Jason opened the door and pretended to be appalled by what

he saw. In Chinese he said to Moby, 'Mr Mubarak, wait please. They surrendered their arms to me. They were not captured with them.'

Moby looked round as if in surprise. 'Captain Rance! Are you sure?'

'Yes, Mr Mubarak. I am sure.'

'In that case, the charges of carrying arms and wearing enemy uniform are dropped. They will not be shot because of it.'

He ordered his squad to withdraw from the firing position and Jason went up to the three men. 'Lucky I came here at this time. What is your trouble? Didn't you believe me when I said nothing would happen to you? Did you change your minds?'

'Can you save us?' all three asked, ashen faces witness of their fear.

'Yes but only if you say you'll work for me or for anyone I detail instead of me.'

'We will, we will,' came the chorus.

Jason turned round and told Moby that the three men would obey him and please revoke the death penalty.

Moby made as though to consider the request. 'Yes, revoke it I will.' He told the three policemen to 'ground arms' and go and undo the captives whose faces resumed their normal colour.

Unbound the three Chinese came and knelt in front of Jason and Moby and said 'We will obey your orders.'

Moby then said, 'Say after me: "I swear that the statement I made is the truth. If it is not and if I have acted against my conscience, deep in my soul I shall be tormented and I shall be subject to legal sanctions."'

This they repeated in unison.

Moby turned to Jason and said, 'You are the witness to what these men have sworn to. Say after me "I swear I told the truth. If any statement that I have made about what I know is false, I hold myself responsible for all legal consequences and moral condemnations."'

Jason, in turn, followed suit. The oath was now official.

The three men stood up and all shook hands. Before being allowed to join other 'Q' squad men, Moby said, 'This is our secret. Keep it quiet.'

'Yes, we will. Yes, we will,' they echoed as someone came to lead them off.

'Jason, that is our secret also. You will be court-martialled if that is known and I will be jailed.'

They shook hands and the police vehicle took Jason back to the bridge below the 1/12 GR camp.

19 August 1954, The funeral of Lieutenant Colonel Edward Ridings was solemn, simple and sad. The long-wheelbase Land Rover carrying the coffin was followed by a staff car in which his widow sat, stern-faced and tense, her two children beside her. The Brigade Commander followed in his vehicle, bedecked with flag and one star in front and one in the rear. Both sides of the road were lined with soldiers standing to attention, gazes fixed fiercely forward, all men vowing to 'get our own back' on the dishonour done to their battalion. Gurkha pallbearers unloaded the coffin and carried it to the grave and interred it. The senior army chaplain in Malaya quickly but gracefully conducted the service.

People dispersed and after Mrs Ridings had been driven away to Major Gibson's house the soldiers lining the route marched back to camp.

The Ridings family was flown back to England at government expense on 21 August, mentally shattered, Mrs Ridings only slightly comforted on learning that her late husband's name had been 'retained but disguised' as the operation to be undertaken to avenge his death was Operation *Red Tidings*.

2

19 August 1954, Seremban: Before Moby left his house for the office he was rung up by his school friend, a Tamil named Vinod Vellu. 'Moby, we haven't met for years and I know its short notice but can I come and see you now as ever is?'

'Vinod, what a surprise! Delighted but why not in my office?'

'Better in your house, please.'

'Okay. Know where I live, do you? Behind the police station. How long will it take to come here?'

'I'll be round in a jiffy as I'm at the Rest House.'

Slightly mystified, Moby sat down and thought back: Vinod Vellu, a strong, dexterous, intelligent man, full of face, with a ready smile. Born and brought up on Lavender Estate where his father was the comprador of the labour force. Married and moved to another part of the state, became a successful businessman when his wife and daughter had been raped then killed by a group of terrorists when he was away on business.

A car drew up. Vinod stepped out and briskly made for the front door which Moby opened as he reached it. They embraced warmly. 'Come in and have a cup of tea,' Moby invited him as he took off his shoes.

'Yes, I'd like that,' and Moby called out for his wife to

arrange it.

'I'll come to the point right away, Moby, as you're a busy man. You know my background, I'm sure. I must get my own back. None of the Communists know my name and the gang who raped and killed my wife and daughter never knew theirs. Can you, with your various secret contacts, get me accepted by the MCP as an ardent politico whose one aim in life is to act against the colonial government?'

Moby thought for a long time before answering. 'Tell me how you want to take your revenge.'

'It is a long-term project I have in mind, one that might take me a couple of years or more. In outline, once I am accepted and believed in, I will try and manoeuvre a group of guerrillas to go for food collection on Lavender estate. As it is near the jungle edge I'll lead them into a Security Force ambush and, while so doing, make my own escape.'

'Now that really is something.'

'It is. I will try and keep tabs with you, quite how I can't say now or, when the time is ripe, how get the details to you. Once you know the time and place you can arrange the military ambush and I will spring my plan.'

'I commend you. Something like this needs bags of guts and even a slight mistake can put your life in jeopardy.'

'I know, Moby, but I've made my mind up. Have you any advice on survival?'

Moby leant back in his chair, a distant look in his eyes. Vinod saw he was concentrating so kept quiet.

'Vinod, I know someone here in Seremban who intimately

knows another someone doing what you want to do. Let me get his advice...'

Vinod shook his head and was on the point of disagreeing but Moby continued, '...theoretically only mind you, on how his friend has managed to keep safe for many years.'

The Tamil hesitated then, rather reluctantly Moby thought, agreed. 'Yes, I'll go along with that.'

Moby looked at his watch. 'Vinod, how long can you spare? I have to go to the cemetery for a funeral at half past nine. I can't not. There I will meet the man who can give you your answer. I won't be back till lunchtime as I have a deadline to meet in my office. Can you have lunch with me? By then I promise you'll have a full answer.'

'If that's my only option, of course, thank you,' Vinod answered with a smile.

After the funeral Moby beckoned to Jason and took him to one side. 'I need your advice. I have a man who wants to be a mole in the MCP coming to lunch today. He has asked me for advice on survival. I thought of Ah Fat and you knowing how he has managed to carry on successfully.'

Jason looked serious and nodded. 'Give me time to give you an answer.'

'Can you join us at lunch today as ever is?'

'No but I'll drop in at a quarter to two, if that is convenient?'

Convenient it was and Jason, after being introduced to Vinod, said, 'basically he is still alive because he has a firm base, an alternative and a reserve. By that I mean living the part he's acting, having a cover plan to answer any suspicions and a get-away-cum-hidey-hole plan for emergencies – and tying a cloth under his chin and over his head at nights to stop him from sleep talking. Survival is an infinite capacity for suspicion and never taking anything for granted.'

Vinod took all that in. 'Anything else for me?'

'Yes, three points of jungle lore: if you find yourself adrift and lost if you have no compass, follow streams as they will lead to habitations; if you are hungry and want to eat a fruit, beware if it red, as red often means it's poisonous. To make sure, take off a bit of peel and rub the fruit on the inside of you lip and if it burns that means it is poisonous; and if you're chased by an elephant, try and run downhill. If you've got all that I must leave you and get my company ready for an operation.'

He stood up and shook Vinod's hand. 'I wish you the best of luck' and went back to his company

By themselves, Moby said 'All good advice indeed. And as for you I will back you up to the hilt and until fruition, apart from Captain Rance, only you and I will know about it at this level but of course ambush planners will have to know in good time and then only in outline, on the "need to know" principle. You will have to have a code name which my boss in Kuala Lumpur must give so it doesn't clash with any other.'

'Who is your boss?'

'An erudite Chinese who has a dedicated Tamil as one of his closest advisers. I'll let you know how to insert yourself and the code name...wait. I have a secure line.'

With veiled speech and 'only when we meet', the code name given was 'Dover'.

1 September 1954, south Thailand: The Central Committee members were discussing how to handle their worsening situation. One ever-present problem was the slowness of communicating with guerrilla units in Malaya. It often took months for a directive to reach its destination and twice as long for any answer to find its way back. Some never arrived when couriers were killed or captured and that seldom came to light.

'Comrade Ah Fat,' the Secretary General called out. 'I have not had a proper session with you since,' and he looked at his notes, 'the 13th of September 1952, two years ago, after you returned from trying to bring back that renegade British officer. You did wonderfully well to get as far as you did although you did not succeed.'

'Comrade Secretary General, thank you for your kind words. We very nearly did succeed. It's history now so let's leave it at that. Since then as you know I have not been idle,' and he went on to describe how he had been helping the printing section with their cyclostyling copies of Voice of the People, Red Flag and Truth. 'As you know, Comrade, ever since our Klyne Street publishing house in Kuala Lumpur was shut down, production of our newspapers has been a fulltime job here.'

'I know, Comrade, and I am grateful for what you and the others have done. However, now is the time for fresh thinking. There is a need to produce another newspaper, unknown to our enemies, with which we can keep our comrades in Malaya informed with what I am trying to plan, an amnesty, which means a ceasefire, and becoming a recognised political party,' said Chin Peng, nodding as he elucidated his points.

Ah Fat, knowing better than to disturb his train of thought, sat still, cogitating how best to react to whatever came his way. What did was unexpected: Chin Peng took a piece of paper out of his pocket and showed it to him. 'Commit this name and address to memory. Mention it to no one else. This is one of my sleepers in the Police HQ in KL who will know if anything hush-hush is being planned. I want you to go there as my secret emissary to find out about any amnesty talks or peace plans.'

Ah Fat took the piece of paper and saw the name was Chan Man Yee. *A woman's name.* His mind raced with a far-fetched idea as he gave it back. 'Comrade, if that is your order of course I will obey it,' he answered, unconsciously rubbing the palms of his hands together.

'Yes. After your return you must start publishing this new newspaper. Try and persuade this contact to give you some paper with a government watermark which we can claim as government propaganda. Our cadres must be ready with any good news we can offer them after all their efforts over so many years. I can remember being put off going to a Catholic school when young, with all their "good tidings" and I don't know what, but that word "tidings" for news sticks in my brain,' and he broke off beaming. 'So let that be the name of our new secret newspaper, *Red Tidings.*'

'That's a wonderful name,' said Ah Fat, in as a toadying tone of voice as he could get himself to make, for once keeping his hands still. 'That is a clever move, Comrade Secretary General,' he added, smarmily as he inwardly exulted. *That is a game two can play at. I'll make trying to sow confusion in the ranks my* Operation Red Tidings. *Once in Kuala Lumpur I'll meet mole Chen and C C Too. My secret code words will be something to do with Jason's and my childhood nicknames.*

'Comrade Secretary General, do you really think that our comrades will look for a watermark? Also, the typing paper we have been using doesn't have a watermark.'

Chin Peng, never wanting to be shown wrong, looked peeved. 'You may be right but in our first issue we can tell them to look for one. Also, we can make our own "government" stories on such paper. Now, to hide our real plans we will adopt the mainland system for encoded communications. Do you know it?'

Ah Fat shook his head. 'I have only vaguely heard of it but not in detail. As only an observer, not a full member of the Politburo, I have not been indoctrinated into the system.'

'Then I will tell you about it. We write out our messages so that when they are read their true meaning is lost to non-indoctrinated readers who waste their time in trying to understand them. They may think that the writer has been lax and made mistakes with what characters have been printed; they may think that it is in what the British know as "veiled speech". In a way it is "veiled" as the real message in the article is only every fourth character. No one expects such an article,' and he chuckled gleefully. 'Our code-books are based on and adapted from the openly available standard Chinese Commercial Telegraphic Code book where each character is represented by a group of four numbers. For example, the commercial code numbers for my name, Chin Peng, are 7115 and 1627. In our codebooks 7115 is not Chin nor is 1627 Peng. The codebook users have an understanding between them as to which codebook to use.'

'That is wonderful,' Ah Fat gushed. 'Won't that be too sophisticated to use for *Red Tidings*?'

Chin Peng did not immediately answer the question but took another piece of paper from his pocket and gave it to Ah Fat. 'Show the mole this permit signed by me for permission to tell you everything. To start with, your *Red Tidings* can tell our comrades what they only need to know merely using the fourth character method. I am sure our – what shall I call them? – normal publications are all sedulously monitored but that way yours won't be so we can hoodwink our enemies.'

'That is a clever move, Comrade Secretary General,' said Ah Fat, unctuously with his secret thought in mind. *I'll work on that later, best done with Mr C C Too down in Kuala Lumpur...*

The Secretary General noticed a far-away look in Ah Fat's eyes. 'You do understand, don't you?' he said slightly sharply, 'because there is one other point I wish you to make clear to the person whose name is on that piece of paper. From now on whenever the mole sends me anything, for security reasons she must only sign her letters "Ng Heng, Representative of the Malayan Races Liberation Army". This is especially important in any document that refers to peace talks and amnesty.'

'I fully understand, Comrade,' Ah Fat answered, poker-faced. 'I was just digesting all the implications. I congratulate you on your resourcefulness.' Chin Peng looked smug. 'I expect you would like me to go sooner than later.'

'Yes. Go on your Thai passport and fly to Kuala Lumpur on Thai Airways. I won't lay down how long you will be away but try to come back within a couple of weeks.'

'Comrade, with your permission, I'll take my Bear with me. In these times it is always best not to be by oneself.'

Chin Peng considered that without answering for so long that Ah Fat sensed danger but he need not have worried. 'I was wondering about the budget for two weeks for two of you. Go and see the Comrade Paymaster and work out the cost for the two of you for ten days. If it too expensive you must go by yourself.'

'Comrade Secretary General, I'll go and make arrangements and report to you before I go.' He stood up and saluted but by then Chin Peng was talking to someone else and did not notice, or if he did, he did not bother to respond.

Listening in to the conversation were the Head of the Psyops Department, Lee An Tung, and his Deputy, Chien Tiang. They exchanged glances, nodding slightly. That meant that there was something new to keep tabs on. Neither man had any sense of humour and both took life seriously, as opposed to the MRLA who took life as and how it could. The senior Political Commissar also took it all in but said nothing. *Basically sound but too early for comment.*

2 September 1954, central Malaya: After the withdrawal of A Company from the Jelebu pass area, Brigade launched a three-battalion Operation, *Red Tidings*, against 2 Regiment, MRLA. 1/12 GR's task was to concentrate by helicopters in an area north

of Bahau to search for contacts around various 'gardens'. It was a vast area and even if no traces of guerrillas were found, crops were to be destroyed by uprooting, a laborious and unmilitary task not all that pleasing to the soldiers. Jason's company was sent to the northernmost area, one map sheet of which had not been surveyed so most of it was white, so indicating places pure guesswork. His platoon commanders looked at it dubiously. 'How will we pin-point our grid references?' one asked.

'By keeping a record of the direction of our axis of advance and of covering one map square in one hour of normal movement.'

By Day 3 they had found that the two gardens located by aerial recce had already been harvested. That evening Jason once more called Corporal Kulbahadur Limbu to him. 'Kulé, Chakré and I were told that the daku know that the area to our north is a white map and they could well go there, hoping that we won't find them there. Tomorrow take your section and see what you can find. If you come back with NTR, "nothing to report", that will mean not a twig, blade of grass or leaf is out of place.'

'Saheb, when have I come back with NTR?'

'Not often!' and both of them smiled knowingly, with a wealth of hidden knowledge.

Late that evening the section returned with a grin on every man's face. 'Tracks for at least twelve men found moving north, Hajur, into the start of the white map area,' he reported. 'They can't be more than two days old.'

'Well done. Give me the grid reference and I'll tell Battalion HQ tomorrow morning.'

'Send in your airdrop demand soonest for another five days'

rations and any clothing requirements then follow up,' was the reply. He was also told that Major Henry Gibson was now the new CO and a lieutenant-colonel,' so don't refer to him as Sunray Minor any more.'

Two days later the airdrop had been distributed among the men. One of the joys for the soldiers was the tins of fifty cigarettes that came for each man. The great joke was 'Seven a day and one extra because the Sarkar doesn't make tins of forty-nine sticks.'

By then CT tracks were only occasionally visible and movement with full packs was slow. By noon next day the tracks had disappeared.

There were two main methods of patrolling: one, 'fan' patrols, moving on the pattern of 'ribs' of a fan, usually ten degrees apart, and the other used in hilly country along the ridges and down on either side, 'linear' patrols. Jason's orders were '2 Platoon will move east and 3 Platoon west, 1 Platoon and Company HQ stay here and quietly prepare an overnight base. I'll move with 2 Platoon.' He looked at his watch. 'It's nearly 3 o'clock. We'll patrol for a couple of hours and be back by dusk at the latest.'

About half a mile along the ridge, Jason said 'let's go downhill from here' and halfway down the hill the lead man held up his hand and then put it on his shoulder: OC. *Come forward.*

'Saheb', the soldier said softly, 'look through the gap in the trees at the top of the next ridge.'

Jason saw several pairs of trousers hanging on a vine, presumably drying after being laundered.

'Back we go,' and they cautiously went back to their

overnight camp. When the other patrols had returned, Jason held another 'O' Group. 'There's a guerrilla camp at...' and he described it. 'I have been told not to attack it but to put up a marker balloon...' He was interrupted by a 'stray' Auster aircraft, which unpredictably flew overhead and circled twice round where the trousers had been seen.

Blast it fumed Jason, knowing that the guerrillas had to 'stand to' if an Auster overflew their camp and to evacuate it if it flew round more than once. 'No time for a marker balloon. We'll have to surround it now.' He detailed two platoons to approach from opposite directions and the third platoon and Company HQ to stay where they were and be ready to move forward at short notice.

It had, unusually, not rained for some days so the undergrowth was cracklingly noisy. Not to alert the guerrillas to their presence, movement was, therefore, slower than normal. After nearly an hour with nothing happening, Jason became impatient. 'Chakré, tell you what I'll do. I'll go to just below the camp and signal to the surrounding troops who can't be far away to move in quickly. You and the LMG gunner with Company HQ, stay by the stream at the bottom. Keep me covered.'

When about fifteen yards below the edge of the camp, Jason crawled upwards and slowly lifted his head to see if he could see the encircling troops. Nothing. *On up higher for another look.*

The last two guerrillas were on the point of leaving when one of them heard a suspicious noise. He went to the edge, rifle ready cocked and slowly lifted his head to see what was causing it. He saw nothing but recognised the noise of foliage being crushed. He put his rifle to his shoulder and waited, expectedly.

At the bottom the two soldiers saw an armed guerrilla peering over the edge. They then saw him put his rifle to his shoulder and wait. *The saheb, too brave at times, is only just out of sight,* both of them thought.

Jason crawled a bit higher, not seeing where the camp edge was from his prone position, lifted his head once more and was momentarily stunned when a bullet was fired at him from about four yards' range, so close to his right ear that he was deafened. At the bottom the LMG gunner opened rapid fire at the guerrilla and Jason saw bullets hitting the trees only inches above his head.

At the first pause in the firing he yelled, 'Cease fire,' voice shriller than normal. As the firing ceased, the surrounding platoons charged in, amazed to see the OC unsteadily getting to his feet and the camp empty. One of the soldiers said, 'Saheb, we heard a voice shouting "cease fire" and thought it was a female daku,' grinning broadly as he did.

Jason subdued his feelings and merely said, 'I saw the man who shot at me limping away. I'd like to follow up but it's too late.' They returned to their overnight base.

The guerrilla who fired at Jason was hit in the leg and so afraid of being captured and tortured was he that, using his rifle as a crutch, he caught up with the others who were waiting for him to join them, hoping he had not been killed. They examined his wound by the light of a fire and one of them gouged out two bullets, put on a rough bandage and bound it as well as he could. 'Are you sure you hit him?'

'Couldn't have missed,' he averred. 'Must be dead. He was the *gwai lo* commander.'

'That was good work killing him. First thing tomorrow morning we must move away quickly, even if it means carrying you,' and they settled down to an uncomfortable night.

That evening's sitrep reported the incident. ''96 Foxtrot overflew an occupied camp twice during our patrol just after seeing some pairs of trousers hanging up to dry. Despite your standing orders about not attacking camps, I judged the situation needed immediate action as it was late in the day. Roger so far, over.'

'Acorn speaking. Wait out, I'll fetch Sunray.'

Jason 'waited out' until he was told Sunray was on set. Coldly, Jason thought, he was told 'Say all again.'

This Jason did, adding that one of the guerrillas was wounded.

'Your reason is accepted until I have a full report. Your task is to follow up the guerrillas. With a wounded man progress will be slow. If you come across a camp you will not, repeat not, attack it but put up your marker balloon. Out.'

No arguments there!

That night, as he lay down to sleep, he rehearsed what had happened earlier on. *The corporal in charge of the shorter encircling group has recently come from the Signal Platoon so was relatively untrained.* Then his thoughts drifted to his near miss...*I may have lost a wife but I still have my life*...he was walking up the aisle and his best man beside him leant over and whispered,

73

'Why are you wearing jungle boots?' He looked down and saw he was bare-footed. 'Your shirt is hanging out at the back,' came another frantic whisper' and he felt around and found he was wearing jungle greens and not his Number 3 Tropical Ceremonial Dress. He woke up, Chakrabahadur's hand on his shoulder. 'Saheb, are you all right?'

'Chakré. Why aren't you asleep?'

'Saheb, I heard you moaning and so came to see what the trouble was.'

'Oh that is kind, very kind,' and, overwhelmed, he said, 'Chakré, you as well as everyone else knows that my woman has run away. In my dream I was to get married and it was going wrong.'

In the dark he did not see Chakré's grin. 'Saheb, don't worry. No river only has one fish,' and he went back to his place. Jason drifted back to sleep with a smile on his face.

6 September 1954, Police HQ, Kuala Lumpur: The phone rang in the office of Too Chee Chew, a.k.a. C C Too, the brilliant propagandist in Special Branch. He was a short, balding man with large horn-rimmed specs and a serious expression which belied a nice sense of humour.

'Too speaking.'

'Mr Too. I'm a friend of yours from up north. You can recognise my voice, can't you?'

'Yes, yes, of course I can. Where are you now?' It was obvious to C C Too that Ah Fat wanted to keep his identity quiet.

'Ten minutes' walk from your HQ.' He changed from English

to Mandarin, not Cantonese. 'Have you got a Chan Man Yee working anywhere near you?'

'Yes, but not in my office. She is in Registry.'

'If I come and see you can you ensure she does not see me?'

'Hm. Like that is it?' Without waiting for an answer, 'You know where I live, don't you?'

Ah Fat did.

'Come and see me this evening at 7 o'clock and I'll give you a meal.'

'Yes, I'd like that. Is there any way you can bring Chan Man Yee's address with you?'

'You don't want it over the phone?'

'Better not. By the way, I've got my Bear with me but, unless you want to see him, I'd like to send him home for a couple of days. He has not seen his family for too long.'

'Understood about the address and let the Bear go home. See you later.'

It was nice for both men to meet up, which they seldom did. After pleasantries and with a drink, 'Tell me all. It must be something serious for you to be here and ask such a question, especially in Mandarin,' said C C Too, chuckling.

'It is. The main cause of my visit is that the Secretary General has asked me to produce a new newspaper, the name of which is to be *Red Tidings* and it is to be printed on paper with a government watermark. But before I go into details of that, what do you know about Chan Man Yee?'

'We have had her vetted and she has nothing against her.'

Ah Fat took the piece of paper Chin Peng had given him out of his pocket and showed it to his host. On seeing her name and Chin Peng's signature, he turned pale. 'Can't believe it, can't believe it,' he whispered to himself. He wiped his brow and took a long pull of his whisky. 'Okay, tell me everything but first of all how do this woman and the Secretary General manage to combine?'

'I do not know the background. I did not want to probe about it in any way but I am to approach her and find out what she has gleaned, unofficially presumably, about any ceasefire and amnesty.'

'So she is in as deeply as all that, is she?' Too said to himself, cursing as he did so.

'Must be if she comes under the direct sway of the Politburo.'

Too cleared his throat. 'With that as a background, tell me everything but before you do, here is the address she has put in her personal file and her telephone number.'

Ah Fat glanced at the scrap of paper on which it was written and then started his brief, first the Secretary General's plan, then his own counter-plan and how his idea of using, or rather of misusing, his and Jason Rance's Chinese nicknames as initial markers that any edition of *Red Tidings* was Ah Fat's special rendering of the Politburo's intentions and instructions.

A servant girl said that a meal for him and his guest was laid so they moved to the dining room. As the Chinese prefer not to talk during their meals, they quickly finished so they could resume their talking back in the other room.

With a brandy in his hand Ah Fat finished his narrative, which had included an up-dating on the general situation of the MCP. C

C Too said 'With that we need to decide how to take advantage of what you have told me.'

'I have a further three more points for you: first, I will go and see Chan Man Yee at her house. I expect her husband, if she has one, or whoever she is living with, has similar ideas as she has. She must not know that you and I have met. Chin Peng thinks I can get some more paper for his new journal from her...'

C C Too broke in. 'Tell her to try and use our paper store rather than buy anything in town. I can keep an eye on the amount of stationary we have and, if I can nab her stealing any, I can give her the sack.'

'Then that answers my second point, which was how will you "play" her now you know her real role?' Ah Fat looked at his watch. 'I must be moving off soon. My wife knows I am back here and is waiting for me so can you briefly tell me how far any ceasefire talks and amnesty plans have reached?'

'There certainly are planning papers circulating but one thing is certain sure, even if there is an amnesty during which the Security Forces observe a ceasefire – and I'm sure the guerrillas will take plenty of advantage of one – the MCP will never be accepted as a legal political party.'

'Talking about peace talks and amnesty, the Secretary General has told me to tell Chan Man Yee from now on whenever she sends anything, especially in any document she might find that refers to peace talks and amnesty, sign it as Ng Heng, Representative of the Malayan Races Liberation Army.'

'How very, very interesting. A tremendous bonus point for us.'

'That makes me happy,' said Ah Fat rising. 'Tell you what, if I were to ring this mole from here, is there any danger of the call being traced?'

C C Too shook his head. 'None whatsoever. In fact, do use my phone so I can listen in to her reply. There it is, in the corner on that table.'

They went over to it and Ah Fat dialled the number. After a few bells, a sleepy voice answered. 'Allo, 'allo.'

Ah Fat used the Cantonese equivalent, '*Wei*,' and continuing in Cantonese asked for her by name at the address on the piece of paper. Yes, it was Chan Man Yee at the other end and briefly, using coded nicknames only the Politburo and one or two others knew, introduced himself as wanting to see her and give her a message from the top. 'It is too late now,' she said, using the same coded words where necessary. As she did, Ah Fat and C C Too exchanged glances. *Proof!*

'Is there any chance of coming to see you tomorrow morning before you go to the office? There is much that I want to say but then there may not be enough time for you to listen to me.'

There was a long pause. 'No. Tomorrow morning is not suitable. Tell you what, when I get to the office, I'll pretend I have to go to the doctor and at, say, around 10 o'clock, you can come. But before I tell you anything, I'll want proof you are who you say you are.'

Ah Fat laughed good-naturedly. 'I'll show you all the proof you want when we meet,' and rang off.

C C Too said, 'It will be interesting indeed if that happens. If she does leave when she says she will it will give us a good chance to search her workplace for any clues. By the way, how will you get back home? It is a bit late for a taxi.'

'Blast. Yes, it is, isn't it?'

'I'll run you back in my car and if there are any points that occur to me, I can ask you as we go.'

'What does she look like and how can I recognise her before she sees me?'

'Short, squat, wears high-heeled shoes. You said you had three points: what is the last one?'

'Yes, of course. I rather got carried away. Sorry. Can you produce about two hundred sheets of the new newspaper's cover? That is something I will find almost impossible to do properly by myself.'

'Have you a motif?'

'Yes, the name was chosen by Chin Peng saying he did not want to go to a Catholic school because of all the preaching of "good tidings" so we hit on the name of *Red Tidings* instead. As for the cover, I'd like to see the Secretary General invoking a congregation, not with "good" but with "red" tidings. That will please his by-now rather deflated ego.'

Mr Too laughed. 'That will give me much pleasure.'

7 September 1954, No. PS 150, Restaurant-cum-bar, 150 Jalan Petaling, Kuala Lumpur: At 8 o'clock Ah Fat went into the cryptically named bar and greeted the owner, Ah Hong, a childhood friend. 'A coffee, please. I'll sit at a table near the window.'

'Back at your old tricks, I suppose,' Ah Hong said with a lopsided grin. 'I stopped playing that game after Mr Rance left for India as, I presume, the intelligence man he always was.'

'Quite right, my old friend, but I have to keep extra special quiet about it.' A waiter took the cup of coffee and put it on the table by the window. 'I'm looking to see if a certain woman leaves from a house just down the road on the other side. If I do see her, I'll call you over to see if you recognise her.'

Ah Hong merely nodded and went to serve a customer who had just come in.

Most office workers were leaving and he did see a short, squat woman come out from the block and look around before going to the bus stop. As she went past on the other side of the street he saw that she did wear high-heeled shoes. He beckoned to Ah Hong. 'There she goes. Know her?'

'Know of her would be more correct. Some of the people who visit her at odd hours come here for a beer afterwards. I never seem as though I am listening in to what they say and that's the way I've been trained. I don't think Jason's father would have allowed them to wander as freely as they seem to be doing.'

'Interesting,' counted his friend. 'I have an interview with her around 10 o'clock, so I'll stick around.'

At a quarter to ten he relieved himself, ready for action. At just before 10 o'clock she came back, looking around as though a bit flustered, and let herself into her front door. Ah Fat waited five minutes to see if there was anyone following her. *No.* He got up, paid the bill, said good bye to Ah Hong and left. He sauntered across the road and as he got to the door of her house it opened and there she was, Chan Man Yee herself. 'Inside,' he hissed at her and, in the hall, pressed Chin Peng's authorisation into her hand. 'Look at this and do not doubt me in any way from now on.' He spoke in exactly the tone of voice someone as senior as he would to one such as her.

'Come with me upstairs to my room,' she said, leading the way. She opened the door into a cheap bed-sitting room, with a small kitchen and wash room to one side. 'Let's have a glass of tea while we talk,' she said, talking off her shoes and going barefooted.

Tea ready and sitting down, Ah Fat told her about his visit and the new newspaper, *Red Tidings*, the need for paper and how much could she tell him about a ceasefire and an amnesty. 'The Secretary General has the greatest faith in you and is sure you can bring him up to date with what is happening in that busy office you work in.'

She was pleased with his praise and started to go into detail, echoing almost exactly what C C Too had said the night before, using certain phrases that could only have been read from any reports he had made or received. 'Thank you, that is most interesting. And the Secretary General has asked if you can get enough paper for cyclostyling our first edition and also others.'

'How much does he want?'

'How much can you get?'

She looked doubtful. 'I can't get too much from the office otherwise they will notice. If you can lend or give me money I know where to buy the type of paper you need. Will that be all right?'

'What the Politburo is looking for is paper that has a

government water mark in it. Paper from shops won't have that, will it?'

'No. And now I think about it, not all our paper does have a government watermark.' She looked out of the little window in thought. 'Tell you what. Come back here tomorrow evening and take however much I will have brought back. I can't do more than that, much as I'd like to.'

'Good. That will certainly be a great help. Thank you for the tea. I'll come back tomorrow at dusk. If anybody were to ask you why you need the paper, please, for Lenin's sake, keep the Party's name out of it.'

'As always, however hard it is,' she said through clenched teeth.

'I have a special message for you from Comrade Chin Peng: whenever you send a report on any proposed amnesty and peace talks, just to make sure that no one finds out your name, sign it "Ng Heng, Representative of the Malayan Races Liberation Army".'

Her eyes glistened at the delicious secrecy of that message.

He bid her farewell, took a taxi back home and rang C C Too. He told him how Chan Man Yee had echoed his words and how she was going to collect some government watermarked paper for him. 'If you can let her have some, it will make my life easier the other end. Oh yes, I have learnt that she has visitors you and yours would not approve of.'

'No, I'll catch her as she leaves and not allow her to return. I'll drop some paper off at your place some time tomorrow or the next day.'

8 September 1954, Police HQ, Kuala Lumpur: At closing time people locked their office and went to the janitors' office to give the keys in. Chan Man Yee wondered why people were taking so long about it and saw to her horror that there was a spot check. Three policemen were searching the bags of the staff. She froze but was pushed on by those behind her, who were grumbling at being late. *'I'll have to think of an excuse,* she fretted, having, in her bag one 'long ream' of government watermarked paper, five hundred and sixteen sheets. As one policeman searched her bag another stood in front of her and the third behind her. When asked what she was doing with so much paper, she became flustered and said something about having homework to do. 'Not good enough,' said the senior policeman and gave the sheets to another policeman before marching her off to see the Duty Officer.

Unsatisfactory answers followed probing questions until the Duty Officer said, 'You will have to spend the night in the cells, I am sorry to say,' not looking at all sorry. 'It is too late to hear your case now. I'll arrange a session for early tomorrow.'

9 September 1954, central Malaya: A Company had managed a follow-up of the group the Auster had alerted as they came across tracks for several men, one of whom was dragging his leg as he walked. *So he was hit.* It was on the third day of steady patrolling after the unsuccessful contact, with the countryside becoming steeper, thicker and more rugged that the patrol Jason was leading heard the sound of someone cutting a tree. By then there was such a depth of knowledge of jungle lore that by the sound made they knew it was a 'palm cabbage' tree that was being chopped down for its delicious fruit. There was a small stream in front of them. The cutter could be no one but a daku. They were not near enough to hear any voices. *Back*. Trying to leave as few foot prints as possible they returned to their overnight base where they waited for the other patrols to return.

During that time Jason thought he ought to warn Sunray of the situation. He sent a message in key, not voice, 'Charlie Tango located. Golf Romeo uncertain because no features on map.' *This grid reference lark is a puzzle.* 'Will make close recce later today. Marker balloon only to be placed later.' *If that does not satisfy His Highness, nothing will.*

Once all were back and a brew of tea was being prepared, Jason held an 'O' Group and told them what he had discovered. 'Corporal Kulbahadur Limbu, Chakré Rai and I will do a close recce, starting,' he looked at his watch, 'in half an hour at 1445 hours. No jungle boots, only canvas shoes, no equipment, only bandolier and weapon. The rest, under the Company 2ic, will be ready to make a frontal attack in the direction of any firing should it be opened against us. Don't worry about hitting us as we will squirm away to a flank.'

'Saheb,' asked the 2ic anxiously, 'are you sure you yourself should go?'

'Gurkha Captain saheb, yes. We have practised this enough times. Also, if I hear any Chinese spoken it could mean we know more about who and how many are in the camp.'

Appreciative grins showed they understood. After their brew, the three of them, putting leaves into their jungle hat and a camouflage net over their lower face – 'If an enemy appears to look straight at you, freeze and he will probably not see you' – with Kulbahadur in front, set off. They knew what to do: on a compass bearing leading to the camp site, five to ten yards apart, they slowly moved to where the tree cutting had been heard. Inching their way forward, they found a cut palm cabbage and saw tracks for three. These they followed until Kulbahadur stopped. 'Can you see a sentry?' Jason quietly asked.

Kulbahadur nodded to a flank. 'Back fifty yards.'

They then cautiously started to circle the camp clockwise, keeping ears and eyes on high alert. After an agonizingly slow two hundred paces, they stopped, waited for ten minutes, then again moved in, this time more like seventy-five paces, their having gone too far to the left. Once more they hid behind trees and listened. *Yes. Voices.* Back again and carry on with the encirclement. Four times they approached the camp and by then they had fully marked its boundaries, where the sentry posts were, where the water point was, not that either mattered if the place was to be bombed, but did matter for putting up the marker balloon. Only once did Jason pick up what was said and that was that the CT had no idea that any Security Forces were in the area.

'Back we go,' said Jason and, by dusk, they had reached their overnight base. Jason called 'Sig-nel ustad, bring a message pad,' and he wrote a short message. 'Camp fully recced. Details tomorrow,' and gave it to the radio operator. 'Send this by key.'

After it was sent, 'Anything for us?'

'No, Hajur, except a "Roger. out" from Sunray.'

After their meal Jason said that, at first light, he would take three men and the marker balloon 'to a place I have already chosen. As you know, there is a canvas bucket for water into which we put the powder. The hot air that comes out from the wet powder must be put under the open mouth of the balloon which we first unroll. As the balloon fills up, we must make fully sure that it does not fly away so its neck must be firmly held but not so that the gas cannot get into it. Once the balloon is full, we tie up its base with its opening still above the bucket then cut off the end. Make sure our khukris are sharp. The water, bubbling and probably making a hissing noise, must be tipped away. We tie the string, knotting it really tight at the base before letting it fly up above the trees. We then tie the end of the string to a tree and it's back here quickly and quietly. Let's check the balloon now.'

The three men to go with Jason did a 'dry run' on what to do on the morrow and felt confident. Once again only weapons would be taken, no equipment. Following them 2 Platoon would move to an observation position to cover the balloon party. 'Just in case,' as Jason put it.

The guerrillas had no idea that their camp had been surrounded. It was a new one and they were tired. 'It was that enemy plane that alerted us,' the commander said, looking at the wounded man. 'Now we will probably be safe for a while.'

10 September 1954, Kuala Lumpur: In the early hours a three-man bug-fixing team entered the block of flats in which were Chan Man Yee's rooms. It was easy work because there were no special security arrangements. One man stayed to put a bug hidden in the phone, activated on sound, to record 'open' speech and the two others went down to the basement. Using their torches, they went by a little-used tunnel to where the telephone cable came into it and followed it along the wall to the central panel near a wire mesh storage space. The senior man opened a metal tool kit and took out the induction tap and cable. The junior man was told to unscrew the cover on the central panel and attach the induction clamp to the line and tap the device into place without touching the wire so making it difficult to detect. The two men wedged a small battery-powered transmitter between a beam and the ceiling then ran a black cable from the induction tap behind a pipe and plugged the end into the transmitter. The induction tap, now clamped, would broadcast to any truck parked not far off where it would be recorded on tape. They connected one end of the antenna wire to the terminal and, unreeling it, taped it to the side of the beam then activated the transmitter and hit the 'Test' button, ringing the phone number in Chan Man Yee's room. The man there answered.

'Tidy up and get out,' he was told. It had not taken long: 'Said it was only a short job, didn't I?' said the senior man in a low voice, grinning with satisfaction at their handiwork.

Next morning the phone tappers gave their report to C C Too. 'You will be able to record and monitor any calls back here, will you?' he asked.

'We hope so but if not, we can always go back and recover the recording device, putting another in its place.'

'That was good work. Thank you' and they were dismissed.

Two hours later the woman was brought out of the cell and,

thoroughly frightened, taken by the Security men to C C Too's office. 'Undo her handcuffs but stay close to her to see she does not do herself any damage.'

'Explain yourself,' C C Too told her, wondering what story she would come up with.

Whimpering, she said that she had promised to take some books she had borrowed from a friend and, in a hurry, she had put in the paper instead. 'Imagine my surprise when it was found,' she gasped, finding her courage rising. 'I could have explained that yesterday but I was so frightened I became tongue-tied.'

Mr Too stared fixedly at her for a while, saying nothing. She dropped her gaze, wondering if her excuse would be taken as valid.

The two guards were surprised at C C Too's verdict. 'I'll accept your story this time however unlikely it sounds. It's a pity the owner of the books came to your office to take them away before we searched it.'

She tried to control her gasp of relief when the guards were told to let her go. She certainly had not expected to be let free. *So I am under no suspicion* she crowed.

She had a fine story to tell Ah Fat that evening. '...and so I have no paper for you. Do you think you can get some from any other source?'

No, sadly, that was not an option. 'I'll tell you what. Now we are together, tell me all you can about what is going on where you work. I know that the Central Committee will vote in your favour if I can tell them what fine work you are doing.'

And out it all came, faithfully recorded on the tape in the basement as well as in Bluff Road. Avenues of misdeeds, of penetration and of finding out of where guerrilla sources lurked were revealed.

At a quarter to midnight Ah Fat said he would have to leave her. 'I will let our comrades know just how well you are doing,' he said as he left. As he reached his house he heard his wife answering the phone. 'Here he is,' she said, handing it over to her husband.

'Well done, you've hit a gold mine.' C C Too was jubilant. 'When will you go back north?'

'I have permission for a few days yet. I can't tell you how marvellous life here is after my other ...'

'No need to say it. We are richer by far for what you're doing. We owe you a large debt. I'll get the paper delivered to your house tomorrow.'

11 September 1954, Kuala Lumpur: 'Tell me what you have in mind about this watermarked paper,' Mr Too asked Ah Fat.

'At the back of my mind I have an idea: you and I only to know how to put a, what, warning at the start of any publication that it is I who doctored the text.'

'Sounds intriguing. Tell me more.'

'Jason and I are pals from way past and if I can involve him somehow in this it will be a "feel-good factor" for me. How to? I will use our nicknames. However, I have never forgotten how my nickname had been known to some of the comrades when Jason saved my life back in 1952. I can't take chances on still being unknown so I'll disguise them.' He picked up a piece of paper and a pencil from Too's desk. 'Any document that I have monitored my name P'ing Yee, with the Yee 耳, Ear, in P'ing Yee , 平耳, will be miswritten as 宜, 'suitable', the first impression the reader would get is that the writer must have meant 'cheap', Pian Yee, 便宜' as he mentally saw it, writing down the characters as he spoke. 'Or even the character P'ing,平 in P'ing Yee, 'flat' combined with the character Yee for 'suitable', would give a nonsense meaning of 'flat suitable' in English that makes no sense so would be taken as a misprint. As it also makes no sense in Chinese, the reader would probably try and determine the meaning from the context. For Jason's name, Shandung P'aau, Shandong Cannon, 山東炮, make the third character miswritten as B'aau, 包, meaning bun or bread roll, so Jason can hide his name as Shandong Bun, 山東包.

'I don't think it matters if suspicion is smelt as quite often there is no obvious sense where there is no counterpart in Chinese that has to be translated from a foreign language or even when writing a non-Chinese phonetic rendering, the sounds required must have their original basic meanings.'

13 September 1954, central Malaya: At dawn Jason and his three men set off to go as far as the small stream where the cutting was heard to fill the canvas bucket, followed by 2 Platoon. One man filled the bucket to the brim and brought it back. Jason felt that any surging by the chemicals would waste them so emptied about a quarter of the water. 'Get the balloon out, unroll it and lay it flat. Open the end and be ready to hold it over the bucket as soon as I've put the powder in. Hold your noses, it'll stink,' he said softly as he undid the tin and poured the granulated chemical into the water. It hissed loudly and smelt vilely. Quickly two men held the end of the balloon over the bucket and gradually, gradually it filled with the gassy effervescence the chemicals had generated and lifted itself upright.

Once it had started tugging one of the men held on to it to keep it steady. Jason saw the bubbling in the bucket had ceased. 'Grasp the balloon's neck before you double the end back to cut it so no gas escapes, then tie the end as tightly as you can, let the balloon rise to the end of the string and tie it to the lowest branch of that small tree,' he pointed out with his chin.

The water was poured into the stream to try and get rid of the smell and away they went, back to their overnight camp.

Looking at his white map and trying to work out how much ground they had covered, at what speed and what his previously reported grid references were, Jason sent a message to Battalion HQ telling them where he thought it was most likely he had put the marker balloon up.

At midday the set was opened again and a priority message was sent from base. 'Move back four thousand yards now. Bombing will come in early tomorrow. Then advance with all speed to assess damage.'

They packed up and almost untactically fast, back they went.

As there were no guerrillas in the area and it had rained heavily at dusk, Jason told his platoon commanders to gather logs and let the men dry their clothes before bedding down. The RMO had always wondered why A Company's sick rate was less than the other three companies': this was the reason.

In the guerrilla camp it was time to cook their morning meal which was normally around 10 o'clock. Down to the water point the fatigue party went to fill their pots. One man sniffed. 'Has the water gone bad?' he asked.

Another man put his nose near the water and sniffed. 'Yes, it smells of chemical.'

'Go back and tell the Comrade Political Commissar and the Comrade Military Commander to come and see if they agree with us.'

He did but both senior comrades were scathingly recalcitrant but, after insistence, went to the stream. 'Yes, you are right. The enemy is trying to poison us. Go back and bring the Duty Section.'

Off he trotted and brought the Duty Section back. 'Follow the stream for as long as you can smell the strange odour. If you find anything come back and tell us. Go very carefully, it could be an enemy ambush. They are capable of many dirty tricks.'

The comrades moved off, snail-slow, noses stream-wards, eyes jungle-wards. 'Comrade, look at that in the water, 'the man in front turned to the senior comrade. 'Is it a tortoise or what?'

'Three men take a prone position where you are and don't move until I tell you. I'll take the others back to camp and get a force to search the jungle either side to see if there is an ambush.'

The Political Commissar stayed back and the Military Commander took a section to the right and a senior comrade a section to the left. Nothing was found and as they went to see what was in the water, a bright young comrade saw the string of the marker balloon jerk as the balloon was pulled by the wind.

'Comrade, look at this string. What is it?'

The Military Commander went over to it, pulled it and felt a weight. He looked up and saw a large red balloon on the end. 'The cunning swine,' he ejaculated viciously. 'That can only mean they will come and bomb us. Cut the string, go back to camp, get ready to evacuate it then we'll move out, AT TOP SPEED.'

Away they scuttled and by dusk they were several thousand yards away.

A Company spent an expectant night, trying to visualise the bombing. The men said that the aircraft would kill all the guerrillas and how clever it was for the OC Saheb to do what had been done. The radio was opened for the morning call and the message was the same as before, 'Move back fastest and search the bombed area.'

'Wilco, out.'

Before the five Lincoln bombers of the Royal Australian Air Force reached their target, an Auster flew over the suspected area. 'No balloon,' the pilot reported. 'I'll put a smoke marker where I believe the balloon should have been then leave the area to you.'

The message was acknowledged and the bombers dropped their bombs where they saw the smoke. In A Company's position the earth shook as though there was an earthquake.

The pilots then overflew the bombed area and heavily machine-gunned it, 'that'll keep the bastards' heads down, Mate, won't it?' one said.

'Sure will,' he answered, unaware that as A Company was getting ready to move out several empties from the machine gunning were being scattered near where they were.

No movement through the jungle had ever been quicker than A Company's approach march. At the scene of the bombing flattened trees were everywhere...except near where the balloon had been flown, which was still pristine jungle. 'Saheb, look there,' one man excitedly called out, pointing.

Jason could hardly believe his eyes: an unexploded bomb! 'All searching stop,' he called out. 'Go back to the nearest stream. Put out sentries and cook your morning meal.'

As he turned to go he saw that he was where the daku had been in their camp and noticed a patch of white on the ground. *Ash!* He bent down to feel it. Cold. That meant they could not have left when the Auster flew over before the bombers came but yesterday. A thought struck him: *did they find the balloon string, cut it and leave then? Looks like it. There'll be no point in searching locally.* In bitter disappointment he went back and joined his men.

The operator called Battalion HQ and Jason was immediately asked for a report by Sunray. 'My personal camp recce was text book. However the bombers had to be sent for, an exercise in optimism over reality. I quote "some are wise and some are otherwise" unquote. The area where we recced the camp and put up the marker balloon is untouched and where we heard the Charlie Tango is an unexploded bomb. I found some ash in their camp site which is cold so it looks as if they found the balloon and left yesterday. They will be a long way from here now. We are keeping well away from the bomb in case it goes off. Roger so far, over.

'1, roger, but you must control your bitter language, over.'

'I strongly recommend that I leave the immediate area now and search for tracks a day's walk distant. I suggest move north-easterly. Your views, please, over.'

'Open this evening for further orders, out.'

The CO spoke to the Brigadier by phone. 'Henry, you won't believe it but I have been told by the RAAF that one of its bombers had an unfused bomb. If Rance finds that near the guerrilla camp it will show that that is why there are no casualties.'

'He has already found it and is keeping well away from it.'

'I'll have to send in a bomb disposal team by chopper but I'll wait a day or two for that. Any live guerrillas will have, by now, left the area. Top up your men's rations and let them go, I suggest move a map square northeast, and start another search for them.'

'Okay, sir. I'll pass that on.'

Jason's soldiers were flabbergasted by what had happened...after successfully tracking the enemy, after so nearly getting them after seeing those trousers hanging up to dry, after the OC saheb and his group had made such a good recce of the enemy camp, then putting up that balloon, all difficult and skilful to do really well... who would have thought it would turn out like this? As they were cooking their meal, the radio operator was told to 'fetch Sunray' so called Jason to the set.

'Submit an airdrop demand for five more days this evening. Prepare a DZ. Your task is to move northeast by minimum one map square. Continue patrolling to pick up any tracks there may be.'

'Wilco out,' was Jason's weary reply.

'Saheb, you didn't try and persuade the CO not to bomb, did you?' his Company 2ic asked, almost unwilling to broach the subject.

'No, Saheb, I didn't. If I had argued you would have had a new OC A Company.'

3

13 September 1954, Police HQ, Kuala Lumpur: 'We've hit gold dust. How can we make it into platinum?' C C Too asked Ah Fat. They were closeted in the former's office.

Ah Fat considered the question. 'The Secretary General has told me he wants me to be the editor of this new paper, *Red Tidings*. The paper we normally use doesn't have watermarks and that is one reason for sending me here. In any case, the rank and file of the MCP are not the type who know what a watermark is, let alone how to look for one or even recognise one. Leave it or what?'

'Before I answer that, where will you do your compilation and printing? In your base camp in Thailand?'

'That certainly seems to be the idea but I don't like it. It's too out-of-the-way for easy access for the couriers from Malaya. I suppose you know that there are two types of courier, a main one or two for long-distance work and local ones who know the terrain like their own back garden. I would prefer to move to somewhere like Ha La[3] village, which is just inside Thailand and has no Customs or police to worry us, nor any propaganda

---

3 The village of Ha La, in map square VE 2126, was no longer traceable when this book was written.

merchants looking over my shoulder. Couriers would also find it easier or I could even set up a place over the border and use *t'o yan* – the orang asli or indigenous people – as storekeepers and to give advanced warning were any Security Forces to be in the area. Unlikely, though possible.'

'Do you think the Secretary General will allow that?'

'Difficult to say off-hand. He might if I make periodical visits to him for copy.'

A gleam came into C C Too's eyes. 'Tell you what. Let me make you some paper like what we have with a government watermark with an MCP watermark. You, in an editorial, can warn the readers to look and see which watermark is on the paper. The MCP one will be touted as genuine government propaganda. You then adapt the version for the Politburo on government watermarked sheets as and how you like, making sure that you keep the two lots completely separate.'

'Have you the funds?'

'Have you the ink?' and both men laughed.

16 September 1954, central Malaya: The daku commander felt smug in foretelling that the marker balloon was indicative of a bombing attack. He had ordered an immediate evacuation, initially carrying the wounded man on a comrade's back with another comrade carrying two packs for speed. They had moved well over a mile before dark and had been thoroughly shaken by the bombing. His men looked at him with admiration, knowing he had saved their lives. 'What we'll do now is what we have practised in the past. Two groups will move off on different axes leaving tracks, while our HQ group will move with the utmost caution in between. Our comrade here,' and he pointed to a young man, 'will make noises like a tiger roaring with this other comrade,' indicating an older man, 'moving at the back, will make the tiger's pug marks. Nobody will ever guess that the tiger is moving backwards, even if they do see the tracks. After all this time no one is better than us,' and he laughed. The others joined in, feeling that they could escape from even the most observant trackers following them. Even so, we will carry out our concealment drill by walking backwards into a stream before making ourselves comfortable for the night, or maybe even longer.'

It had been a bulkier than usual airdrop as by then most of the men's canvas jungle boots, never strong items, were torn and apart from being easy for leeches to get inside, were unsuitable except on flat ground. Another marker balloon had been sent – *let them fly one off their own bat*, thought Jason sulkily – and, because they were higher up, so colder than usual, Jason allowed each man to have his own bottle of rum – he never touched the stuff – as an evening tipple of rum and a handful of heated up tiny prawns was by now the men's traditional and only relaxation.

After moving off from the airdrop, patrols picked up tracks for at least ten men, one who was limping, moving north-easterly. They heard a helicopter to their southwest, most likely carrying the bomb disposal team and escort.

It had been four days since they had heard the palm tree

being cut. At his orders the night before Jason had stressed that he did not expect to catch up with the daku easily or quickly, so movement, now that the tracks had been found, need not be as slow as if they were near. The jungle was prime, the trees tall and undergrowth scant, so tracking was done by ground signs, not top signs. Some of the former are foot and boot marks, bruises or 'bleeding' roots, disturbances of insect life, mud left from footwear, while some of the latter are broken twigs or bent leaves, scratches, cuts, bruised moss or handholds on trees, big spiders' webs with spiders as big as a clenched fist, broken, changes in colour and natural position of vegetation.

Halfway through the day the tracks were lost so a halt was called and more patrolling initiated, this time the 'fan' method, even though going sideways across the grain of the high ground was a penance and left traces as feet slipped. 'They are skilled operators and know their jungle lore backwards,' Jason said. 'They are as keyed up to danger as are wild animals.'

That evening 2 Platoon and 3 Platoon reported tracks. Each had taken a compass bearing of the axis and they were 15 degrees apart. The white map was no use for showing any high ground where there might be caves to hide in or swift rivers difficult to cross. Corporal Kulbahadur said, 'Saheb, I have an idea. It is just possible that those tracks are decoy tracks leading us away from their real position. One lot of tracks was moving at 12 degrees and the other at 27. They were more obvious than normal. Suppose the main axis is 18 or 19 degrees and tomorrow, say, those radial tracks will merge. All those angles are difficult to follow exactly on a compass as none has a thick black line opposite it.'

Listening heads nodded appreciatively. 'The only problem is what will the middle group do to get the other patrols back? They don't have any radio.'

Jason stared with a 'thousand-yard' look in his eyes, trying to envisage how to react to what Kulbahadur was suggesting. Even if he was wrong in his estimation, ground would be covered so any tracks could be picked up. How long before tracks had been made could often be gauged by the state of the bent foliage that had brushed against: the dryer it was, the longer the time of movement had elapsed.

'I know it's unpopular but an early meal tomorrow.' He looked up and saw disappointed faces. Gurkhas are not 'good' early eaters. 'Cancel that. Start cooking at 0430 hours and carry your food in your mess tins to eat later. We'll move after our morning brew. Full water bottles.'

They stopped at their normal meal time. 'Saheb,' Jason said to his 2ic. 'Get the men to fill their water bottles at the next stream but not, repeat not, wash out their mess tins in it.' The Gurkha Captain looked at Jason quizzically but said nothing. *The saheb never gives an order without a reason.* 'Let us say, Saheb, that the daku smelt the balloon stuff in their water downstream from us. I ordered that it be thrown into the water to keep the smell from the land. I've learnt my lesson the hard way. Just suppose they are not far away downstream and again smell us through their water before we have a chance to deal with them?' Recognition came into the Gurkha Captain's eyes. 'Maybe I am too cautious but...' and he left the rest of his sentence unsaid.

At two in the afternoon the leading scout stopped and,

with a hand signal, called his platoon Sunray forward. 'Look, tiger tracks.' At that very moment a tiger was heard calling not so far away. Jason was sent for. Looking at the tracks he was doubtful but, so that any suspicion could be resolved, he sent for Kulbahadur.

The corporal silently came up and Jason pointed to the ground. With obvious glee he said, 'Saheb, that tiger is moving backwards! Look,' and, moving in front of it, he turned and, bending down, splayed his fingers over it. They fitted nicely. 'The end man is turning and making them.'

'But the roaring?'

'Saheb,' he grinned wolfishly, 'if you practised, you could do better!'

'So the noise and the fake tracks are the guide to get the other patrols back on course?'

Another huge grin and a nod; 'Yes.'

'That means they can't be far away.'

'Saheb, let me take one man and I'll find out just where they are. It shouldn't take us too long.'

Jason allowed that and told the others to take up all-round defence positions while they waited for the two men to make their recce and return, which they did within the hour.

'We have found out where they are and their tactics. With the tiger tracks behind them they moved downhill to a large stream and before they went into the water, they turned round and went in backwards. The prints of the balls of their feet were deeper than their heel prints.'

'Very well done, Kulé,' Jason congratulated him, thinking

that if his work so far didn't deserve a medal, what did? He remembered what the CO of the Nepalese battalion he had been seconded to, to teach sniping, during the war in Burma had written about one of his men: 'He is not a man but a superman.' *So is Kulé.*

'I am sure we would have been successful if we had not been ordered to use that marker balloon. You think the same, don't you?' Jason asked his platoon commanders at that evening's 'O' Group.

Yes, they did.

'What if we find the daku in their camp this time? Go through that balloon and bombing all over again?' and he answered his own query with a Gurkha saying, 'In the house, uncle die; in the trap, fish to fry.'

The CSM added his own adage, 'Monkey's tail, neither walking stick nor weapon,' untactfully referring to the failed bombing raid.

His 2ic and platoon commanders pondered on those unexpected words of wisdom. 'So, Saheb, what is your answer?' one of them asked.

'Report that we have found a camp and attack it is the second thing I'll do, though, in fact, calling in the bombers is the second last thing I'll do. I'll send Corporal Kulbahadur Limbu and his squad to find out exactly where the daku are hiding. Once we know that, I'll send two platoons behind the camp to lay a linear ambush on one side of the stream and the third platoon to open fire from in front but not attack. That will make them run away into the ambush. As they will only have been there a short time there won't be any proper defence positions so that will make our task easier. My report will be correct, that we laid an ambush for them and it was successful, although of course until we have killed or captured them we cannot say we have had success.'

They talked around that and found they liked it.

'Saheb, shall I go now?' asked Kulbahadur.

Jason looked at his watch. 'No, I don't like the idea of even you moving through this type of country at night. Go first thing tomorrow. The remainder will stay here until you return and then I'll confirm my orders.'

Unusually, the place where they had stopped was relatively open, with no tall trees for a hundred or so paces. Jason looked at it with a practiced eye and thought, *if we do have casualties we can quickly make this into a touch-down, not a hover, LP.*

By noon on the morrow Kulbahadur returned. He and his men looked strained, as well they might, as doing any recce in such a roundabout manner is never easy. But there was an exultant smile on his face. 'Saheb, the camp is not far away. There are good ambush positions on either side of the stream on the far side of their camp. We know they won't want to stop and fight it out like they used to a couple of years ago so your idea of frightening them away means they can only escape downstream.'

'I fully agree, Kulé. I can now plan my orders with confidence.'

Jason called for his 'O' Group: 'It will be a rough night for all of us. 1 Platoon will open fire from in front but not attack the camp. Flank sections move out at 0550 hours to be ready to move forward when I give our battle cry at 6 o'clock. 'That means lying up just out of earshot of it. 2 and 3 Platoons will move to take up positions along the stream, giving the camp site a wide berth. If anyone snores, his mate must wake him. Insect repellent can be used as the stream flows down from the camp so any smell will go downstream so 1 Platoon upstream will be the mosquitoes' and the leeches' overnight meal.'

Details were discussed and commanders quizzed as to exactly what to do. 'You will decide, 2 and 3 Platoon Commanders, among yourselves, where to lay the ambush, which platoon will be ahead and which behind. Place the men in pairs, not singly. No following of any daku over the stream if he tries to escape. Let the LMG team look after anyone who tries his luck that way.' After tea and biscuits, much quicker than cooking a meal, away the ambush group went, as quietly and slowly as 'a moving ambush'.

'Sig-nel,' softly called Jason after the last man had disappeared, 'Open your set and I'll give you a message to send in key. While the radio operator was hanging his aerial Jason wrote: 'Have good chance of ambushing enemy group. Will observe radio silence until earliest 0800 hours tomorrow.'

After the attacking platoon's meal was cooked and eaten, by turns, well in the rear and to a flank of their position to prevent downstream air permeating the CT camp, Jason said, 'We'll move forward to near the daku camp just before dusk and lie low all night, 2 Section left, 3 Section right and Company HQ with 1 Section in the middle. When we attack tomorrow morning we'll do it as we did in Burma against the Japs. I'll shout "ayo Gurkhali chaaaaaarge" but give the daku time to bug out into the ambush and only then in we'll go. By then the camp will be empty but we may have to shoot a couple of idle men.'

The older soldiers grinned at that.

At dusk 1 Platoon moved slowly forward, on a compass bearing of 18 degrees. Just before last light, talking in the camp was heard. Jason oozed forward and listening intently he heard whom he presumed was the Political Commissar congratulating the man who roared like a lion – 'he says he has a sore throat' – and the track layer – 'he says he has a stiff back' – and there was a muffled response of suppressed laughter. 'No one can find us here. We are so safe there's no need to put out any sentries. I know that that is against all orders but we have a long way to go tomorrow and our wounded comrade needs carrying so we all need a good night's sleep.'

Creeping back to where 1 Platoon Commander was Jason told him what he'd heard. 'Saheb, in a low voice pass it around your men.'

The other two platoons reached the stream half an hour before last light. 2 Platoon Commander, the senior of the two, moved with OC 3 Platoon and silently pointed out where the first two men of 3 Platoon would take up their positions, with ten to twelve paces between each pair, depending on the ground. Section LMGs were sited as the column slowly moved forward. The ambush would only be sprung when 2 Platoon Commander opened fire. Then every man would fire at an enemy target in front of him.

It was a long night for everyone. Chakré was by Jason's side and, turn by turn, each nodded off. At 5 o'clock Chakré shook Jason and woke him. At a quarter past 5 Jason said to 1 Platoon Commander, 'Saheb, if anyone has to go into the bushes, send him fifty yards behind.'

The ambush platoons were also ready at dawn. Could this, at last, be a successful ambush? They all hoped so. It had been an uncomfortable night and the men were keen for action. 'Only fire after you hear fire opened,' was passed down the line.

We're ready!

When it was light enough to see, Jason looked left and right. Men were standing up, weapons cocked and ready. He signalled to move slowly forward and when he saw the camp he shouted 'ayo Gurkhali chaaaaaarge' and forward they went, keeping their line, shooting. 'Shoot anyone you see in front of you,' he yelled and once again, 'ayo Gurkhali chaaaaaarge.'

In the guerrilla camp there was pandemonium. Daku standing orders were to sleep with pack and weapon always in reach. The Political Commissar and the Military Commander both shouted at once 'move downstream quickest. Assemble only on a tiger call.' The daku, rubbing their eyes and cursing, grabbed packs and weapons scuttled away precipitously...from in front, heavy fire was opened, by LMGs and rifles. Screaming and yelling reverberated. 'Now move forward,' yelled Jason, 'but be ready in case any daku try to come back this way.'

Two men had taken up kneeling positions behind trees at the

far end of the camp and saw two daku stumbling away in panic. Both were killed by the ambush.

One man lying in the camp was still alive so Jason went to look at him. 'Who are you? What unit are you?'

'2 Regiment,' he gasped, sobbing. *So these are Ten Foot Long's men*. Taking his First Field Dressing out of his front pocket, Jason opened the daku's shirt. The death rattle 'gargled' in his throat as Jason's hands were on the man's skin, about to cover the wound. Jason stood up and put the dressing back into his pocket, not realising that as the man had died his soul had entered him. He would not find that out for a little while.

The Platoon Commander at the far end of the ambush had waited until the leading daku were opposite him and, shouting 'fire', opened up. Immediately everyone else also did, except in the case of, it so happened, the company's Goalkeeper who, in the dim light, thought the man in front of him was a *gora*, so pale was he.

Instinctively he held his fire. There had been rumours of a *gora* among the daku but no one had taken it seriously but, hard to believe, there he was. *Is he there because he can't escape or what?* flashed through the Goalkeeper's mind as he stood up in a mistaken attempt to call him over.

The *gora* turned and, in one skilful shot, wounded the Gurkha with a bullet in the side of his neck. He fell, bleeding severely, unconscious. Men to his right and left felled the firer before quickly patching up the wounded man with their First Field Dressings.

In five minutes there was no more daku movement and the order to cease fire was shouted down the line.

'Is it safe for us to move forward?' Jason bellowed loudly when the firing from in front had ceased.

'Yes, we're checking enemy casualties. Our Goalkeeper is badly wounded.'

Even so, that's a great relief. Phew, and what a gamble. Jason felt elated. His venture had paid off thanks to Corporal Kulbahadur's superb tracking. *I'll most certainly put him in for a decoration. I've said that before and I'll say it again. I must go and see the wounded man.*

There were ten daku bodies, no wounded and no captives. Three of the bodies were of a much paler skin colour than the rest. *They don't look Chinese*, thought the searchers. The first man to have fallen was the lame man, the one who had shot at Jason. Jason looked at him. *He's only a kid, poor fellow.* 'But you joined the wrong side, didn't you,' he said aloud. He saw each corpse had a mattock or an axe. *So they left the Jelebu area to go deep into the jungle, shielded by the white map, to make a garden.*

The unconscious Gurkha was being tenderly looked after

The bodies were centrally dumped and searched for any documents. Several 'rolled slips' were found on one body, presumably the Political Commissar's. These were documents written in tiny characters on diaphanously flimsy paper and rolled up like a mini-sized cigarette for ease of concealment. Jason thought it better not to open them as no tactical benefit would accrue.

When the radio operator had his set ready and contact was made with Battalion HQ, Jason said, 'Sunray call sign 1 on set. Fetch Acorn, over.'

He was answered with 'Wilco. Wait out.'

While waiting Jason took out his note book and to see what he thought was the grid reference of their night-stop before the action.

'Hullo 1. Acorn on set. Send, over.'

'1. We have ambushed and killed ten Charlie Tangos part of figures two regiment, I say again, we have ambushed and killed ten Charlie Tangos. Three do not look like Chinese, too pale. Several rolled slips found. No other docus. Own troops, one wounded in the neck. Casevac heli needed.' He gave the grid reference. 'Heli can land, no need to hover. Over.'

'1. Jolly good show about the CT but bad news about your man. How will you dispose of bodies? Over.'

'1. I have a camera, can take photos and bury. If you want bodies out send heli and bring body bags or equivalent.'

Acorn told him to wait out while he fetched Sunray, who came on set a quarter of an hour later, full of congratulations but concern for the wounded man. 'Casevac heli already asked for. Take wounded man to LP soonest. Keep on listening watch for ETA. How did you manage such an extensive kill? Over.'

'1. Good patrolling and good marksmanship. Details later.'

'1. Have you camera and sufficient film?'

Yes, he had. 'I particularly want photos of the three non-

Chinese corpses,[4] then bury them. Bring out any papers and identification material. How long will it take you to walk out?'

'1. With patrolling, about a week. I'll send an airdrop demand within figures one hour. Over.'

'1. I have been asked by Big Sunray to confirm that you did not attack camp. If you did, he will be angry and you will have to answer.'

Jason grinned. '1. The daku were flushed from a camp site that was too difficult to surround and attack. They thought they were to be attacked, tried to escape and were ambushed as they fled. If this is not good enough, sorry. Too late to undo damage already caused. Over.'

'1. Roger. Careful with your language. Big Sunray says this phase of Operation *Red Tidings* is over but will wait for news of Ten Foot Long's death before terminating it. Send resup details when required and report when bodies buried. Wait out.'

Half a minute later, Sunray was back on the set. '1, how will you manage to dig a communal grave? It will be too difficult with khukris. Over.'

'1. The aim of the group must have been to make a garden for there were many mattocks and axes left for us to pick up and use, over.'

'1 Roger, out.'

Jason sent his Company 2ic and one section to take the wounded

---

4 They were Japanese. About thirty moved to the guerrillas after the war and only two, Hashimoto Shigeyuki and Tanaka Kiyoaki survived and returned to Japan in 1998.

man to where they had waited the day before to make the place suitable for a heli touchdown rather than a hover. 'Saheb, get your men to light a fire and be ready to make smoke when you hear the noise of the heli engine and also put out panels to make an H, pinning them firmly into the ground. Detail a couple of men to go with the Goalkeeper.' The casevac chopper had a medic plus life-saving equipment so, to everyone's relief, the Goalkeeper did not die – *and* saved what would have been a winning goal six months later!

After their meal the digging of a communal grave started. With eight mattocks eight men took it in turns to work on it and, three hours later, the grisly business of interring started, after photoing the dead men's faces. Jason had to hold the eyes of one man open with two fingers as he took the photo with the other hand. *I'll bet any money they will think I was torturing him before killing him,* he mused – which they did! The soldiers did not like the lifting of the corpses and throwing them in the large hole and everyone was glad when it had been re-covered by soil. As the last eight men returned to the overnight base, one rifleman vented his disgust on the trouble the daku had given him by pissing on the grave. It so happened that the Company 2ic saw him and, being of a religious bent, was afraid that, as the corpses had not been interred with any customary religious marks, something might happen to the man who pissed on it. He remembered a story his grandfather had told him about a pre-war column on the North-West Frontier of India when a soldier of 1/4 GR had, during a ten-minute break, not looked where his jet was aimed and had, accidentally, wetted an unconsecrated Muslim grave. The man had become unconscious and, when revived, only spoke Pashtu, a language he did not know, nor did he answer to Nepali. The battalion's Indian doctor did know Pashtu, had managed to talk him out of his temporary insanity. Only then did he return to normal, not knowing a word of Pashtu and speaking Nepali again. *I'll have to watch that lad,* he thought.

And indeed, that night, the soldiers were woken up by screams of Chinese invective. 'Stand to,' yelled the sentry, although he had heard no movement from outside the camp area. The 2ic went to where the screams were and saw they came from the man who had pissed on the grave earlier on in the day. He shook him and spoke to him in Nepali, only to get a Chinese answer. The Company 2ic knew that there was one man, a shaman in fact, who could put matters right, Corporal Kulbahadur Limbu. He called him over – by that time there was no security in the camp because of the noise but, luckily, there were no enemy around to hear it – and explained what had happened and why.

'Saheb, there's only one thing to do. We need a Chinese speaker to talk the spirit out of him. That will have to be the OC saheb.' By then Jason was with them and Kulbahadur explained what had to be done. 'I'll tell you what to say, then let him sleep. Tomorrow morning it will be my turn to exorcise the Chinese element and he will return to normality.' It was a bizarre session that followed and it was too dark for anyone to see the strange look on Jason Rance's face.

Next morning Corporal Kulbahadur, acting as a shaman, exorcised the Chinese spirit out of the soldier who, once the effect of the 'magic' words had taken place, was back to normal, only speaking Nepali and knowing no Chinese.[5] Meanwhile the company moved to the site of the casevac and prepared more smoke for their airdrop. When it came around noon, Jason stood stock still, staring at the parachutes dropping, Chakré at his side. Chakré sensed something was wrong and asked Jason if he was feeling queer? 'I am cold, Chakré, cold. Something in my stomach is trying to get out. I can't breathe properly.'

The batman, who had never left Jason's side during the attack on the camp, remembered the saheb having his hands on the daku's body at the time of the death rattle. *It's a* syañ, *the dead man's soul must have got into the saheb when he had his hands on the body. It's trying to get out but can't.* 'Sit down on that log. I'll fetch help,' he said, helping Jason settle down, noting he had started shivering with cold although the sun was hot. Jason lent forward and held his head with his hands.

The Company 2ic went to see what was wrong and said, 'Go and fetch Corporal Kulbahadur Limbu and bring him to me. I'll arrange a place for the saheb to lie down.'

Kulbahadur came and saw Jason lying on a poncho cape, looking pale and breathing roughly. 'What's the matter with our Saheb?' he asked.

'I think he has a *syañ* but surely a *syañ* doesn't go into one who goes to church?'

---

5 There was a similar case in Seremban in 1958, when a Gurkha pissed on an unsanctified Chinese grave of men the Japanese had killed. In your author's case a Church of England padre told him that that is what happens when 'evil spirits were exorcised'.

'Captain saheb, our saheb has been with us so long that the church is no protection for him. I can fix it,' he said. Sitting by Jason's side he started muttering then put a finger tip on one of Jason's jungle boots and scratched a small piece of mud off. Blowing on it he smeared a piece on Jason's forehead. 'Put out your tongue, Saheb,' and daubed some mud on it, then on the back of Jason's hands. 'Chakré,' he called. 'Sit next to your Saheb and if he tries to catch hold of you, let him.'

The two men sat together and, with a groan, Jason put his arms round Chakré, moaning, 'I'm cold, I'm cold,' shuddering as if, he explained later, a hand inside him was pushing something up and up from the bottom of his stomach and out through his throat. Jason let go of Chakré and tried to stand up. He fell down. 'I'm weak, I'm weak,' he muttered.

Kulbahadur looked at him. 'The *syañ* has left him. He'll be new-baby weak for several hours. I'll tell the Captain saheb we can only move on tomorrow.'

The Company 2ic said, 'Saheb, shall I ask for a heli to take you back?'

Jason looked at him with a crooked grin and whispered, 'Saheb, if you do that I'll demote you,' and fell back into a deep, deep sleep.

On the morrow he was his usual self and the company started off back to the main road for a motor pick up. *If it had been any other battalion British saheb we would have had a major panic but with our Rance saheb, matters are easy to put right* were the thoughts of most of the company, *but even so, two 'near misses' because of the dead men!*

When Special Branch perused the slips, they found a name they already knew, Ng Heng, a Representative of the Malayan Races Liberation Army. When the rolls of paper had wended their way up to the top, to C C Too's office, he stood up and gave a little jump of joy. *We're ahead of you and you don't know it,* he gloated.

17 September 1954, Kuala Lumpur: Ah Fat went to Mr C C Too's office hoping that the MCP-watermarked sheets of paper were ready. 'Sit down and listen to an idea I have,' he was told. 'The sheets are ready. In order to get your new paper looked on as something special you must appeal to our countrymen's historical leanings. After all, Chinese culture is more than three thousand years old.'

Ah Fat looked on quizzically, wondering where this was leading to.

'What do you know of the Heavenly Stems and the Earthly Branches?' and he wrote out the characters as he spoke and showed them, 天干 and 地支.

Ah Fat had to admit he was lost.

'Their origin is as early as about 2700 BC. The ancestor of the Chinese nation, the Yellow Emperor, sent Da Rao Shi to create a calendar system. Da Rao Shi explored the rule of changes between sky and earth, as well as that of the four seasons. Then he created ten heavenly stems and twelve earthly branches to make combinations representing a sexagenary cycle, sixty years. A year can be represented by the composition of two characters, one from the heavenly set, and one from the earthly one. That is believed to be the start of the stem-branch calendar. Thus came a way of counting time which has been passed down since then.'

'That's one large mouthful,' Ah Fat said, smiling wryly at his elder's erudition.

'I know it is but if you put something like that in your first number, and this year's zodiac, 马, ma, a horse,' although there was no need to write the character, he did so automatically, 'you will be looked on as a scholar so your articles will be accepted.' He took a cigarette from a box in a drawer and lit it. 'I seldom smoke but I have to have one when such exciting ideas get hold of me.'

Ah Fat looked at his watch. Time enough. 'Anything to say about any ceasefire, amnesty or meeting?'

'Nothing definite at this stage although you can tell your boss that the Security Forces will be told to stop all operations a fortnight before any meeting can take place.' He inhaled a large gout of smoke and coughed. 'Excuse me. I've been thinking how we can best keep in touch. Either Chan Man Yee can be secretly used to send you something by her own couriers or I could leave a phone message...no that is too risky. I have someone who can feed Chan Man Yee with a message for you...' He broke off. 'Your nicknames. How about only using yours adulterated for downward traffic and Jason Rance's for upward, my, traffic. I can use the four-character system that way.'

Ah Fat considered it. 'With respect, sir, I think that is too intricate to remember so why not merely use them together indiscriminately? Also, wouldn't it be kinder to let Jason know?'

'Okay, I won't tamper with it and I'll see that Jason gets to know about it if you really think it matters. Have you thought of putting any surrender leaflets in the issues of *Red Tidings* going south?'

'No, I hadn't,' Ah Fat admitted. 'That is an extremely good idea. If you have any in your office, please give me about fifty or so.'

'This is easily done.' He went to a cupboard and brought out a handful. 'Here you are.'

Ah Fat took them and packed them in his case. Armed with the surrender leaflets, the cover for *Red Tidings* and the watermarked paper, he stood up and thanked C C Too. 'It won't be easy to phone you from Thailand. Too many stool pigeons in the exchanges for safety. Have you got a simple code, asking for various articles for instance, that I can use? Also, if you had an unlisted number I could call, it could just make my life that bit easier.'

Yes, always ready for the unexpected, C C Too did have a book code, 'but I don't want to use this method as I think it unsafe for you. Let us try another simpler ruse, say the opposite of what we mean. I'll give you an unlisted number. We'll talk in Chinese. I don't speak Thai and either Malay or English would make the operator suspicious.'

Ah Fat thanked him. They shook hands and said their farewells, not knowing if or when they would meet again.

21 September 1954, south Thailand: Chin Peng welcomed Ah Fat and his Bear warmly, suspecting nothing untoward in what had happened during his non-voting Politburo's member's time away. 'Let's have a session tomorrow midday, with just my Military

Commander and the propaganda representative. There's no need for a plenum yet.'

And so, on the following day, Ah Fat told his story, how he had met Chan Man Yee, who sent her loyal greetings to all... He was interrupted with 'Does she feel lonely, do you think?'

'No, Comrade Secretary General, she is fully accepted by all in Bluff Road and is regarded as a bit of a star performer,' *and butter won't melt in my mouth, a phrase Jason once taught me,* he said to himself.

'Good, Comrade, proceed' and Ah Fat produced both types of watermarked sheets of paper, explaining how Chan Man Yee had arranged both with the idea of using one or the other for pro-MCP and the other as anti-Government.'

'Yes, she does sound like a star performer.'

Ah Fat allowed himself a small joke, 'No, Comrade Secretary General, a red star performer,' which made Chin Peng laugh.

Ah Fat went on to say how watermarks were not usually thought of, even if known about, so how he hoped to use the Heavenly Stems and the Earthly Branches background in the first issue of *Red Tidings*. 'If that doesn't draw their attention to the perspicacity and erudition of you, Comrade, not much else will.'

Chin Peng allowed himself to simper.

'I have also been thinking logistically, Comrade,' and Ah Fat went on to talk about the disadvantages of producing the new newspaper in the MCP camp area, so far from couriers, but 'better by far would be to set up a small base in Ha La. Couriers already stop there to relax.'

He stopped talking to let Chin Peng catch up with that new

thought.

'You mean you go to Ha La and work matters from there, leaving me to arrange the other periodicals with my own staff?'

'Comrade, under the circumstances, that is what will have to happen. When you asked me to look after this idea of a new periodical and go to Kuala Lumpur to work out the details, I took it to mean that that was over and above any other periodical work that was already in place. I doubt I can give my full attention, at least not to start with, to this new venture if I can't concentrate on it.'

A long silence ensured. 'I'll have to talk this over with the Central Committee as it is such a new venture' and thanking Ah Fat, dismissed him.

A plenum session of the Politburo was called for the morrow and Ah Fat was invited to give a full account of what he had done. Po-faced and solemn, he gave as one-sided a statement as was necessary. He was asked if Special Branch had any idea of Chan Men Yee's commitment to the party and he said that, as far as she knew, none at all. She was in Registry and managed to see sll documents that were not kept in office safes. 'I have instructed her to use the name Ng Heng and she certainly will do that.'

'What about our new journal, *Red Tidings*?' asked the Director of Psyops.

'I am coming on to that. Not only have I managed to get our agent to give me some government watermarked paper, I have also managed to get her to do the same with MCP watermarked paper.'

That elicited a gasp of surprise and 'how do you propose to use both at once?'

Ah Fat had his answer off pat. He explained about Heavenly Stems and the Earthly Branches, and that elicited another gasp. Reaction was positive, even the Psyops Director and the Political Commissar saw no harm in that, so Ah Fat explained how he foresaw how he would produce his newspaper, '...and so I propose to form my printing base in Ha La, making it much easier for couriers to collect the material. If, after a couple of issues, I find it too far, I propose crossing the border and using the *t'o yan,* all of whom are on our side, both as storekeepers and an early warning system, just in case any enemy does come that way.'

They debated the issue and took a vote: a base in Ha La was the verdict, using his own squad, commanded by the Bear, as security and also using them to send copies of the newspaper back up to the main MCP camp in Betong. 'How will you prepare the cover?' someone asked.

Ah Fat had a copy of it in his pocket. He took it out and showed it to the members. Hands were clapped in appreciation and the Secretary General came to as near blushing as he ever had. The only other question for Ah Fat was how could he get any urgent news from 'our agent in Bluff Road' to the Central Committee?

'She seems to have her own method of making contact,' he said, adlibbing skilfully, 'but, for security reasons, I did not ask for details.'

'That was wise,' opined Chin Peng, 'but now you have made contact, what are your plans, just in case the agent' – not letting on that it was a female – 'can't get through.'

'I can make arrangements with the couriers once they know where I'm working. We have arranged our own secret contact details,' he said, unblushingly.

'I congratulate you,' said the Secretary General and dismissed the meeting.

As Ah Fat went back to his own quarters in deep thought, remembering the games of tennis he and Jason Rance had played as schoolboys, '40 15, my serve.'

21 September 1954, central Malaya: The guerrillas' other two platoons had moved north of Bahau and, in deep jungle, established themselves near cultivations which the local *t'o yan* had made for themselves. The crops already sown were chiefly tapioca and yams but, with the seeds that the guerrillas already had with them, work on enlargement of the cultivations was not a large problem. Tan Fook Leong called his Deputy to him and told him to take a select few to go and search for the third platoon, those in the white map area. To their satisfaction they found A Company's tracks as no large a group of men can move without leaving any.

They were still a couple of days behind them when the air raid occurred and, luckily finding a nearby *t'o yan* settlement, took refuge there. A Company's position was pinpointed by their airdrop. Leaving the *ladang* they cast about. 'We are not far from them, now,' said the guerrilla commander. 'They seem to be going southwest to the main road. Once we are within contact, I'll make my plans.'

None of A Company had any idea that other guerrillas had found their tracks and had been shadowing them since their airdrop. The euphoric soldiers were, somewhat naturally, less keyed-up than they normal. It was early afternoon and Jason saw that his men were tired. 'Captain saheb, let's have an earlier halt today. Once we have made our night-stop, the men can relax just that little bit.'

The Company 2ic's lit up. 'Saheb, that is a good idea. Anywhere around here will do as the stream we have been following is good water and a pleasure to drink. I'll arrange it.'

A 'clearing' patrol was sent out on a circuitous route about two hundred yards from the overnight base to see if there were any traces of movement. The guerrillas, maybe three hundred yards from the Gurkhas, saw the two 'clearing' patrol men moving to their front. 'Lie low. Do nothing,' the leader said. They then saw a sentry move out to a flank, about fifty paces distant and take up a position not in their line of sight. 'We'll wait till it is dusk, the sentry is recalled and then, by the light of the fires they are sure to have, we will select the most juicy target, their running-dog leader. Till then we'll wait here.' They nibbled some almost tasteless dried tapioca, mouths watering as they smelt the cooking just beyond them.

Jason suddenly felt the urge to defecate. 'Chakré, I have to move out and hide behind a tree for a few minutes. No need to escort me. I have my rifle. You tell the 2ic and I'll warn the platoon as I walk through it.'

Off he went with his water bottle (no green toilet paper had been issued since Burma) and was seen by the Deputy. 'Got you,

you blasted imperialist capitalist,' he mouthed quietly. 'Get ready to kill him as he squats.'

His men tensed expectantly. Here, at last, was wonderful revenge.

'Chakré,' the 2ic said. 'Follow your saheb at a distance that doesn't embarrass him and escort him back.'

Unseen by the guerrillas, Chakré moved to a flank and took up a position behind a tree. As Jason squatted, a bird flew past him. He didn't notice it. Then another. Notice it he did. He heard monkeys screeching, beating branches with sticks. *Unusual in the evening,* he mused. A tiny mouse deer rustled past, unworried by Jason's immobility. *Bear, tiger or men on the move? If so, not ours.*

Fully relieved he lay forward to do up his buttons and picked up his rifle but he stayed bent over, as though he were still relieving himself. A few feet to his front was a stick of wood. He reached for it, took his jungle hat off his head and put it on the stick. Slowly he raised it as though he were standing up, arranging his clothes.

Chakré, too, jungle-wise, had fully understood the signs of men. Still standing by the tree he peered in the direction of the monkeys' noise. *Men moving towards my saheb?* He left his tree and something moving caught his eye. He stopped and peered into the gloom. His sharp ears caught the sound of a foot hitting a fallen log. *Men!* As though pulled by some invisible magnet, he moved wraith-like towards the noise. Out of the corner of his eye he saw his saheb's hat moving slightly, as though its wearer were about to stand up. He switched his sight to the noise, saw three men stand up and aim – *at the hat! At my saheb!* Chakré aimed at the middle of the three and fired just before the man stalking Jason did. A bullet went high over Chakré's head as the shot had startled the firer and disturbed his aim. Simultaneously another daku shot Jason's hat off the stick. Chakré again fired and heard a loud cry. Firing stopped and he heard a rustling as the two unwounded guerrillas pulled their wounded comrade away.

The company had 'stood to' on hearing the shooting and heard Chakré shout, 'Saheb, it's Chakré here. Come to me and we'll go and see if we can capture the daku.'

Jason, picking up his hat, shouted out, 'the section on the perimeter this side come out and join us,' and, seeing Chakré, joined him. It took just too long to react at such short notice that by the time the section joined Chakré and Jason, it was too dark to go any farther. 'What is that?' asked one, pointing to the ground. He bent down and picked up a cap. He squinted at it and saw it had a red star in the front. He looked inside but by then it was too dark to see if there was any blood.'

'Back to camp,' Jason called.

The 2ic came up to him. 'Saheb, any damage?'

By the light of a cooking fire Jason showed him his hat with a bullet hole each side. 'I heard the sounds of birds and monkeys make on men or a wild animal approaching so I put my hat on a stick and kept low myself so I was in no danger,' he said, 'but without Chakré the result could have been different.'

I'm glad I sent the lad out the 2ic thought.

'Saheb, I doubt they will come back but we cannot take that for granted. Double the sentries and have a proper stand to at

0545 hours tomorrow. Once it's light we'll go and see if we can find those daku who fired at me.' A few minutes later Chakré brought him a brew of hot tea. Jason said, 'Chakré, I owe my life to you. I'll never forget it.'

That night, in his troubled state, he had another dream: he was walking up the church aisle, having put on his ceremonial uniform. His feet felt cold and he looked down, he was barefooted. 'Stay as you are,' said his Best Man. Then 'do your shirt up, it's open,' the Best Man whispered. Jason turned and saw everyone in the pews either side were looking at him. Then the padre, whose face was like a guerrilla's, came down and shook him. 'Saheb, it's Chakré here. You have had a bad dream. Don't worry, all will be well now.'

The next morning 'fan' patrols went out on bearings from 10 to 90 degrees and one of them, after only twenty minutes moving cautiously, saw a body – *is it in a firing position?* – at the base of a tree. 'Don't go any farther forward,' murmured the patrol commander. 'Let us watch it closely.'

After ten minutes of no movement at all, the patrol commander softly said, 'It's dead. The daku don't leave their dead behind like that. The other daku who were with him will be in an ambush position, thinking we won't think of that.' He considered his options. 'You two,' he detailed them, 'go back to the company base and tell the saheb what we've found. Bring back enough men to get behind the corpse but only bring the commander to where we are. Off you go.'

Hidden close by and watching the corpse, one of the two remaining guerrillas said, 'we'll give them another two hours to find it. We have a long way to go and we can't take him with us. Great Lenin, we were sent away with too few men,' and he relapsed into stony silence.

Within the hour Jason and his 'O' Group of two platoon commanders, with phantom quietness, reached the watching patrol. The corpse was pointed out. 'I haven't seen anyone else,' admitted the patrol commander, 'but it is so unlike the daku to leave a body behind, there may be an ambush.'

'You couldn't have done better,' Jason breathed his reply. 'I'll take my men back and go round to the rear of the corpse, keeping well out of sight. Once I have decided that the area is empty, I'll emerge to where the corpse is, so don't open fire. If there is anyone else and we can deal with them, you'll know soon enough.'

His 'O' Group silently withdrew and, one platoon to the right and the other to the left, moved to a position about three hundred yards to the rear of the corpse. Then, having met up, they moved forward in extended line, weapons ready, eyes a-quiver left and right. It was the section commander next to Jason who saw two bodies, lying down facing in the direction the Gurkhas were moving, about ten paces away. He put his arm up, the signal to halt. All eyes were on them: everyone saw that they were either dozing or had fallen asleep,

Jason signalled to right and left, gesticulating by moving his fingers as though walking quietly and opening and closing his arms as though to hold on to, that is say, capture the two men.

Four men on each side went forward, quietly as though on tiptoe and, standing above the men, who they saw were dozing, were just about to pounce on them when they both 'felt a presence' and turned round. It was their last free movement. They were overpowered by the Gurkhas who hauled them to their feet. Jason went forward and spoke to them in Chinese. 'Are you the men who fired on us last evening?'

One of the daku spat in disgust and said, 'filthy imperialist running dog.'

Jason then damned them both, with the most devastating curse known to the Chinese, '*Ch'uan Jia Chan*', May your entire family be wiped out.

'Who are you? What are your names? Although I have cursed you I am not a bully. I'll take you back to our camp. You look tired and hungry. If you tell me truthfully who you are, where you are based and other questions that I ask you, I'll cook food for you and let you rest.'

The older looking of the two spat again. 'Curse you, too, *gwai lo*.'

Jason took his rifle, loaded it and pointed it at the man's foot. 'Say that again...'

The man was about to speak when the other man cried out, 'No, no. I'll tell you all...'

His companion told him to be quiet and Jason fired, missing the elder man's foot by a quarter of an inch. The man jumped back in alarm, pulling his captives with him.

Through clenched teeth, he told Jason who he was, finishing up with being Tan Fook Leong's deputy.

'Were you in the ambush that killed that British officer?'

No answer.

Jason loaded his rifle. 'I won't kill you. Just make it impossible for you to be a father ever again and leave you here to rot.' *I can't actually see myself doing that...*

The man sighed deeply and muttered, 'Yes.'

Jason ordered them to be bound with the toggle ropes that men had hanging from the belts. 'Take your khukris and cut down a branch. Hang the corpse from it and our prisoners will take it to our camp. I will make my way back separately and get on the blower and ask for a heli to take them away. This man has admitted he was in the ambush that killed the Commanding saheb.'

Back in their overnight camp Jason put a call through to Battalion HQ and, once Acorn was on set, told him what had happened and who they had captured. 'I want a heli to take them out as they are Ten Foot Long's number 2 and two others. Instead of my searching for a good place for a Lima Papa, suggest you send 96 Foxtrot to overfly my area which is...' and he gave a six-figure grid reference.

'1. Here is Sunray. Wait out.'

Lieutenant Colonel Gibson came on set and for once his tone seemed to be friendlier than normal. 'I understand you have captured Sunray minor of figures two regiment. Is that correct? Over.'

'1. That is what he says. I believe he is telling the truth. The dead man tried to kill me last night when I was having a rear. He'll smell badly soon. Request a heli urgently here, unless you want me to make my two captives bury him. Over.'

'1. No, do not bury him. Send him with the others. I'll arrange for 96 Foxtrot to be over you within the hour. Roger so far, over.'

'1, roger, over.'

'Well done. Congratulate the men from me. I will now get Acorn to arrange heli and an LP recce while I appraise Big Sunray. Out.'

An Auster aircraft flew over the camp site within the hour and, ready on the set, told Jason where a Landing Point was. 'Six hundred yards to your north-northeast,' the pilot said.

Jason thanked him. He did not ask him if he knew when a heli would be there as he knew that the pilot would have told him if he had known. He heard the pilot call Battalion HQ and waited for a call from Acorn. It came five minutes later to tell him that the heli would take six passengers, that the pilot insisted that the corpse be wrapped up – 'he will bring a body bag' – and that the two prisoners would be tightly bound. 'Send three soldiers with the daku, weapons not, repeat not, loaded but khukris drawn once they have emplaned. ETA 1430 hours. Over.'

'Wilco, out.'

Jason and Chakré, with an escort, accompanied the two daku, still carrying the corpse, to the LP, getting there in good time. They heard the machine before they saw it and Jason marshalled it in to where panels, always a burden to carry but, today, of great use, had been fixed into the ground. The crewman threw out a body bag.

Once the body bag had been stowed in the heli, Jason, ducking under the idling rotors, climbed up to tell the pilot the body bag was filled and stowed.

'Good. Please show the prisoners to the crew man who will ensure that their bindings are strong enough. Three of your men as escort?'

Jason nodded.

'You look tired and you pong but that is not your fault.'

Jason grinned at him. 'I'll wash at the next river,' he chortled back and climbed down onto the ground. He went round to where the crew man was inspecting the prisoners' bindings.

'They're okay so in with them,' the crew man called out. They were physically hoisted aboard and rolled on the floor before being put in the sitting position in a corner by their Gurkha escort. The door was shut and Jason went in front of the heli and signalled to the pilot with his arms outstretched, hands upwards. Inside, the crew man tapped the pilot's leg.

Rotors speeded up and away it flew. Jason and his men went back to the camp and reported that the heli had left with the prisoners.

That evening, looking at his map, he reckoned that, using normal speed, they would be out of the jungle onto a main road ready to be picked up in three days so another airdrop was not needed.

23 September 1954, south Thailand: Ah Fat and the Bear, along with the rest of his escort, planned to move down to Ha La.

They would need to take a cyclostyle machine with them, a lot of ink and the two types of paper. It would be a slow and difficult journey through the jungle. They could have moved to the east onto a secondary road but that was considered an unacceptable security risk so the slower, more laborious route was mandated. Ah Fat knew that he had his work cut out to find the right balance between what was needed in his 'mole' mode and not to cause Politburo suspicion in their edition. It would take time before the couriers would know where to find where the new journals were to be collected. *I'll play it by ear. What was it Jason had taught me? Oh yes, Order, counter-order, disorder.*

Just in case he had a bad dream that last night, he tied a cloth round his head, under his chin, to stop any likelihood of his talking in his sleep. *I am so near to starting Operation* Red Tidings *in earnest.*

25 September 1954, Seremban: A Company was finally back in camp, tired but delighted with their successes. The other three rifle companies had also been withdrawn and a week's 'rest and relaxation' followed weapon cleaning, re-clothing and re-equipping so as to be ready for more deployment. None had had any contacts and the redoubtable Tan Fook Leong was still in charge of a considerable force.

Big Sunray told the CO to debrief Captain Rance, who was to write a report of 'what went wrong' with the marker balloon prior to the bombing, as well as to find out exactly how the ten CT had been killed when they were in an overnight camp. Not only that, how were those captured and sent out by heli able to come so close to Captain Rance's overnight camp without being spotted? Were Captain Rance's tactics really that good? 'Quiz him, get him to include that in his report, and then send it to me,' were the Brigadier's orders.

Jason felt that he was being treated with unfair suspicion but finished his report by writing four citations, a Military Cross each for all three platoon commanders and a Military Medal for 21138176 Corporal Kulbahadur Limbu.

At a meeting between the Brigade Commander, his battalion commanders and Head of Special Branch, the talk turned to how Tan Fook Leong could be eliminated. 'Brigadier, I have an idea,' said Moby. 'I have told those four men who surrendered to Captain Rance last month how to eliminate their one-time commander. It is a good plan and I am sure it will work. They are ready to undertake it but, however, there is one stipulation that is not in my hands.'

'And, pray, what is that?' asked the Brigadier.

'Sir, they will only go if Captain Rance goes with them.'

4

27 September 1954, Seremban: 'The SEP will only go back and deliver the radio if Captain Rance goes with them?' queried the Brigadier with more than a tinge of frost in his voice. *Quite ludicrous!* 'Without doubting your word, Mr Mubarak, are you sure you are correct?' He used the shorthand SEP for Surrendered Enemy Personnel, rather than CEP, captured dittos.

Before being posted to command an active service brigade in Malaya, the Brigadier had served only in Africa and Europe during the war and UK and Germany afterwards, always with British troops. Asians were a 'closed book' to him. He was not against initiative but knew that the Army, like the Royal Academy, desired docility in its children and even originality had to be stereotyped. Thus any officer under his command, especially a young one whom he thought had maverick tendencies, was military anathema. His opinion of Rance was 'too impulsive and too unconventional for promotion above major'.

The good-tempered Moby answered as politely as he could. 'Sir, if I had thought otherwise I would not have mentioned it.'

'And why is that a condition, do you think? It is most irregular and I am sure the Director of Operations in Kuala Lumpur would not allow us to risk such a venture.' Moby said nothing.

'Henry, what are your views about sending one of your company commanders away on such a far-fetched and irregular jaunt?' asked with a decided sniff. 'I've never heard such nonsense,' he added with a pout.

'Brigadier, I agree with you but, in his own way, Rance is a remarkable man. You may not realise just how talented a linguist he is, far above the normal standard of Chinese speakers. I am told a Chinese thinks he is a Chinese if he hears him and does not see his face. But why the four men are so insistent is beyond me.'

'Mr Mubarak, will you interview the four men in front of me without Captain Rance being present?'

'Certainly, sir, if that is your wish. Here and now?'

'Yes, it shouldn't take too long if you put a call through on my phone.' He twisted round in his seat. 'Henry, send for Captain Rance, will you. We'll keep him out of sight at first then let them see him.'

As soon as Moby had finished his call, the CO made his to the battalion. 'Give me the Adjutant,' he told the exchange operator.

'Adjutant speaking.'

'Oh, Peter, CO here. I am in the Brigadier's office. Get Captain Rance down here quicker than normal,' and peremptorily rang off.

Waiting for their people to come, the Brigadier asked Moby, 'what exactly is the plan you have sold to the SEPs?'

'Sir, the day after the ambush was sprung Ten Foot Long gave his useless portable radio to one of them to get it repaired or to buy a new one. My idea is to get a new radio and put a bug in it so that when it is switched on its location on the ground can be picked up from the air. If we can get a bomber overhead once he has been pin-pointed he, and the men with him, could be eliminated any day suitable to the RAF.'

'Hm,' grunted the Brigadier, 'neat but unsporting. How did you think this one up? Wouldn't they be suspicious about such a move?'

'I doubt it. How did I think this up? Two years ago it was used by an Auster to locate a renegade British officer of 1/12 GR who was being escorted by the guerrillas up north to the MCP HQ. Captain Rance and his small team of Gurkhas were involved in the chase to re-capture him. Subsequently bombs were not used but a voice aircraft was. I very much doubt if any CT knows anything of such a ruse, as those of the CT escort not killed by Rance's follow-up are working for us now.'

'Yes, I can understand that and a fine piece of work it must have been. But my question is how and why the SEP think they can give their one-time leader this new radio with a British officer standing around. I've never heard anything like it before. Doesn't make sense to me.'

Moby gave a large inward sigh. 'Sir, not to get our wires crossed, please ask the SEP yourself.'

Jason was the first to arrive. The Brigadier had not had a close look at him before and now saw a tall man with a taut, lean body and the indefinable air of a natural commander. *On first sight I like what I see: here is a man who keeps himself fit and looks as if he knows his own mind, maverick though he be.*

'Rance, tell me why the four men who surrendered to you won't go back into the jungle without you.'

'Sir, this is news to me. I can't tell you as I have no idea. Sorry.'

Moby came back to say that the four SEP were outside. 'Shall I bring them in now?'

'Wait till Captain Rance goes into the ops room,' and to Jason, 'Only come out when I call you.'

Dear God, send me some soldiers, wooden ones would do, the frustrated sergeant major's tag came into Jason's mind.

The four surrendered guerrillas were brought in. 'Mr Mubarak, please ask the senior man why he won't go without this British officer?'

Moby did and was appalled when told that Rance had saved him from being shot. Moby, thinking that Goh Ah Wah was referring to the mock execution in the Police Station, translated it, almost against his will.

'What does he mean?' queried the Brigadier, lamenting that he couldn't understand a word of 'that damned lingo'.

'Sir, please call Captain Rance,' Moby replied, managing to keep his voice even. 'He can tell you.'

The Brigadier gave vent to his frustration by bellowing 'Rance'.

When the SEP saw him, they all started talking to him at once, smiles on their faces. Jason answered them with a Chinese proverb, 'Feigning to be a pig he vanquishes tigers' and told them to keep quiet. The Brigadier looked on with amazed curiosity.

'What is this about nearly being shot?'

'Sir, I heard them coming towards me and hid behind a tree, threatening them with the oldest known Chinese curse, always effectively used by emperors in times past once uttered. They did not try to shoot us and so probably be shot by us but surrendered to me.' He stared straight into the Brigadier's eyes, the elder man thinking *young pup, that's almost a case of pre-World War 2 of 'dumb insolence'.*

Moby, breathing his biggest inward sigh of relief ever, took over before the Brigadier could answer, 'Sir, he says that he knows he will come back safely only if they go together.'

'And your answer to that, Rance?' the Brigadier snapped, thinking *bloody heathen nonsense.*

'Sir, it is up to you. I am perfectly ready to take a small party of my Gurkhas and go with these four men if so ordered.'

'Mr Mubarak, tell me how they can know how to meet up with their one-time boss in such a large area of jungle? It doesn't make sense to me.' *How does a man like this become a brigadier?* Moby wondered

Moby put the question to Goh Ah Wah. The answer was a long one and the Brigadier was not good at hiding his impatience.

'Sir, there is a secret cave he knows that Ten Foot Long uses as a resting area. He told this SEP when he gave him his useless radio to take it and, repaired or a new one with plenty of batteries, go there and dump the package in the cave. The sentries there will give it to him when next he goes there. These four do not want Captain Rance to go into the cave with them or meet any sentries, merely to be with them until they reach it and come back with them because were they to bump into any Security Force unit, being with a British officer would save their lives.'

'Yes, that last does make good sense, I can see that. And where is this cave?'

There followed a long rambling discourse with many hand gestures and, at last, 'about three days' walk north of Bahau, at the top of some high ground. Once he's in the general area he will recognise it.'

'Does he approve of what we are doing?' asked the CO.

'Colonel, with respect, you have yet to understand these people. Approval doesn't come into it. They have surrendered to us so are now on our side, not the guerrillas', and that is that.'

'I'll think it over and let you know,' the Brigadier directed. 'Take them away and you, Rance, can go back to the battalion.'

Jason saluted and left.

1 October 1954, Ha La, south Thailand: The difference in the tempo in Ha La and Kuala Lumpur always struck Ah Fat as needing mentally to change gear from 'mod cons' to basic. The courier system was uncontrollably slow and unreliable but, amazingly, seemed to work more often than not. How much the recipients understood when they got their propaganda sheets was an unknown but they were probably the only reading material they managed to get sight of so should merit at least a cursory glance if nothing else. By now so many comrades were disillusioned they probably didn't believe what they read even though 'lip service' would be paid to any senior comrade who asked about the contents. Ah Fat was no academic but had a lively brain. *How best can I write something in the 4-letter code that will play into our hands, not theirs?* haunted him.

In Ha La there were no frontier posts and no police in the small village and supplies were limited. The villagers were used to seeing such people as him and his group and were not worried. In fact, they were mostly Muslims, speaking Malay as well as Thai, who had little time for the government in Bangkok and, thinking that those strange visitors were also anti-government – though quite how they were not sure and they never asked – were not worried by their presence. The nearest towns were Betong to the northwest and Songkhla farther away to the north. The road to Songkhla was the better.

Ah Fat settled down to work. *Operation* Red Tidings, *you are about to be launched.* He found that the best method of arranging the four-letter code was to write out the main message in the simplest way possible and then filling in the gaps afterwards. At times that meant his original made little or no sense so that it had to be re-written. After several days' hectic work he had his first draft, 'from a "deep throat" in the MCP itself telling the truth' for comrades in Malaya ready for printing on MCP-watermarked paper. *Will it really work?* he constantly asked himself, 'yessing and noing' like a weathercock in a stiff breeze. His message then, and later, was 'so many people are now fed up with the incompetence of the leadership and the hard and hungry life in the jungle that they want to go home and are willing to receive a reward for surrendering, so trust no one but yourself.'

That done he laboriously re-wrote the sensitive sections in a way to please the Politburo, this time to be printed with government-watermarked paper, telling them that the other, all similar, copies were being despatched by courier to take south. 'So far no courier has come but I am sure one or two will arrive shortly,' he wrote. He made arrangements always to have someone ready to tell him if anyone from the MCP camp came to visit him. *If they do, they can take their copies back with them and I will have hidden mine.*

Two couriers arrived the following week, both from the Bekok area of north Johor; one said his name was Ah Chong; the other refused to give his name and glowered like an eagle when spoken to. *A man impossible to break,* Ah Fat summed him up.

'Here are twenty copies for each of you of the new newspaper, *Red Tidings,*' Ah Fat told them. 'I don't want to give you any more as, what with all the other stuff you will be asked to carry, your loads will make you too slow.'

Ah Chong thanked him but 'Nameless' said nothing as he put the copies in his pack. Off they went and it was only long afterwards that Ah Fat learnt that his childhood friend, Jason Rance, had met them.

After Ah Fat had started to compose his second edition, he sent the Bear with one man to Songkhla to look around and to buy a few goodies. He already knew that there was a telephone exchange there. He gave the Bear a piece of paper with C C Too's unlisted number on it and a message, 'My son has had his school report. It is not a good one. He doesn't want his friends who live to our south to see it. I'll just have to wait and see what happens. Tell my school friend there's no need to go to the Bekok area as there won't be any mail.'

'Don't tell the called party who you are as the number you are ringing is only ever used by expected people. Once you have given the message, burn it and the phone number,' Ah Fat cautioned.

2 October 1954, Director of Operation's Office, Kuala Lumpur:
The Director of Operations, a Major General, was a tall, bluff man, well decorated and who had had a 'good war' as a battalion commander of British troops in Africa, followed by a brigade in Italy, France and Germany. Senior ranks in the British army go where there is a vacancy, not necessarily where their previous knowledge is a bonus, so now in Malaya, the Director relied more on other people's advice than he instinctively preferred but, being a wise man, he knew such was best. He was intrigued by and relied on Mr C C Too's knowledge of how his Communist-minded compatriots' minds worked, to say nothing of his subtle sense of humour. He had been in a quandary when first asked if a Captain Rance of 1/12 Gurkha Rifles should go into the jungle with a small group of SEP on some hare-brained mission of giving the Commander of the MRLA's 2 Regiment a new radio: it was such an unusual, so unheard of suggestion it had to have some merit somewhere in it but quite where to look for it was lost on him. He had therefore called Mr Too into his office and asked him for his frank advice and had been surprised to learn that Captain Rance's linguistic abilities, especially in Chinese, put him in a category of his own. 'General, if he is ready to risk his life in what, basically, is a simple operation that can pay great dividends, my advice is to let him go, especially if the senior SEP refuses to go without him.'

Final permission would only be given if the Director of Operations personally was fully satisfied that that was the best option and, if only to satisfy his curiosity, he had called both Mr Ismail Mubarak and Captain Rance to help him make up his mind one way or the other. There was a quiet knock on his door. 'Come on in,' the General called and his Military Adviser said, 'Sir, your three visitors have arrived. Are you ready for them?'

'Yes, and arrange for coffee and biscuits to be brought in after a few minutes.'

'Yes, sir,' the MA said and, opening the door wider, showed his three guests in. The General stood up to welcome them. 'Mr Too, I know. You must be Mr Mubarak, Moby they call you, and you,' he looked at the tall man with a taut, lean body and the indefinable air of a natural commander, standing to attention in front of him, 'you must be Captain Rance.'

'Yes, sir,' Rance answered, his clear blue eyes and almost hawk-like features making a good impression on the elder man.

'I notice you are wearing the Burma Star. I never got there. Also you are wearing a General Service Medal. What was that for?'

'Sir, and a bar "Southeast Asia 1945" for when my battalion went to Cochin-China to disarm the Japanese. The surrender terms were such that I found myself commanding, in name anyway, a battalion of the Imperial Army against the Vietminh.'

The General raised his eyebrows in astonishment. 'Now, that's something I've never heard about. Do you like the jungle?'

Jason answered after dwelling on the question. 'I think, sir, we all like the place we grew up nearest to, jungle, mountains, wherever.'

That answer pleased the General. 'And you like the jungle, uncomfortable, sweaty and all the rest of it?'

'Sir, my mind changes gear when I am under the canopy. It's

a, what shall I call it, a parallel life, a challenge and yes,' with a smile, 'I can cope with it.'

'I mustn't bang on. Sit you down.' He indicated some comfortable chairs around a small circular table. 'I wanted to make your acquaintance not only to pick your brains but also to meet someone who is said to have a capability for the unusual.'

He broke off as coffee and biscuits were brought in. The guests sipped and munched dutifully.

'I will open the discussion by asking how it was that you, Moby, thought of such a trick, if I may call it that, of putting a bug into a small radio that an aircraft can zone in on and drop bombs on?'

Moby swallowed his mouthful of biscuit and said 'Sir, I will go back to 1952 when Captain Rance went on an operation we knew as *Janus*. It concerned an officer of 1/12 GR who tried to defect to the Communists. We managed to put a bug into a radio and an Auster picked up the absconding group's position that was being tracked by Captain Rance and a few Gurkhas and relayed it back to them. As it was successful I thought why not do it again but this time with a bomber?'

The General looked at Jason and asked if he had anything to add. 'No, sir. That is what happened and to go into chapter and verse would only be otiose.'

Mr Too broke in. 'General, there is an added dimension here that I must tell you about but before I do, may I have your permission, Jason?'

With a wonderful open smile Jason said, 'provided it won't result in my court-martial, feel free.'

C C Too grinned back and continued, 'Captain Rance's background is unusual in that he was born and bred in pre-war Malaya and his boon companion, almost like a brother, was a Chinese boy of the same age, one Ah Fat who is now a non-voting member of the MCP Politburo and one of our most trusted moles.' He looked at the General whose face was a study of incredulity.

'Captain Rance reads and writes Chinese and was, through a trick of ventriloquism, able to rescue Ah Fat when he was shortly to be killed by the group taking the renegade officer to the MCP HQ. In other words, he can "read" the Chinese mind to such an extent that they think he has an almost magic power ...'

'Mr Too, please,' interrupted Jason, embarrassed, a blush showing on his sunburnt features.

C C Too took no notice and blithely continued '... he was responsible for making four of the CT belonging to the group that killed Lieutenant Colonel Ridings surrender to him but,' and he paused almost theatrically, 'what he said then and how he did it, only he, and the guerrillas, know.'

The General looked at Jason with a respect that was not there before. 'That is most uncanny,' he said, 'can you enlarge on that?'

'Sir, I first of all frightened them out of their wits by cursing them with the most savage Chinese curse that there is, after which I frightened them even more with a dummy krait. There was, after that, only the need to let them know they would not be tortured in any way if they worked for us.'

The General called the MA and told him to bring a fresh pot of coffee. 'And, Rance, where is your friend Ah Fat now?'

Before he could answer, C C Too said, 'Sir, I briefed him

only recently here in KL. He is now in south Thailand editing a new newspaper that the Central Committee wants to impress their comrades with and is even now trying to edit them in such a way that the copies that the Central Committee get say one thing and the copies that the couriers are in the process of distributing another, with anti-Communist articles designed to get them to surrender.'

'You never told me that,' said the General accusingly.

'I had it in my diary to tell you today, General, after your return from visiting units,' was the soothing reply.

The General nodded but said nothing.

C C Too continued. 'I have just had a thought, one to keep inside this room. I am sure that peace talks will be on the menu next year. There are no details yet but just suppose we can get Captain Rance, in some guise that does not offend political protocol, to be at them or near them when he can contact Ah Fat who will know what Chin Peng *et al* won't say at any meeting so get the actual low-down on what the Central Committee is really thinking.'

'I like it, I like it,' beamed the General, 'you have sown a tiny seed in my mind. That is for the future, nothing this year but, hopefully, sometime next year. We must continue to squeeze them so the accent stays on food denial and leaflets for surrender.' He looked at Jason questioningly as he clearly had something on his mind. 'Rance, you are now in your early thirties. I presume you have passed your Captain to Major Promotion Examination.'

'Yes, sir. I took it when I was in UK early this year when on my long leave.'

'And how about the Staff College Entrance exam?'

Jason gave a rueful smile. 'Sir, I am told that to be staff officer is the only way to climb the promotion ladder. Quite frankly, the tempo of operations has prevented me from studying for it. In any case, so many take it and pass, so few get to the top. Even twins have an elder and a younger.'

The General blenched at such an unexpected reply. *Rance's answer doesn't as sound though he's sorry about that.* 'And how about marriage?'

'General, my Gurkhas tell me that marriage is an unsolvable mystery. Everyone should marry but after marriage there is always trouble.'

The General looked at Rance in blank amazement, made as though to say something but held his tongue. His own marriage neatly fitted that unexpected definition and he thought of his wife as 'my little whiff of grapeshot'.

Rance continued, 'I got engaged on my last long leave. My wife to be, who had come out to Malaya for marriage, was so frightened by Colonel Ridings' death, sir, she secretly left. The ceremony would have been the following week.'

'And, if I may ask, what was your reaction?'

'Sir, deeply hurt and bitterly angry so decided that the best tonic to get back to normal and get my marital snub out of my system was by physically tiring myself out after a hard day in the jungle for a good night's sleep. To achieve that I take my company out myself and I go on more patrols than my section commanders do. It has become a habit! On consideration, if she was uncertain, better before than after. I read somewhere that "a good wife is a harbour in a storm but a bad one is a storm in a harbour".'

The General gaped and, recovering his wits, asked 'So morale's back to normal?'

'Yes, sir. It's high.'

'And how do you describe "high morale"?'

Jason answered immediately: 'To be able and willing to give of your best when the audience is of the smallest and you are far from base, out-numbered, tired, hungry and maybe unsure of your position.'

'So you are prepared to go with the SEP and a small group of your own men?'

'Yes, sir,' Jason answered as soberly as he could.

'I grant you permission, only 51 percent pro and 49 percent anti.'

4-10 October 1954, central Malaya: Moby's workshop had secreted a tiny bug with a fixed frequency in a new radio and had had it tested with the help of a friendly Auster pilot. Contact could be made and the radio's position on the ground easy to zone in on.

Jason detailed Corporal Kulbahadur Limbu, Rifleman Chakrabahadur Rai and Lance Corporal Minbahadur Gurung as radio operator to go with him with the guerrillas to the cave area. Goh Ah Wah insisted that only gym shoes be worn: 'any sign of a jungle boot within a day's walk could wreck our plans,' he said. Jason knew that was an open invitation for leech bites: to lessen their impact he decided to buy sixteen strips of oil cloth to wrap round their ankles under their socks and for all of them to carry some pieces of the flannelette used for cleaning rifles made into little bags to contain the salt, tied to the end of a stick which, wetted, were completely efficacious against the most determined leech when dabbed on it.

To keep cooking to a minimum they carried four days' tinned food, ready for heating, tea and sugar, as well as biscuits and chocolate for calories and as a couple of days' reserve. The four SEP were equipped, armed with pistols and rationed similarly, with noodles to eat dry instead of biscuits and, as a treat, Ovaltine instead of tea. Jason reminded his three men of their names, Yap Keng and Sim Ting Hok, who had been working in the 'garden' and their rescuers, Kwek Leng Ming and Goh Ah Wah, the senior of the pair who carried the doctored radio and batteries carefully wrapped and in a manner that Tan Fook Leong would recognise that a comrade, not an enemy, had prepared the package. He also told the SEP his men's names.

Goh Ah Wah told Jason that he and his men needed to take two sets of clothing, one to make them look like a member of the Security Forces in case any of them was met and the other to look like a comrade when the placing of the radio was to be done.

Early that morning as they left camp it had, unusually, rained for a few minutes. Jason reminded his men that during the war any draft that left their depot for the front when it had rained that same morning or in the rain, regarded it as an exceptionally good omen.

A helicopter was arranged to fly the eight men to as near to the target as Jason had thought expedient. He had already had clearance that there were no other military units operating in that area. There was flat country in front of the hilly area where the cave was: there should have been no problem for the pilot to have found a suitable LP near the given grid reference, and if not a landing, then a winch-down would be made.

As Jason put it later, it must have been a case of 'Sod's Law, not God's Law' that caused the pilot to take a map a quarter-of-an-inch-to-the-mile rather than an inch-to-the-mile. He noticed it when he had climbed up the outside and showed his map to the pilot, pointing out where their intended LP was. The pilot traced the way there with his finger on his map and seemed satisfied.

Once over what he thought was the correct target the pilot flew around until he saw an area open enough and clear enough of trees to land. He lowered his machine and the crewman signalled all out. On the ground Jason waved to the pilot, who waved back and, lifting off, flew away.

The four SEP looked around with increasing doubt: they had landed on an old 'garden' that they knew was three days' walk from their cave, not the one day's that had been planned. Goh Ah Wah told Jason that they were in the wrong area and Jason had no option but to believe him. 'I'll scout around to see if there are any clues. You stay under those trees and we'll be back as soon as we're sure there's no unfriendly movement.'

Jason let them go, feeling it was, indeed, a tense moment. *Would they come back? Are they bluffing me?* But he need not have worried. Back they came with a negative report. Goh Ah Wah looked at the sun and said, 'I know where we are. It would be wise to tell your people that we have landed in the wrong place and ask if there are any of your own troops in the area between us and our cave.'

Yes, now, before tonight's sitrep. Minbahadur rigged up his radio and made a call. When he got through and an as-near-as-possible grid reference of their position had been passed, Jason took over and asked for Acorn, who had to be called from his office. *What is it this time?* he asked himself and was disconcerted to be told that the heli pilot had dropped them in the wrong area, two days too far, as he had been using a small scale map instead of a larger one. 'Tell Sunray to report this upwards and to ensure that the correct scale of maps is carried by pilots in future.' The British Army listens to the 'man on the ground' in a way other armies do not and, after a lot of chuntering about too many sheets to look at while flying, such came about.

'1. Wilco. Any more? Over?'

'1. Yes. Let me know Alpha Sierra Papa' – as soon as possible – 'if there are any Sierra Foxtrots – Security Forces – 'between my Golf Romeo' – grid reference – 'and my target area. If so get Big Sunray to order an immediate freeze on their movements until I am where I should be. Call back and confirm.'

'1. Wilco. I will stress that to my utmost. Out.'

Confirmation was given that same evening and the SEP were satisfied. They spent the night there. Before dark they picked some small chillies, split them lengthways and, with thread from a reel of cotton Jason always carried, tied them by their ends and bound the thread round their head, always a sure way to keep the small stinging 'eye flies', always present in such places, off them, otherwise sleep would be almost impossible.

The next three days' movement was a total eye-opener to Jason and his three men. The SEP's fieldcraft was on a standard none of them had previously seen: their constant alertness, the way they seemed to listen with their eyes, careful and caring the whole time and sometimes glancing at their Gurkha companions' jungle skills almost as if censuring them. The time and trouble spent to make their night stops 'invisible' when they left them was without parallel.

Corporal Kulbahadur, who already knew that he was the best tracker in the battalion, learnt something new every day. Luckily the two groups got on well together and the Gurkhas' mangled Malay meant that one-to-one contact was possible.

The first two days passed with no incident and they made their rough camp before the customary evening rain shower. Goh Ah Wah's jungle lore was animal-like in its perfection and he knew, by looking at the sun, by studying the streams and once by climbing a tree to have a clear view, where they were almost all the time. On the evening of the second day he said to Jason, 'we are now in the target area. I now know where the cave is. I would prefer Tan Fook Leong is not there so cannot detain me. We four must change into our old uniform and go forward. I will find a place for you, with our packs, to stay until we return.'

Jason had no option but to agree.

The cave was in thick jungle near the top of the highest point in hilly country. At that height the noise from the cicadas in the surrounding jungle was, at times, so loud it was difficult to hear what a person said in a normal voice. When the cave was occupied, a strong defence post was sited with the one Bren light machine gun, neatly hidden, with rifle positions around the perimeter.

On the flatter ground guerrilla outposts were responsible for the safety of the cave by patrolling and ambushing any Security Forces, in order to draw any attacker away from the cave to enable an escape by the senior men.

The four SEP silently approached where they thought the most distant outpost from the camp would be. Flitting from tree to tree, with Kwek Leng Ming in front, they smelt fresh human ordure, always a give-away unless it is buried immediately. Inching their way stealthily forward the next give-away was the faintest smell of unwashed bodies. To the expert, sweat and a dirty body smell of what the person has eaten: British troops with their own rations smell differently from rice eaters and it was rice that tainted the air. *Our outpost*!

Yap Keng, of the 'garden', was beckoned forwards and Goh Ah Wah, putting his mouth to the other's ear, said, 'You are the best at making frog noises. Do so now.'

Yap Keng made frog noises, varying in pitch and tone, until told to cease. The four men listened for an answer. None. 'Forward!' and they eased themselves about ten yards to their front, taking all of two minutes to get there. 'Try again.'

This time there was an answer, a frog answer, with Yap Keng answering similarly. Then a voice from in front, 'Whoever you are you are clear to come forward.'

To his great relief Goh Ah Wah saw that there were two of his old friends hiding in a camouflaged position. Goh put his fingers to his lips for silence as the two sentries stood up and came forward. Hands shaken and bear hugs apiece, Goh took the conversational initiative. 'Is Comrade Tang in the cave?'

'No, but he is expected from the north later on today or early tomorrow.'

'A pity I can't wait that long so ...' rummaging inside his shirt, he produced the wrapped radio. 'I don't know if you heard Comrade Tang talking to two of us about his radio that was not working properly. He had wanted me to try and have it repaired or get a new one from Seremban.'

The sentry nodded. 'Yes,' he said, 'I did hear something about it but as I was not involved I took no notice of it.'

'My group was ordered to the most westerly part of our area to rescue two gardeners. I knew all the Security Forces would be drawn away from Seremban so we took a chance and went back there. Lucky we did as Sim Ting Hok was wounded so we four stayed together. We were very daring and, claiming to be civilians – and keeping well out of the way of the police – did manage to buy this new one.' He handed it over. 'There are a lot of batteries, the little pen-light type I think they are called, in the package to last him quite a long time. Take care of it all, won't you?'

'Of course but won't you stay and give it to him yourself?'

'I had thought of doing that but the fewer people who clutter the place up the better and I also want to get back to my own group. I've been away from them too long.'

The sentry considered that. 'A pity you can't stay. Tell you what, at least I can get you a drink of tea, surely? I can go to the cave and bring you a mugful or go yourself?'

It was tempting but *no I'd better not* so Goh thanked the

sentry and said he had to move off to make the most of the daylight. 'When Comrade Tang comes, give him our fraternal regards and tell him that in our part of his regimental area, we are holding our own and managing our gardens. We have enough to eat. We are all waiting for his, and your, return.'

'So you can't stay?' Goh shook his head. 'That's a shame; we are bored stiff here but if you have to go, we understand.'

They bid each other farewell and Goh's four drifted into the undergrowth. They came to a small river and, although the water came to above their knees, continued down it for about a hundred paces before joining Jason in their hide-out.

'Follow me. We need to hurry. Comrade Tang is not in the cave but is expected from the north later on today or early tomorrow. He may order a search of us but,' pointing to their wet trousers,' we have walked along a river so they can't easily follow us. After we have changed into other uniform, let's be off.'

There was time, that evening, to send a message to Battalion HQ, telling of the safe delivery and their speedy exodus. 'I hope to give you our golf romeo much farther south by midday tomorrow and once I have found a suitable lima papa I request a heli pick-up soonest. Must move now to avoid being chased. Out.'

When the news reached the CO, his Big Sunray and the Director of Operations, to say nothing of C C Too and Moby, all heaved a sigh of relief. The whole concept was against their better feelings and sending a British officer and his Gurkhas to help in a man's death by such a subterfuge embarrassed them. *Will the scheme work?* they asked themselves.

On the morrow's early opening schedule, Jason was told that an Auster was due to overfly where he had reported his last position. 'Get to an open space, light a fire, put up smoke and 96 Foxtrot will get a message to you, telling you where the heli will land or hover,' he was told.

Jason told Goh who, knowing the area like the back of his hand, led them to an old garden only an hour's walk distant. There, with Lance Corporal Minbahadur Gurung with his set watching over their packs, the others collected as much kindling and damp foliage as they could find ready to fan into smoke when they heard the Auster. As soon as they heard it they put the damp foliage on the fire and the smoke rose thickly. The Auster flew overhead and around twice. Jason, netted in, spoke to the pilot.

'1 for 96 Foxtrot. How do you read me, over?'

'96 Foxtrot for 1, read you loud and clear. A heli is standing by at Seremban and I will guide it back here. The pilot is carrying a mile-to-the-inch map, do you roger that?' the pilot radioed.

Jason answered with a happy, '1 for 96 Foxtrot. Roger, roger. There was a young lady of Lod, who thought all good things came from God, it was not the Almighty who lifted her nighty, but Roger, the Lodger the sod. Out.'

The Auster flew over once more, flapped the wings in response and flew off. *That's a happy-go-lucky bloke if ever there was one* smiled the pilot to himself.

They heard the heli droning in the distance earlier than they had expected. 'Make more smoke and get ready to emplane as soon as the chopper pilot gives us the signal,' Jason called out, first in

Nepali and then in Chinese. 'Also don't forget to bend down as you run below the blades or you'll leave your head behind.'

The four Chinese had a good laugh at that weak joke. Although they had not shown it, they had been on tenterhooks until the package had been handed over and now their relief was obvious so all small jokes were larger than they deserved to be.

The heli landed, the pilot gave them the thumbs up and, heads bent, they clambered into the back, helped by the crewman. Once in and the door shut, the crewman reached up and slapped the pilot's leg to let him know they were ready for lift-off. It was too noisy for any conversation so they closed their eyes and, as best they could, dozed till touchdown on the football pitch outside the camp. As soon they were on the ground the heli continued on its journey to Kuala Lumpur.

A police vehicle, ready to pick up the SEP when the heli was heard, drove up, with Moby sitting in the front. He expansively welcomed their return and slapped his men on the back in appreciation. 'Jason, great to have you back. We'll have a long chinwag later.'

7 October 1954, Ha La, south Thailand: A couple of couriers came into the village looking for Ah Fat. 'Comrade, we met two, Ah Chong and his nameless friend, the one who never talks and has a face like a bird, I don't know its name but I once saw a picture of it. How long ago did they leave here?'

'Comrade, only a couple of days ago, now I come to think of it.'

'Ah Chong said how much easier it was to collect the material from here than having to go all the way to the main camp. That is a most depressing place. I've only been there twice but no one ever smiles there. At least here, as far as I have so far seen, life is more or less normal. I think I'll exercise my male human rights in the village tonight!'

Ah Fat let him rattle on while he collected some more copies of *Red Tidings*. 'Here you are. Look at them. Classy, what, compared with the other rather drab stuff the Central Committee normally sends out.'

The courier examined the cover closely. 'Yes, I like it but I'd like it much better when we can get back and lead a normal life.'

Ah Fat was always careful how to answer such remarks. *Never know of any unfortunate rebound.* 'So, you'll stay in Ha La a day or so for a rest then be on your way?'

'Comrade, that's right.' He raised his right arm. 'Red salute!' and off the pair of them went.

The Bear came back soon afterwards and gave Ah Fat a smile and a nod. 'We'll talk after our meal,' was all he said then. Later he said, 'I made a phone call but it had to go through the exchange at Bangkok. I had an answer after the fifth, or was it the sixth? ring. The man who answered gave a name I didn't know but I recognised the voice. I gave him your message. He thanked me and merely said he was disappointed and put the phone down. That was not much of a conversation was it?'

'No, it wasn't but it was exactly right,' was the enigmatic answer the Bear had to be content with.

Same day, Central Committee, south Thailand: Chin Peng was looking at his copy of the new newspaper. His chief confidant and propaganda expert, Chien Tiang, was also reading his copy. After a while, he said, 'Comrade Secretary General, Comrade Ah Fat has made a good job of this, hasn't he?'

'Comrade, yes. I approve. I am a little mystified by 平宜平宜 and 便宜, also 山東炮 seems out of place but our comrade in Ha La is new to the game and the four-character method is not easy. But there is something I can't quite understand about it.'

Again, the inherently suspicious psyops duo wondered if there was any secret meaning there that they had yet to understand.

'Comrade Secretary General, you are trying to read sense into something that sometimes reads as nonsense. It is all right. Now, let's get back to thinking about the amnesty we want to be announced.'

October 1954 to April 1955, central Malaya: Operation Red Tidings, now virtually finished, there was a change of policy from searching for guerrilla 'gardens' to food denial. This meant that companies were engaged on boring and routine tasks of stopping vehicles and people on the highways and, as the battalion diarist put it, 'pre-dawn to locked and barbed village gates where arc lamps throw a sickly white light on the straggly groups of men and women, buckets and bicycles gathering to go and collect latex, the arrival of the police in an armoured vehicle, the search, of people by the police, of bicycles, tins and bottles by the soldiers, and finally the opening of the gates and the release of the flood, tins clanking, bicycles bounding over ruts in the road, coloured scarves flying in the pearl-grey half-light ... and then the weary searching throughout the day of all who pass.'

People tried to hide rice in secret compartments at the bottom of buckets of night soil, into the handles of bicycles, in places of women's bodies that certainly no Gurkha soldier could ever imagine or would ever look for. It was impossible to tell how much stuff was smuggled through road blocks and how much was kept back through fear of being discovered.

Life was so comparatively quiet that Jason Rance felt he ought to start studying for the dreaded Staff College Entrance Exam but, when he was true to himself, he knew that he was not interested in that type of soldiering. His seniors had warned him against such a short-sighted outlook. *Dame Fortune will come up with something interesting instead he mused. I'm sure she won't desert me.*

And, in the immediate future, desert him she did not: towards the end of December the Director of Operations felt that Tan Fook Leong should be eliminated. He had asked Mr C C Too to do some homework about the man and had found out he had been in the Victory Parade in London after being of great value to the British stay-behind groups during the war. *I wonder if we can save his life by getting him to surrender. It would be a real propaganda coup and the psyops boys would love it.* That idea tickled him. *But how to? Why not get the same group that went and put the radio in the cave to try and physically contact him?* The more he thought about it, the more he liked it.

He called his Int and Psywar staff in and told them about his ides. Heads were scratched, throats were cleared and eyebrows raised till eventually 'it's worth a try' was the accepted answer. 'He won't come over unless there is a more than good reason,' declared C C Too, 'but, General, I can tell you this that the SEP who went with Captain Rance to deliver the radio will not go with him on such an operation.'

'And why not?' asked the General abruptly, not wanting his brain child put to one side so easily.

'Because were it to rebound against them, they would be dead men after a most painful death, eyes and testicles missing.'

'Is it worthwhile trying to contact his wife or son, do you think?'

'To do what, sir?'

'Broadcast to him to surrender over Radio Malay?'

'Sir, I somehow think they would rather have him dead than to be seen by other comrades as government lackeys.'

'So what's your answer?'

'Do it secretly by sending Captain Rance and his Gurkhas with the rest of his company, or even another company behind them as backup. He's up to his neck in all this and he'll just have to go.'

'Do you think he'd do it?'

'And spoil his time for studying for the Staff College Entrance Exam?' and he laughed at his own joke.

So it was decided that, Captain Rance being willing, that's what would happen.

As everyone had expected, Captain Rance was willing. The first detail to ensure was, obviously, where was his target? So, for the next few days, two Austers flew over an area to the east and south, in one case, and the north and west in the other, of the cave area. Not to attract undue attention, planes only flew every alternate day and, after five days, the gizmo in the plane flying east and south of the cave picked up an answering 'peep'. On the next day the same pilot flew towards where he had heard the 'peep' from the other direction and it was much louder, loud enough to pinpoint the position within one map square. It was three days' foot journey from the road leading to the northeast from Bahau.

Jason remembered he had Ten Foot Long's phone number, wife's and son's names. *I'll risk it and call Penang.* A man's voice answered, giving the phone number.

'*Wei*, is that Tan Wing Bun, Tan Fook Leong's son?'

'Yes, who are you?'

'Is your mother, Chen Yok Lan there?'

'What is it to you? Who are you?'

'Just someone telling you that I'll be talking to your father and unless you tell me to tell him you want him back home alive, he'll be dead within the week.'

As Tan Wing Bun put the phone down he told himself he'd never forget that voice *but whose is it?*

Rather than risk an airdrop, thereby jeopardising security, part of A Company would be used to carry more rations than usual. Once the target had been pinpointed, night movement would be necessary to get to within hailing distance of the daku camp. Then, with his close bodyguard around him and his face covered in case a light was shone his way, Jason would start calling out. He would make his next move depending on the answer. His back-up platoon would be far enough away not to spoil the ambience and near enough to take what counter-action might be needed.

Jason briefed his company. 'This is a great honour for all of us. No other battalion is thought good enough ...' and he went on to give out details, finishing up with, 'luckily it is the full moon period but, even so, fire discipline must be tighter than a miser's clenched fist. My bodyguards will be Corporal Kulbahadur Limbu and my batman, Chakrabahadur Rai.'

They found the camp on a slight rise on the fourth day after entering the jungle. Three men of the close escort platoon made a recce of the position, cautiously, oh so cautiously, spotting where the sentry posts were as well as the general lie of the land. The water point was on the far side of their approach. Jason decided that forward movement was the only answer as that would mean the quickest withdrawal if the worst happened and they were attacked. 'But they won't move at night, I'm sure,' he said.

They kept well hidden after the recce group returned and, as daylight ebbed, inched their way forward to a position between where two sentry posts had been detected. Jason hoped that if the daku thought they were completely safe, they would have a sing-song after their evening meal; it would cover any noise they might make going through the jungle at night as it hadn't rained for three days so the undergrowth was liable to crackle. Once they were within earshot they heard a monotonous lecture so Jason and his two men moved as silently as they could until he could make out what was being said. At last all was quiet.

'Cover your face and I'll cover mine,' he said softly then called out, 'Comrade Tang, Comrade Tang, can you hear me?'

Nothing but stirring was heard as though the guerrillas were suspiciously alert.

'Comrade Tang, it is Goh Ah Wah here, come to talk to you. I have brought comrade Kwek Leng Mong with me. Comrade Kwek, tell them you're here.' In another voice, 'Comrade Tang, this is Kwek Leng Mong. There are four of us, the other two are comrades Yap Kheng and Sim Ting Hok.' Another change of voice and twice came 'Yes, Comrade Tang, here we are.'

'I am comrade Tang. What do you think you are doing in the jungle at this time of night? You haven't come with any *gwai lo*, have you? If you have, they and you will regret it.' Tan Fook Leong sounded suspicious and inordinately surprised.

'We are on our own, comrade. No *gwai lo* can move in the jungle at night as we can.'

No answer.

'You got the new radio and the batteries, didn't you? The sentry gave you our names, didn't he? He never made mention of any *gwai lo* did he?'

'No, no, he did not.'

'On our way back from giving the sentry the radio we were captured. The *gwai lo* were many, we were only four but resisted until we were overpowered and captured. "Surrender, come over to us and be civilians or we will kill you here and now," Jason adlibbed, 'but they did not kill us and we have been treated well. We have not been tortured. We have been allowed to visit our families. We have been well fed and rewarded with money. We have had a good medical check up and our jungle sores have been cured. We were homesick. We have been given an amnesty. The armed struggle is futile. Why sacrifice your life for the party when the Secretary General and his clique have gone to Thailand and are living in safety with all the rations and comforts they need and you are missing. We have dangerously come back as we respect you. You treated us well and we want you to live at peace with your family. I have telephoned your son, Tan Wing Bun in Penang, to tell him I'll be talking to you but he rang off without an answer.'

Jason's oratory was in vain. Insults were hurled at them, their families and ancestors. 'Go away you traitors before we come out and capture you. You'll wish you were never born.' A pause, a silence then, 'No, we won't let you go away. Comrades, advance and capture those pigs.' Shots were fired but they were wild and went overhead.

'Back now,' said Jason and they moved back as quickly as they could, blessing and cursing the moonlight at the same time. A voice in Nepali to their front, 'Saheb, here we are. What now?'

'Back, Saheb, bring all your men back and we'll go as far as I think we need to. There is no need to hurry as we will hear the daku follow us if they do.'

They moved for an hour and waited till dawn before meeting the rest of the company. 'Sentries out and let's have a brew,' Jason ordered. 'Miné, open the set and pass a message I'll write out for you.'

The message they received at 0800 hours was stark. 'Go back two thousand yards now as bombers are coming over at 1000 hours. Out.' *I've heard that before, how many unfused bombs this time?*

A bomber flew over and dropped its bombs exactly on target, killing Ten Foot Long and killing or wounding all the men with him.[6] Jason was ordered to return to where the camp had been to inspect the damage. There were six wounded men and fifteen corpses. Jason signalled Battalion HQ and the CO managed to get two helicopters, much against the RAF's better judgement, to go and collect the corpses and wounded. This time it was another company and some SEP who went and arranged matters. As Jason said, 'once is enough.'

With Ten Foot Long's death Operation *Red Tidings* was terminated and 'Framework Operations' came into force. That meant company commanders were given their own area and were responsible for keeping 'boots on the ground' according to their own programme. The aim was to keep the daku guessing so making them unsettled and more likely to surrender. More surrender leaflets were dropped than before, some showing little scenes depicting, in strip-cartoon fashion. In one it was clear that this was the work of a European ill-versed in Chinese etiquette: Father rushes out of the house and falls on the neck of his returning and once errant son who shakes his father's hand.

---

6 It is a historical fact that Tan Fook Leong, Commander 2 Regiment, MRLA, known as Ten Foot Long, was killed by an aircraft-alerted by a gizmo in his new radio set. The author's friend, the late Mr A J V ('Gus') Fletcher, escorted by men of 2/2 Gurkha Rifles, was awarded the George Medal for successfully getting a CT, Wang Hsi, to surrender by talking to him in Chinese at night in the jungle. Wang Hsi thought the speaker was a one-time CT. Mr Fletcher was successful in similar escapades.

Lieutenant Colonel Henry Gibson wrote a letter to Mrs Ridings telling her that her husband's murderer had been accounted for. She never replied.

And, by now, Jason had worked so hard and concentrated so diligently on such different and difficult targets, he had burnt out his hurt feelings of being jilted, so the recurring dream of walking up the aisle to get married and losing his clothes never returned, nor did the 'black at the sides and the white on top' dream of missing a daku. He felt shriven.

Late December 1954, central Malaya: Vinod Vellu was not a consummate actor for nothing. He had been accepted by the group to which he had been sent and, having studied Political Science at university, was well aware of what to say when talking about Marxism and other –isms. Unusually there was a Malay CT in the otherwise all Chinese group and the two of them became close friends, although both knew that showing undue friendship when a true Communist was suspicious. In this case, however, the leaders of the group they were in realised that as neither of them spoke Chinese, a certain degree of amity was to be tolerated.

After only four months the Indian's political advice was often asked, in Malay, although it was difficult for him to know how much notice his seniors took of it. What did intrigue them was how southern Indians, especially those working as labourers on the 'colonial' rubber estates, might be persuaded to show their 'colonial' masters what their true feelings were.

'We would like to co-opt them into our ambit.'

'I have not had much to do with those people, I am sorry

to say,' admitted Vinod Vellu. 'What I can do, were you to wish it, is surreptitiously visit such labour lines when our group gets anywhere near them.'

He let that sink in and a couple of days later he was asked if he was ready to visit such a place. 'With your permission of course, yes. However, as you well know, I am not a military man and so my ability to find my way through the jungle will depend on the comrades you detail to go with me and wait nearby until I have finished my research.'

A week later, after quite a traipse through some stiff country, he was told 'tomorrow is your turn. We believe that you should get to the labour lines after work has finished, say by 4 o'clock. Be with them till six and, excusing yourself in the twilight, you will be picked up and escorted back to us. You will change into plain clothes, oh yes, we have a spare set handy, before you approach the lines. We will give you a piece of the deer we caught to throw at any barking dogs.'

'Yes, I will put my thoughts together and hope for success. What is the estate's name?'

'Lavender Estate.'

Unseen by his Chinese comrades, he wrote a note to Ismail Mubarak, c/o his father, the comprador, as the chief on an Indian labour estate, which he would drop inconspicuously and hope it would find its way back to Seremban.

He was guided to the labourers' quarters and told that his escort would be waiting for him at the jungle edge. 'We expect you not to be more than an hour,' he was told.

When Vinod Vellu lived with his parents he never visited the lines so the labourers were initially underwhelmed at seeing a stranger but, on giving a 'red salute' with one arm and fingers to the lips with the other, the atmosphere quickly changed. Beckoning them to close round him, he told them that he had heard they had grievances and, if these were not met, 'I will bring the comrades to persuade' – said with irony – 'the manager to attend to them. They are also relying on you to supply them with some rice. If you can they can guarantee their support.'

Well within the hour they had told him they wanted better quarters, more pay and better rations, otherwise they would go on strike. 'The comrades will accept that, I know,' he told them encouragingly. 'I will return after reporting to the comrades how to set about your demands.' Once outside their lines he unobtrusively dropped his message, met his escort and they went back to base slowly, blessing an old timber track to help them.

The next morning a meeting was called. Vinod Vellu addressed them: 'That was an excellent idea of yours. I had a really satisfactory talk with the labour force. They were so keen on what I said they told me they would discuss the idea among themselves and let me know their answer.'

'What is their idea?' he was asked.

'Their spokesman's tentative plan is to tell the manager that if he did not double their pay, they would walk out and leave him. I said that if they could get rice for you that would guarantee your support. Once that is confirmed, all that is needed is a date for their coup, as they called it.'

The reaction was better than he had anticipated. He was warmly congratulated. 'We will discuss this in detail and, once our firm date has been decided, escort you back to Lavender Estate so you can fix it up that end'.

The comprador was an astute man. Tall, with thinning hair, he had been an athlete when young and although now in his fifties, he was alert and adept as any man half his age. He had been on that rubber estate for many years and was on good terms with the European manager, a Mr Evan Jones, an ex-officer of the wartime Indian Army, who, most unusually, was fluent in Tamil. Not far from being pensioned, he felt that by keeping in the manager's good graces, it could only redound in his favour. From his separate quarter he had sensed, rather than heard, an unusual amount of conversation the evening before, almost as though someone – but who could it be? – was giving a lecture. He had slipped on his flip-flops and quietly, quietly gone over to where he heard a voice that sounded like his son's and, peering through one of the slats of a window frame, saw it was he. *My son! Can he be in this for real or is he trying to get his own back?* He felt it was the latter but... He nearly called out to ask him who he was but decided against it. After a while, being bitten by mosquitoes for almost as long as he could bear and not hearing any noise or hint of discontent, he had slipped back to his quarter. He rehearsed the main points he had heard, rather disturbingly anti-British and pro-Communist.

'What was all that about?' his wife asked him. 'You don't often bother to go and listen to the coolies' claptrap.' Being the comprador's wife, she knew she was superior.

He didn't answer her but quietened her down by snuggling up to her. However, both were beyond their prime and the warm night would make them sweaty, so, separated, they went to sleep, unexercised.

Next morning the comprador casually wandered around the block where his son had been and saw a piece of paper on the ground. Normally he didn't bother to pick up any dropped piece of paper but this time he did. It was a cheap envelope and the address on it read, Mr Ismail Mubarak, c/o the Comprador, Lavender Estate, Police HQ, Seremban. That really intrigued him. He recognised his son's writing. He had heard of a 'Moby' but had never met him. Momentarily he was tempted to open the envelope but prudence won: *I'll give it to the manager when I go to the office and make my report. Let him do any skulduggery if he wants to. I'll keep quiet about who wrote it.*

And so, later on in the morning, he went to the manager's office and told him what he had learnt the previous night, what he had found earlier on. 'Sir, here is the envelope I picked up,' and he handed the cheap-looking envelope over and waited to be questioned.

'Can you give me a description of the man giving the lecture and what was he talking about?' Mr Jones, a tall, gaunt man, asked him.

The comprador told him as much as he thought was prudent, was thanked and dismissed. The manager had been in the Intelligence Department during the war and 'knew' such things happened although this was the first time he had come across such a case during the Emergency. He thought it over: *either the letter was meant for 'posting' and the stranger's visit was the way he wanted it posted or, perhaps, it was dropped by mistake.*

Probably the former, otherwise why the address on the outside? He reached for his phone book and looked up the number of Seremban Police HQ.

The exchange answered, 'Police HQ, Seremban speaking. Can I help you?' in Malay.

The manager also spoke Malay but he chose to speak in English. 'I am Mr Jones, the manager of Lavender Estate. May I speak to Mr Ismail Mubarak please?'

'Hold on, sir, I'll put you through.' The Malay exchange operator's tone was good.

A ringing tone was heard and 'Ismail Mubarak speaking. Can I help you?'

The manager introduced himself first and said, 'Can I come and see you about something that I can't talk to you about on the phone?'

'Sounds exciting. Yes, any time. Come to Police HQ and we can go into a huddle over a beer in my quarter.' Although a Moslem, Moby felt he would be forgiven taking alcohol in the line of duty.

Later that same day Evan Jones met Moby in his office and they introduced themselves. 'Come into our visitors' room. Beer or tea?'

'Beer, my syce is driving.'

Moby gave his orders and they talked about nothing in particular till 'Cheers and what can I do for you?'

Moby asked.

Evan Jones took the letter out of his pocket and handed it over. 'I'll tell you what my comprador told me,' – and, to Moby's intense interest, the story came out – '... and this morning, this is what he gave to me,' he said as he handed the envelope over. Moby took it and Jones noticed that he did not open it to read it.

'I thank you warmly,' Moby said. 'I can't give you any details, I'm afraid...'

'Don't worry, old boy, I was in Int during the war,' he answered, a touch patronisingly.

'...but what I must ask is, is there any bodily description of the man who left the letter behind when he left and also what he was talking about?'

Evan Jones came into his own and told Moby as much as he knew. Moby lapped it up. *It has to be my Dover, just has to be*, he inwardly chortled.

After finishing their beer the manager was once more thanked. Moby took a gamble. 'Mr Jones, as a responsible army officer...'

'Ex-army, please. I'm a civvy now.'

Moby, versed in British secret necessities, said, 'Mr Jones, you signed the Official Secrets Act, surely?'

'But of course I did. Most essential it was, I can tell you.'

'Have you unsigned it?'

Jones did a 'double take' and suddenly realised that Moby was being dead serious. 'Please elucidate.'

'I ask you to do two things for me, for Malaya, for everyone who is against Communism. Are you prepared for that?'

'Most earnestly' and they shook hands.

Moby leant forward. 'The first thing is, if the man you have described to me ever makes contact with you, accept all that he says and immediately come and tell me.'

Moby paused long enough for Evan Jones to ask him the second point. 'Keep your mouth totally shut and tell no one at all about it.'

Jones dramatically put his hand on his heart and said. 'I sincerely accept both points.'

He stood up, they shook hands again and he left.

Only then did Moby open the letter and read it carefully. He saw that his Dover was on course for a major triumph, *no, don't tempt Fate*, had plans as nearly as firm as were needed, for a food lift at a certain deserted labour lines on Lavender Estate probably on the next full moon. 'I and my friend will be wearing white shirts. The others will be in uniform. I am hoping about thirty bodies will be ready for you. Please prepare your answer. I will try and send you another letter but don't bank on it.'

My gamble surely, surely, will pay off, Moby prematurely gloated as he made his way to see the CO 1/12 GR, whose troops would be used on Operation *Dover* as Lavender Estate was in the battalion's area.

5

1 November 1954, central Malaya: After the excitement of operating against Ten Foot Long, food denial work seemed more boring than ever. But that fickle lady, Dame Fortune, did come to A Company's rescue once more to test the company commander's nerve when 'reacting to the unexpected': a captured guerrilla reported that even while the Security Forces were engaged in food denial duties, stocks of rice had been taken to the jungle in waterproof tins and cashed in such a way that routine patrols would be unlikely to find them. The Brigade Commander had airily said 'Let's swamp the area and find the hidden stocks,' unconsciously aping a conjurer taking a rabbit out of an empty hat!

Jungle lore is something that takes time, effort and much discomfort to absorb properly and anyone, especially senior commanders who have never been on jungle operations, have no idea that looking at a map or flying over the countryside were in any way equal to walking 'under the canopy'. 2/12 GR, ordered to search a large area, claimed they did not have enough troops to do so properly so 1/12 GR had to lend them one rifle company to make up numbers. Captain Jason Rance's A Company was detailed for this task.

2/12 GR was stationed in Bahau where Jason went to be briefed by the acting CO, a burnt-out major due for pension who, knowing he would never go any further, had 'opted out'. When he spoke, he blinked with a nervous tic that being a prisoner-of-war of the Japanese had induced and the military world had left him behind. When he had first seen a 68 radio set, with its flexible aerial raised, it was on the ground. Thinking that the aerial was stiff he had leant against it and fallen over. He had got to his feet, ashamed and with a guilty feeling of insufficiency. He was what the unkinder members of the battalion called 'rice-minded'. The 1/12 GR company was to operate south of a river flowing west to east, as good a boundary marker as any in preventing mistakes in recognition as 2/12 GR were to operate only north of it. The boundary between two states, shown on maps as a dotted line, ran through the area of 2/12 GR's southern company, call sign 1. Recognition of friend and foe was a constant problem: inter-subunit boundaries, so easy to mark on a map but hard to distinguish on the ground without easily distinguishable features, had to be known by all involved.

Jason was told: 'We wear crossed yellow khukris in the front of our jungle hats so are easy to recognise.' 'We wear a white square in the front of ours,' was his response. Unaccountably he was not told that one of 2/12 GR's sub-units had met a guerrilla group wearing exactly similar signs in jungle hats, not their normal red-starred peaked caps, and dressed like Security Forces. One of them had beckoned to the Gurkhas and the senior man had gone forward, only to have his left leg shot off. Since then each man's hat had two signs, the yellow crossed khukris showing when worn in the lines and a red guerrilla star, sown in the inside, showing when worn in the jungle.

Jason briefed his men collectively, it being the first time the company was to work under command of another battalion. He showed them the relevant map sheet: 'Up to this river anyone seen not wearing crossed yellow khukris in the front of their jungle hats will not be 2/12 GR but daku.'

For the first two days A Company, now call sign 5, searched diligently and found no traces of daku movement. Called to the set that evening he was given fresh orders. 'Your boundary is extended north of the river to the state boundary dotted line on the map.' Pre-war an inter-state boundary might have been discerned on the ground by a man-made path, but because of guerrilla activity it had not been cleared since before the war so now impossible to recognise.

'5, wilco. Request confirmation call sign 1 has also been notified of change.'

'5, of course. I confirm call sign 1 has been informed. Out,' but something told Jason that that was not so. In all, to the acting CO 2/12 GR's obvious vexation, he personally checked twice more.

So over the knee-deep river A Company, 1/12 GR, went and normal 'fan' patrols were sent out. Jason had taken a patrol of four men to explore up to the extended operational boundary. They came across a large guerrilla camp, big enough for eighty to one hundred men but now empty. Jason walked around inside it, inspecting a primitive workshop, a sports area and strong defences, and noticed a small hut in one corner with a cooking place. Bending down to inspect the ash, he found it was still warm. On the ground he saw a newspaper and, in idle curiosity, he picked it up. He was stupefied on reading the title, 紅色消息 *Hung Sik Siu Sik, Red Tidings*, with a picture of the Secretary General looking almost as though he were about to give a Christian blessing, except that the expression of mockery on his face belied the original impression. *Red Tidings! What an amazing coincidence*, he thought, shaking his head in disbelief. He read the first line of the text and 'did a double take' at the similarity of his friend Ah Fat's nickname, *P'ing Yee,* 'Flat Ears', 平耳, now written as *Pian Yee,* 便宜, which he knew meant 'suitable', and of his own, 山東炮, *Shandong cannon*, now written as 山東包, 'East of the mountain bun'. He was deeply puzzled and not a little worried. *Is it a one-in-a-million coincidence? Surely it can't be my old friend trying to send me a message?* He put it in his pocket to read it later.

He mentioned the warm ash to his men, emphasising that it meant a small group was still using the camp, could be met with so to stay alert. On they went. At the top of a small rise they heard a noise on the far side of an overgrown stream, now a swamp, about thirty yards wide, below them. They halted. 'Birds,' said one of the soldiers. 'No, man-made,' Jason answered, 'a patrol from the camp returning?' He checked their position on his map: his new boundary was another map square to the north so the noise had to be made by guerrillas.

As they reached the bank at the edge of the swamp they heard the same noise again on the other side, louder and definitely man-made. 'They may not cross over so we must go and meet them,'

Jason said softly.

The five men moved down the bank into the swamp which was ankle deep and thick with aloes, twelve-foot tall 'spikes' with barbed edges that make a metallic noise when brushed against. With extreme caution they started to go across. The mid-afternoon weather was overcast and in the swamp it was gloomily dark.

Halfway across they heard a noise like a tin being pierced, then the unmistakable clink of an opened water bottle's stopper hitting the side. Jason's patrol stood stock still. More noises: a muffled Chinese-sounding voice that Jason could not understand, men moving, sloshing...and coming their way. All five men froze, faced the direction of the on-coming men, lifted their weapon to their shoulder, took aim and waited. One, two, three men came into sight, a dozen yards away, moving diagonally across the patrol's front, dressed like soldiers. On their jungle hats was a red Communist star, not crossed yellow khukris. In an agony of doubt because guerrillas he had met had never been so noisy... *Guerrillas, not Gurkhas* – seven, eight – *but who are they? – must be...have to be guerrillas Yes or no? Yes!* – so he whispered 'Open fire when I do' and tensed himself in readiness, senses razor-sharp.

As if on a sudden impulse the men wearing a red star in their hats turned and saw five unexpected men aiming their weapons at them. They instantly and instinctively came into the aim ready to open fire. The man on Jason's right turned to him and hissed 'second twelfth, second twelfth.'

For a dreadful, loaded second, all thirteen men stood poised, aiming loaded weapons at each other. In a flash Jason saw that the men facing them in the gloom might just somehow be Gurkhas with a guerrilla hat sign, rather than Chinese in security-force uniform and captured equipment. *No, I can't be wrong.* And yet the cold worm of doubt was working overtime in his bowels. In less than a half second he thought *if I shout 'Don't shoot!' in Chinese and they are Gurkhas, they are much more likely to shoot and not to miss than if they are Chinese and I shout 'Don't shoot!' in Nepali.* He chose the latter, took off his hat so that the other men could see his face, lowered his rifle and sloshing his way forward shouted 'Don't shoot, don't shoot,' in Nepali. 'We are A Company, 1/12 GR.'

They were 2/12 GR men. Almost reluctantly they lowered their weapons.

'Why are you in our area?' a Sergeant snapped, angry and clearly frightened. 'Can't you map read?'

'Why have you daku signs in your hats when I was told you wore crossed yellow khukris? That's why we were aiming at you in our area. And why can't you map read?'

The angry Sergeant snapped back, 'Of course I can map read, but you are in our area.'

Both groups, shocked at the awful possibility of so many casualties, tried not to give further vent to their overwrought feelings. 'Haven't you been told of the change in our companies' boundary?'

'Change? There has been no change. It's your bad map reading that's to blame for our nearly killing each other.'

It was now evident that the order of the change of boundary had not been told call sign 1 of 2/12 GR by their own CO so neither patrol had strayed into the others' area in ignorance.

'What was that noise we heard from the other side of this swamp?' Jason asked.

Hesitantly the Sergeant explained that they had found sealed tins of rice which they slashed with their khukris so that rain would seep in and the rice become inedible. By then Jason realised that he had been duped by the Gurkha Sergeant's unusual accent into thinking it was a Chinese speaking. He was not to know that his nickname was 'Cheena' because of his strange Nepali accent.

'Don't let's quarrel. I'll go back to my overnight base and you go back to yours,' said Jason and both groups, each still convinced that they were in the right and the others were in the wrong, departed.

Back in his base Jason learnt that there had been three other instances of patrols clashing, none opening fire. Determined to voice his deep concern, he went to his radio set to talk to Sunray 2/12 GR, only to hear Sunray call sign 1 complaining bitterly that the map reading prowess of call sign 5 was nil.

When it was Jason's turn he started by saying '5, by the grace of God you have just been saved the responsibility of many Gurkhas' unnecessary deaths ...' giving details.

An exculpatory but almost apologetic 'Roger' was the only answer.

After his evening meal Jason called the soldier who had been on his right in the swamp and asked him why he had urged him not to open fire.

Came the devastating reply, 'Because I recognised my brother.'

The operation was called off immediately. Back in Seremban

Jason complained bitterly to his CO about the boundary change mix-up but how Gurkhas, not being trigger happy, had not had a massacre, unlike an unfortunate British company who, seeing their Chinese JCLO in front of them, mistook him for a 'baddy', had opened fire, killing nine of their own troops.[7] 'Sir, our men are wonderfully observant and steadfast. Their fire-discipline is second to none.'

The CO agreed wholeheartedly. Later still he realised that he wouldn't have found that *Red Tidings* newspaper, the name an extraordinary coincidence, to say nothing of those two misspelled names adding an extra dimension to the enigma if the boundary had not been extended.

Meanwhile efforts were being redoubled to prevent stores and supplies leaving towns, so meriting a new code name, without which the planners feel naked: 'Key', to open the door to the end of the Emergency, was chosen to put on the surrender leaflets. The leaflets were all printed with 'Quay' – same sound! – so the code name was changed to 'Pibroch', which made sense to nobody, probably not even to the name givers. The actual air drop of leaflets to let the guerrillas know their hungry fate coincided with municipal elections. The tape given to the voice aircraft to warn the guerrillas about their expected starvation so surrender was advisable, was inadvertently changed with the one warning people to cast their vote for town councillors. The good citizens of Malaya were indignant at the slur on their probity; nobody ever did hear what the guerrillas thought but Jason, on learning about

7 1st Battalion, Queen's Royal Regiment.

it, expected that the message to vote properly gave them a giggle or two that raised their morale. That was needed as, despite such staff idiocies, Government was, in fact, by then winning the war.

25 January 1955, Rompin, Negri Sembilan: Rubber tappers, those sympathetic to the guerrilla cause and those threatened if unwilling, were one tenuous source of resupply. It was impossible to look at each latex-collecting bucket to see if it had a false bottom, however hard troops and police tried to. Bits and pieces, dribs and drabs, jots and tittles of this and that and hidden in unexpected places, were carried by tappers whose 'task' lay by the jungle edge and so could the more safely be collected by the CT.

A Company, 1/12 GR, had been sent on detachment to Rompin, quite some distance from Seremban. The nearest estate, Rompin Estate, was in two parts and managed by a man named Peter Cox who was just about to retire on pension, He was a desiccated little man of uncertain years and more uncertain temper, had been a prisoner-of-war of the Japanese, was 'jumpy' and felt superior to all military who 'had let us down in 1942'. The detached part, several miles distant and colloquially known as Rompin South, was looked after by a Geoffrey Fremin, a one-time National Service corporal of a British battalion, who had served in Malaya. He had so liked the country and the people he'd returned as a rubber planter. Bumptious and swollen-headed, he still had a lot to learn.

One day he rang Jason and told him that one of his staff had given him a tip that a group of CT were to visit his part of the estate's northern boundary in two days' time to collect rations.

'They will come between half past six and nine o'clock. Are you interested?'

But of course!

In Geoffrey Fremin's office Jason was shown on an estate map where the guerrillas were expected. He mentally related that to his own operational map before the conversation turned to details of how he intended to set about his task. The door was open and Chinese clerk in the outer office heard details of place, date and timings. His brother was in the local guerrilla group. *I must warn him* the clerk decided. *The Gurkhas will make a good target.*

Jason briefed the platoon he himself would take out. 'Our task is to ambush some daku who are planning to pick up some rations on the corner of Rompin South rubber estate,' showing them on the map where their target was. 'They are expected from the northwest and we will reach the ambush area from the northeast. They won't show their faces till the tapping starts so we'll take up our positions just after dawn, well before any tappers can see us. We'll go the first five miles from camp by transport with our evening meal in our mess tins, move through the jungle where we'll spend the night by a stream near the estate edge. Once in position just after dawn we will camouflage our jungle hats with pieces of the cover crop. If nothing happens by nine o'clock that's it so back to base. If they do come, try not to shoot any civilian tappers.'

The ambush was on a slight rise giving a clear view of the dull red laterite estate road that ended by a stream some fifty yards to their front and a large area of rubber to be tapped. The ambush would be invisible from the road only if heads were kept down.

The cover crop between the trees was less than six inches high.

Before lying down and sticking greenery into his hatband, Jason saw that his men were spread out like a half-moon, with the nearest trees to be tapped only a few yards in front.

Meanwhile the guerrillas had decided not to take any supplies but to ambush the Gurkhas when they lifted their ambush so they took up a position to a flank, surreptitiously, well after dawn by when the Gurkhas were in the prone position, watching their front.

At about 8 o'clock Jason saw three men walking down the estate road towards them, Cox, carrying a shot gun and followed by a large Alsatian dog, Fremin and in the rear a Malay Special Constable with a Sten gun. The guerrillas also saw them. At the end of the road, just in front of the stream, Fremin said, loudly enough for every soldier to hear, 'Captain Rance and his Gurkhas are ambushing the ground in front of us.'

Cox turned on him and, bitter reproach in his voice, said 'I never gave permission for the military to come onto any part of my estate. How dare you let them?' and, so saying, he brought his shot gun up into his shoulder, unwittingly aiming straight at Jason, and said, 'If I see Captain Rance I'll shoot him.'

Out of the corner of his eye, at the far end of the ambush, Jason noticed a woman tapper leave the last tree, put her latex collecting bucket on the ground and move to where he knew the left-hand soldier was. A couple of paces from him she turned round, lowered her trousers and, stepping backwards, squatted down out of Jason's sight.

Looking ahead once more, hoping against hope that what was happening on his left flank would not result in the soldier remonstrating and so giving his position away thereby rousing Cox's ire any more, Jason saw Cox bend down to his dog and sick him on up the rising ground. The dog jumped over the stream and came directly towards where he lay. *All we need now is a roll of drums*, flashed through his mind as the dog came straight towards him. A non-church goer, he mumbled 'God help us' and, to his astonishment and great relief, God did because the dog turned round and went back to his master, having been only about five yards from his unseen quest. At the same time, squinting to his left, he saw the tapper woman rise, pull up her trousers and resume her tapping duties.

Angry voices clearly reached him from below. 'Fremin, what rot you talk. No one could hide in the ground to our front without our seeing them and the dog would have found anyone there, so would the tapper.'

'But, Mr Cox, Captain...'

'Close your damned mouth. Nobody can hide there without being seen here. Nobody could hide here with the dog searching for them. Nobody could be here if the tappers don't give the game away.'

'But Captain Rance never told me he'd cancelled it,' Fremin expostulated.

'I said "shut your mouth" so shut it.'

The guerrillas were also privy to the unexpected scene. The leader was in two minds, whether to ambush the Gurkhas – *but could they be there if the dog found nothing and the woman tapper behaved normally?* – or kill the three men as they walked back up the road. Knowing that Fremin and his clerk were friends he decided that it were better not to attack them. As soon as the three men were out of sight the guerrillas disappeared back into the jungle.

Jason thought it highly unlikely any daku would make an appearance now so, after waiting half an hour, he lifted the ambush. He called the flank soldier over to him and asked him about the squatting woman. 'Saheb, I turned my head away but I had never seen "it" from that angle before.'

They made their way back through the jungle, met transport ordered for 1030 hours and reached base in time for a late morning meal.

Back in his office, smarting at the rebuffs, Fremin fumed about the Gurkhas not telling him they wouldn't be coming. *I'll have it out with that Rance chap next time I see him* he promised himself but the two never did meet up again.

That evening Jason rang Mr Cox in his house. 'Captain Rance here, Mr Cox.'

'I was told you were in ambush near the jungle edge over the stream, Captain. If you had been there I'd have shot you I was so angry that you had the impertinence to go there without my permission.' Jason let him blow off steam and then said, 'But I was there. I heard what you and Geoffrey said,' and he repeated them, almost word for word.

After a hush, broken only by heavy breathing, a chastened Cox said, 'but the dog? It could not have made a mistake.'

'It came within five yards of me and turned back of its own accord.'

Another pause and then, apologetically, 'what troops other

than Gurkhas would have remained so quiet?'

There was no need for an answer so Jason rang off and ate his supper, happy at the high standard of his men's discipline but never knowing how their skill had unintentionally also foiled the guerrillas.

15 February 1955, central Malaya: Food denial efforts were strict enough for some guerrillas to defect. One was a courier who described how deep jungle courier 'letter boxes' were selected; couriers never followed the same route between pickup and delivery but they had to 'post' their correspondence in designated 'letter boxes'. This was confirmatory information. One such he loosely described as 'a large tree by a stream junction' was assessed to take a day to reach from the nearest village, Bekok. Jason's company was detailed to go and find it. *Rifles or crystal balls to the fore?* Jason asked himself.

The soldiers wondered why such tasks always came their way. They felt proud of their OC's skill, tactically and linguistically. *He is sure to get a* bahaduri *in the next list.*

It would be hard put to plan on a vaguer description Jason thought as he studied his map. By dint of elimination, he decided to search one area less unlikely than others to look for a tree that couriers could recognise as a 'letter box'. His reasoning was based on what lovers of military appreciations call 'time and space' factors. The area had to be far enough off the beaten track for safety, near enough the outside world for convenience and so situated that it could be of use in the main north-south guerrilla courier route, or rather corridor, and a prominent enough tree to be easily recognised. *Near running water so deep roots so tree more conspicuous?* Jason mused.

At 2 o'clock on the day chosen he was awoken to a large mug of tea before as unlikely a mission as any he had ever undertaken – *and that's saying quite a lot!* They were in the jungle by first light and moved all day on a compass bearing taking them northeast.

By evening they had reached the target area and small patrols were sent out to make sure there were no guerrillas in the vicinity before starting to make camp. One reported that it had seen a large tree by a stream junction.

Next morning Jason went to see it: once it had been a very large tree, sprawling around a small rocky outcrop in the junction of two streams. The Gurkhas recognised it as a *chhatiwan*, no English name but Devil Tree in Nepali. It had been struck by lightning and now only its large bole was left, entwined with creepers and encased in lichen. Even so it would be too much of a coincidence to have found the correct place so easily, so more patrols were sent out at 10 degree intervals to cover all the territory in the target area. In the forenoon eight patrols searched to the north and later on in the day six patrols went searching to the west, Jason having surmised that there was little likelihood of there being any courier movement to the south or east. No similarly positive tree had raised the men's suspicions or hopes, so ambush positions would be put around the old bole. 'My plan is to have an outer ring some two hundred yards from the tree and an inner ring actually watching it,' Jason told his men. 'If and daku to come try for a capture rather than a kill.'

By half past eight next morning all were in position and two hours and ten minutes later two guerrillas came into sight and were engaged by three soldiers. Jason ran to the scene of the firing. Both guerrillas had been wounded and were running away. Jason and Corporal Kulbahadur Limbu chased them.

Jason glanced at Kulbahadur as they surged forward and saw his eyes were completely bloodshot. The lust to kill was in him and he would not be deprived of his prey. They found the first man trying to hide under a bush, flesh wounds in his legs and upper body. Jason stopped moved the man's weapon out of reach before putting an emergency dressing on the worst wound.

As he did so he heard the other guerrilla open fire and Kulbahadur return it. It sounded as though he was engaged in a running battle so Jason went to help him and found that by then Kulé had captured his man and, to do this, he had wounded him in the leg so he could not run away. On approaching him, he had been fired at from thirty yards' range so Kulbahadur had gone forward another ten yards and been shot at again so had aimed at the guerrilla's right arm to prevent him from firing any more. He had then gone forward and captured him. The guerrilla was furious. He refused to talk, trying not to wince as he had a First Field Dressing put on his leg, glowering fiercely, like an eagle. The Gurkha's blood-red eyes were slowly returning to normal.

After both men had been carried to Company HQ they had their wounds the better seen to. Jason spoke with them both while the Company 2ic called for a heli to evacuate them on the morrow and a patrol was sent to discover the nearest LP. Jason asked what their names were and the man wounded in leg and arm, aged about thirty, lean and strong, refused to give it and stared stubbornly ahead, saying nothing when spoken to. The other said his name was Ah Chong. While interrogating him Jason told one of the soldiers to examine the guerrillas' packs. One of them found some newspapers, thought that the OC Saheb would be interested, so took them over to him. Jason scanned the title, 紅色消息, and asked 'Where did you bring these from?'

'Ha La, in Thailand.'

Jason took a gamble: 'Comrade Ah Fat gave them to you, didn't he?'

A look of amazement crossed Ah Chong's face. 'How can you know that?'

'I know many things you think I don't know,' was Jason's equivocal answer. *I haven't heard of Ah Fat for ages. Moby and C C Too will have to learn about this as soon as I get back.*

Flicking through the pages of the paper Jason found a surrender leaflet. He called over to Ah Chong and asked him why he had not carried it in his hand in case he bumped into the Security Forces?

Motioning to the other guerrilla, he mumbled 'he didn't let me. He never would. He told me he'd rather die than surrender.' And indeed that night the man who had not spoken and who was not fatally wounded did die, almost as though he had willed himself not to live. Before being flown out with the corpse, Ah Chong, clutching a surrender leaflet, told Jason he was grateful for what had done for him and said he would no longer be a Communist but a civilian instead.

He was debriefed when in hospital and both Moby and C C Too were delighted when they learnt how much effect on guerrilla morale that issue of *Red Tidings* had had, and, having read it for themselves, felt that the author had scored a bull's eye.

Mr Too was vastly impressed at Ah Fat's subtle use of the nicknames, which he already knew about. *I must find out if Captain Rance has twigged that subtlety.* He phoned Moby and, in veiled speech, asked him to contact Rance to find out. He was pleased, but not surprised, to learn that, yes, Jason had cottoned on to it but had not understood why. 'Unless he is trying to send me a message' he had suggested.

C C Too met the Director of Operations and told him about the incident. 'Sir, your seed of an idea has fertile soil in which to grow.'

'Mr Too. I like the idea even better than before,' the General replied.

Back in camp, Jason was called to the CO's office and given his annual confidential report to read. 'Sit down, read it and initial it.' Jason took that most important of personal documents and read *'This officer has a taut, lean body and the indefinable air of a natural commander. He is very active. Outwardly he is always cheerful and irrepressible in spirits, but I believe that beneath it all he is sensitive and easily depressed.'*

He's got it wrong, Jason thought. *I must have looked gloomy when my wife-to-be ran away but that was only temporarily.* He continued reading:

'He is an excellent company commander in the jungle. His appreciations are sound and he works methodically and tirelessly in his efforts to obtain success. He is also not afraid to take

personal risks. His men have the highest regard for him and he is a fluent linguist.

'That is all to the good: his main weaknesses seem to be a lack of tact with senior officers he does not agree with. There are people like him in every army - a brilliant Roman 'Centurion' leading his hundred men, fiercely defending their interests but unable to adapt to the hierarchical structure which an army must have if it is going to win wars. Men like Rance win battles but they cannot conceal their contempt for their more conventional superior officers. It is a major weakness.

His military background and knowledge of staff matters are too unbalanced in the peacetime army for me to recommend his promotion to major.'

He was graded 'Average', a grading never likely to get him above the rank of major.

Jason signed it, not to show he agreed with it but to show he had read it. He stood up, placed it on the CO's table, saluted and left without saying anything. It was on the tip of the CO's tongue to say that, after being promoted for command of a Territorial battalion in England, he had only stayed on to command 1/12 GR until the designated CO, indisposed for several months, was fit to resume military duties and who was coming to take over command at the end of July. It was Captain Rance's unintended brusqueness that stopped him. *I won't forget to make a special note of him for my relief* he slightly maliciously told himself.

The Honours and Awards' committee held its final meeting for recommendations to be sent to the War Office in time to be officially announced for Queen's Birthday. Citations were read by each member. There were only six awards allocated for the Military Cross, MC, for officers and Warrant Officers, and the same for the Military Medal, MM, for the lower ranks. Other awards had their own 'ration'.

The Major General chairing meeting in GHQ FARELF looked at his list and made a cogent remark, 'All these citations are subjective. I know of a case of a man with no imagination winning two MMs and not realising that he had been brave and another man who peed himself with fright on night operations but removed a land mine with great bravery in Korea and was awarded nothing.' The others nodded. They had heard that at the last session. 'We have another problem,' the Major General continued, 'two British battalions left the theatre of operations during the last six months and one will leave next autumn. None will probably have another chance of earning a decoration. Now, this citation,' he picked it up, 'for an MC for Captain Rance of 1/12 GR. It is a good citation but Gurkha battalions are permanently here so he'll have another chance. I suggest we give our allotment of MCs to the British battalions and let the Gurkhas, including this one, a Distinguished Conduct Medal, DCM, for a Corporal Kulbahadur Limbu of 1/12 GR, have another chance later.'

This was agreed. 'Now for the m.i.ds. The Gurkhas must have something so...' and the result was, for 1/12 GR a Gurkha Captain of A Company and Corporal Kulbahadur Limbu a 'mention'. At the end, one of the members said, 'General, 1/12 GR has had a good record. How about a DSO for the CO? When he was 2ic none of us thought all that much of him but, as a CO, he seems to have shone.'

So that was also agreed.

The list was eagerly awaited and scrutinised eagerly by many hopefuls. To his peers, Captain Jason Rance seemed set for an award but when nothing came doubts were raised. Was his unusual temperament seen so tactless in front of senior officers that no citation was put forward? Of course, no one could say and no one could ask.

Jason held a party for the two recipients of the m.i.d. and had them in shrieks of laughter with his ventriloquist dummy, this time with no krait but bombs that didn't explode when dropped. He seemed in no way upset that his name had not been on the list.

His Company 2ic smiled when he said, 'Saheb, you are an unlucky man. In 1954 you lost a wife and a *bahaduri*. But we have a proverb, "Pure gold needs no touchstone or a good man any adornment".'

Jason gave him his brilliant smile and thanked him for the compliment, adding: 'Saheb, until the CO takes me away, I still have A Company.'

1 March 1955, central Malaya: Vinod Vellu was briefed to make another visit to Lavender Estate. Hunger was setting in. 'We can't eat almost anything but leaves for much longer,' said the Military Commander. He detailed his Deputy and a bodyguard of two to go with the Tamil and, if the coast was clear, personally to see if Vellu's talk had been successful and the estate labourers had, in fact, reacted as they had promised to.

They went down from their jungle base cautiously, not realising that the area was purposely being kept clear of any Security Forces during the plan's 'incubation' period. Leaving a guerrilla section at the jungle edge, the four men approached the labour lines. Inside the comprador's house his dog whined, warning its master that something unusual was afoot. The comprador felt he should go and tell his manager as he had been warned to. Without telling his wife, who was in the kitchen getting supper ready, he stole off for the ten minutes' walk up to the manager's bungalow. Jones was single, his wife, not liking Malaya, had gone home.

The comprador tapped on the manager's window, got his attention and told him that there was probably another meeting in his labour lines. Evan Jones thanked him, said he himself would stay where he was but that the comprador was to return to the lines, remain out of sight and if, just if, a Tamil, even in CT uniform, wanted to speak to him, bring him along.

The comprador said he understood and went back to spy on what was happening. By then Vellu had gathered the labourers who told him that they were ready to go on strike for their demands but wanted the comrades to put such pressure on the manager that they would be sure he would do what was wanted. 'Accepted or not, we will not be here,' the spokesman told Vellu who told the Deputy CT Commander in Malay, he not understanding Tamil.

Delighted at the outcome of comrade Vellu's efforts, the deputy said, 'we will be off now but first we'll visit the manager. You, comrade, stay with these people and check that they were not saying what they did just because we Chinese are here. We will not wait for you at the jungle edge but the section will be there to escort you back.'

Vinod Vellu acknowledged that and a guide led the three guerrillas to the manager's bungalow There they dismissed him then cautiously went around the place, saw the French window of the study was open and stepped inside. Jones, pretending to be reading, heard them and put his book down. In Malay they said, 'if you do what we say, we will spare your life. If not, we will have to kill you by disembowelling you.'

Jones was no coward and answered. 'Tell me what you want and, if possible, I'll do it.'

'How can we trust you?'

'Because, secretly, I have been a card-carrying member of the Communist Party since I was twenty years old.'

The deputy proceeded to ask questions which Jones, remembering how he had interviewed Indian Communists during the war, answered with accuracy. His credentials were accepted.

'We want to use your lines for a food lift ready on the 7th, the day before the full moon. The labourers will complain to you about bad quarters, low pay and poor rations and say they'll go on strike it their conditions are not met. We want you to get the accommodation nearest the jungle empty and to provide at least twenty sacks of rice for us to collect. Are you willing?'

Evan Jones played up admirably. 'Of course. I thought we'd already decided I'd do what you want me to do. I will have the accommodation you mention searched for white ants and move the coolies, even if they are still negotiating a walk-out. I will let my work force pilfer my rice stocks and, for the time you want to come, I will not be here'...*and I'll make certain sure the Government repays me what's taken.*

Hands were shaken, 'red salute' with arms raised were carried out and the three guerrillas left.

Vinod Vellu sat and talked with the excited labourers for half an hour then stepped outside. 'Hist, hist,' he heard. 'Son, come here. Mr Jones, the manager, wants to speak with you. Let me take you up to his bungalow.'

So my note was found and I am almost safe. 'I'll come with you but can't stay long. I'm not one of them really but busy planning my revenge,' he answered, embracing his father as they met after so long.

'I am so glad to hear that,' said Vellu's father as they went up to the bungalow. Evan Jones was ready. 'Come in, come in,' he said. 'I don't want to put the lights on. Would you like a brandy?'

'I'd love one but my breath will smell so I daren't.'

'Good man. Listen, I have been visited by your escort, pretended I'm one of them, have told them I'll ensure rice will be ready for pick-up and that the lines will be empty.'

'Really, all that?'

'Yes, you know I'm on your side. I'll also go and tell Mr Ismail Mubarak that the place will be ready, that is rice ready and lines empty by the 7th, the day before the full moon.'

'That's a great weight off my mind,' said Vellu, happy to find a European speaking fluent Tamil. 'Better not mention me to mother,' he told his father as he left. 'She might talk about it.'

The deputy made a full report to the Political Commissar and to the Military Commander saying that he felt all was safe to go to the empty lines and fetch the rice. To make matters speedy up to thirty people – a sack each if lucky – could go.

The Military Commander at first agreed with that suggestion but he was woken up in the small hours of the 7th night by Vinod Vellu sleep talking. In his excitement the Tamil had forgotten to bind his head and was dreaming of meeting Moby again and had called his name. The Military Commander heard words that sounded like the English 'maybe, maybe' – *or was it 'Moby, Moby?* He knew the name. *Flash!* He remembered reading that strange message in the recent edition of *Red Tidings*, 'so many people are now fed up with the incompetence of the leadership and the hard and hungry life in the jungle that they want to go home and are willing to receive a reward for surrendering, so trust no one but yourself.' Such anti-Party rot had upset him and he had not counted on any of his men being affected but... Can *this Tamil be a friend of the writer so a spy trying to affect my men?* The new newspaper had also given him the idea that not all was well up in the north – *it is written as if a secret message is in it I don't fully understand; it could mean that our men should not be made expendable. Cancel the lift? No, we desperately need food.* Before he went to sleep again, he compromised, take thirty men to the jungle edge and twenty to go the lines to pick up as much rice as possible but to keep the Tamil ignorant of his secret knowledge he'd take thirty men as far as the jungle edge. There he would divide his force, twenty to collect the rations and the others as a reaction force if there were any tricks.

Vinod Vellu had told Evan Jones that it would be on the 8th of March, the night of the full moon, so that was the date for which the operation was planned. 1/12 GR was the battalion ear-marked for the operation and the other Special Branch 'plant' was to lead A Company back to the guerrilla camp to surround and attack it. *No Smash-Hit!* Such was the absurd optimism of complete success had been envisaged and the Government's superiority was to be shown nation-wide. With this in view follow-up company was to be accompanied by two Chinese Special Branch men to escort the 'plant', a police Inspector, two aborigine trackers, a British soldier dog handler and his dog, and a Malay Film Unit photographer to witness the guerrillas' closing moments.

When the CO gave his orders he saw such a savage look on Captain Rance's face that boded no good. 'Captain Rance, this is an order so no argument.'

'Sir, I understand but,' not helping himself now or later, unwisely added 'a circus and a zoo never won battles.'

Vellu never knew that by forgetting to bind his head, he had ruined his chances of a full revenge for the killing of his wife and daughter. He and Moby's Malay, who had purposely kept his real identity from the Tamil until then, would put on white shirts at the last moment before slipping away from the guerrillas to join up with the Security Forces during the food lift. Both were to be taken away, unhurt and later Vellu to be announced as dead for public consumption. The Malay 'plant' would guide A Company back to the guerrilla camp despite A Company's proven tracking ability. But no, somewhere near the top of the military tree

There were three tracks in front of the manager's bungalow, one of which went to the labourers' lines where the rice was, the killing ground. B Company crawled into it two hours before dusk. Meanwhile C and D Companies had moved up to ambush positions on possible guerrilla escape routes. A Company was the follow-up company and had been told to collect its 'supernumeraries' from the nearest police station on their way down. The company had to stay in a holding area until firing was heard and move to near the rubber near the manager's bungalow on hearing the firing.

When Jason looked at the motley bunch who, except for the trackers (who were not needed) did not look fit enough to go uphill even without packs on, let alone with, so robbing him of an possibility of his company's normal rate of advance. He felt sorry for the photographer, hapless man, who told him he had just returned from his honeymoon and was obviously in no fit state for any type of jungle operation. *Operation Dover or Damp Squib?*

When firing broke out it was not as heavy as expected. Those in ambush had been told not to open fire until they saw two men in white shirts pass. The men they did see were in uniform. The two wearers had been sent to the back of the carrying party so appeared last. Not only that: alas, for all the intricate planning, high hopes, bravery shown, calculations made and time spent, no one had checked that the sacks of rice were also white. The guerrillas started carrying the white sacks on their backs before the two 'white shirts' managed to slip away to the bungalow to meet Moby, CO 1/12 GR and the rest of the reception committee by when most of the rice had been carried away. Only one guerrilla was killed and another wounded and captured.

Out of sight from the jungle edge, the Military Commander ordered that the sacks of rice be broken down into twenty-eight loads before moving back to their camp, even at night, as soon as that was done. He had taken the trouble to hack a rough path so, he gambled, they would be well away before any follow-up. 'I was not wrong, I was not wrong,' he cursed under his breath, furious with himself to have been fooled all the time the 'south Indian traitor' had been with them. *It was a gamble to have let him go and lecture those men and it failed, failed.* However, there was no need to report it any higher up his own chain of command. *But now we have food.*

What he had not told Vellu was that he had ordered the men not involved in the food lift to move elsewhere while those on the food lift would also not return to their camp but split up before joining them.

By 2 o'clock in the morning when Jason was sent for moonlight was no more. He shook hands with Vellu who was having a meal and a glass of brandy and congratulated him on having done so well and still being alive⁺ before being introduced to his Malay guide. Reaction had started to set in and both men seemed dazed. Yet, despite the obvious dangers, the Malay said he was willing to guide the Gurkhas to the camp. When he was ready to move the CO asked Jason if he had met up with the rest of the people he was to take.

Jason stared dumbly at his senior. *I'll try again.* 'Yes sir, I have. Are they really necessary?'

'I've told you before, it is an order from high up. Obey it and keep quiet,' the CO angrily snapped.

Jason, completely underwhelmed, took the Malay to his Company and handed him over to the platoon commander who was to move in front.

After some time all were ready but, pitch dark under the trees the extraneous people, less the two aborigines, wandered away so got lost. The already tired soldiers were growing frustrated having to search for those missing. Jason decided to cut his losses and only move off in the light, if only to ensure all his 'foreigners' were with him.

At day break off they went. Not having recced the ground from the jungle edge to the pick-up point, he did not go to the place the guerrillas had left the jungle. The leading scout, therefore, could see no tracks. After several hours of very, very slow, stop and start movement the guide told Jason that he had no idea where he was. Hoping to be fighting a battle by 8 o'clock, it was cold comfort to finding an empty camp at half past one. After patrolling for a further four hours, Jason's report on the radio was, sadly, negative.[8]

Down in Battalion HQ, the CO, impatient at hearing no news all day, roundly and unfairly castigated Jason personally for the delay and not killing any enemy. 'It can only be because of your lack of drive and leadership,' he fumed during his long radio call. There was no point in any other answer except 'Roger, out.'

---

8 Operation 'Dover' did take place historically. Here names and dates have been changed for obvious reasons. 'Vinod Vellu' was awarded a George Medal for his undoubted courage - it was not his fault matters fizzled out so disappointingly. He changed his name and went to live out his life in India where he knew he had a much better chance of dying of old age than had he stayed on in Malaya.

It was evening by the time the Company cooked a meal and the soldiers were very tired and hungry. The photographer was nearly out on his feet having had to be pulled up the steeper inclines, his pack being carried for him, neither were the rest of the followers-on in any fit state for further movement. Even the dog had had enough. They were sent back the next day, as thankful to go as were the Gurkhas to be rid of them.

After five days of more fruitless patrolling they returned to their base.

Same time, various places: Plans for a possible amnesty were being thought out in various places. In London, the problem with UK still being in debt as a result of the war would be eased by giving Malaya self-government with a lessening of British support. Politically it would remove the main political plank of the MCP that Malaya was a British colony. The main Malay political party won a landslide victory and asked for an amnesty as early as January 1955, hoping a ceasefire and reversion to a 'normal' situation would follow. In south Thailand, the MCP, with their radio contact with the Chinese Communists in Beijing, were advised to request, nay demand, being accepted as a legitimate political party or go on fighting. In Singapore, still of vestigial interest to the MCP rather than a moribund Singapore Communist party, intense interest and suspicion, and a need to show solidarity were behind its Chief Minister being invited by the Prime Minister of Malaya to attend any peace talks in the event of any occurring.

The current situation could not be maintained indefinitely by either the MCP or the legitimate governments. It had to change, but how and when?

3 March 1955, Kuala Lumpur: Mr C C Too was re-reading one of his files, the one that contained the capture of Ah Chong. He had only suffered flesh wounds and had said that he was glad to be a civilian once more but he thought Moby still had him under wraps. *I wonder if he could be my answer to my getting into contact with Ah Fat again. Can either I or Moby persuade him to go back to Ha La once more?* He picked up his phone and rang Moby. 'Moby, I'm told that in wartime Britain there were notices near telephones that read "Walls have ears". I'd like to have a short change of scenery and come and pay you a visit.'

'Welcome any time, sir, as you very well know. You probably don't want me to be empty-handed: anything on my menu that you'd like to sample?'

'Yes, a Bekok sandwich.'

'You must be feeling hungry. That will be no problem. When can I expect you?'

'How about the day after tomorrow? I'll motor down as the roads are safe enough these days. I'll start early and arrive around mid-morning.'

'And your sandwich?'

'I'm always hungry,' and C C Too rang off with a giggle.

I wonder what the old fox is onto now. Soon find out. He called one of his helpers. 'Go and see Ah Chong. Ask him if he'd like a walk with you. Get him moving and watch his legs.'

'Watch his legs?' asked his helper, slightly bewildered. *Who will ever understand officers?*

'Yes. You know he was wounded. See if he limps or drags his injured his leg or makes any comment.'

'Okay sir,' and the man went out.

When he returned he said 'all he said was how pleasant it was to walk when it didn't hurt and he was lucky that that kind *gwai lo* bandaged him up so quickly.'

5 March 1955, Seremban: 'Moby, I'll come clean with you...'

'For once,' said with a grin.

'As I was saying, I'll come clean with you. I have, as indeed we both have certain contacts, how shall I put it? "up our sleeve" as the conjurer says. You have Ah Chong and I want to use him. How is he?'

'Cured of his wounds, I am glad to say. I had him taken for a walk after you rang and his minder said that Ah Chong had said that the kind *gwai lo* had bandaged him up so quickly, there were now no ill effects.'

'Good. I want him to go to Ha La, in south Thailand.' Moby lifted an eyebrow in surprise. 'It was from Ha La you will remember that he got those copies of the new newspaper *Red Tidings*, whose editor is our common friend Ah Fat.'

'So I am guessing you want to use As Chong as your contact man. Correct?'

'Correct. If I was your school master I'd allow you to give out the new pencils with the green rubber at the end,' and both laughed. 'Please send for him.'

Ah Chong came in. Moby introduced C C Too under a

pseudonym and said that 'Mr Chen' had a question for him. 'Nothing at all to worry about.'

'Ah Chong. Soon you will be a civilian. If you do not have a family, you will want to get married, buy a house and start a trade to earn some money. Am I right?'

Sinsaang Chen was right.

'And have you worked out how much that will all come to?'

No he had not.

'Then, with this piece of paper and this pencil, work it out and tell me.'

Ah Chong, scowling with concentration, set to work. 'Fifty thousand ringgit to start with. If any is left over, I'll bank it.'

'And how do you propose to get it. How long do you think it will take you to earn it?'

Ah Chong had not thought of that.

'Would you like it next month? All of it?'

'Oh yes, I would,' was the answer, eyes a-gleam and a smile.

'You will have it if you first do something for me.'

The smile faded.

'I want you to go back to Ha La.' He saw Ah Chong stiffen. 'Wait, wait. I will arrange for you to be helicoptered in a day's walk south of the border. You will go to Ha La and give a letter to a friend of mine, the editor of *Red Tidings*. He will then ask the Politburo for permission to go to Kuala Lumpur and I will arrange for you to go with him. Once that is done successfully, you will get the money.'

'Yes, I agree if I can have someone to go with me as far as Ha La.'

Hm, that's a thorny one. 'I think that the best way is to take some extra tobacco and cloth with you and give it to a couple of *t'o yan*. From what I know, they'll help you.'

It was only after the reward was raised to sixty thousand ringgit that the deal was clinched.

12 March 1955, Ha La, south Thailand: Ah Fat had been churning out his editions of *Red Tidings* as best he could when he was surprised by Ah Chong's arrival, with, unusually, an escort of two *t'o yan*. He saw Ah Chong take a bundle of tobacco and some cloth out of his knapsack and give it to his escorts who snatched it out of his hand and bolted away.

I'll be told all about it in its own good time.

'Ah Fat *sinsaang*,' – no *'Comrade!'* – 'I have a letter for you,' he said in a low voice. 'Shall I give it to you here and now or after our' – *our!* – 'evening meal?'

'Hand it over now, if you will. We'll talk about whatever is in it after we've eaten,' Ah Fat answered pleasantly.

Ah Chong gave him the letter and said he presumed the accommodation would be as before. Yes, it would. Ah Fat called his Bear over to him and, with a slight wink, told him to look after the new arrival.

Opening the envelope he saw it was from C C Too. *So he's using Ah Chong as a postman. That is clever. How much did it cost him, I wonder?* The letter asked him to come to Kuala Lumpur as 'I really want to meet you. No details now but bring some copies of your *Red Tidings*. I will leave it with you how you fix it with your boss.'

After their meal Ah Fat and Ah Chong, with the Bear listening in – 'his ears are my ears' – Ah Chong told his story, included being bandaged by a *gwai lo* who spoke Chinese. At the end he said, 'now you can tell me how you can get me back to Seremban so I can start my new life.'

'That shouldn't be too difficult. What we'll do is this,' and he explained that he would have to go to MCP HQ farther into Thailand. 'I have my own squad and I'm expected to go there now and again. You will come with me and stay with my squad who have their own place. You will not leave where they put you. This is only in case there are any inquisitive snoopers who might wonder who you are and why you have reported in without their permission.'

Yes, that was fully understood.

'When will we leave?'

'After you have had a good rest. Say in four days' time?'

And that too was agreed.

16 March, south Thailand: The Politburo was in session when Ah Fat's group reached MCP HQ. Ah Fat went to make his presence known. He saluted them and sat down at the edge of the group, waiting to be asked what had brought him there.

The meeting finished and Chin Peng welcomed him back. 'We were wondering when we would see you again. We have had no news of the efficacy of our *Red Tidings*. Have you had any news from your couriers?'

'No, Comrade Secretary General. It is really too soon for any of them to return. I am expecting one or two of the ones who had a nearer destination any day now.'

'Comrade, from what we have read, we all believe you have done a thoroughly good job and we congratulate you. That will be in the minutes of this meeting.'

Ah Fat put on his false smile as he expressed his total satisfaction.

'So why have you come back here, Comrade?' Chien Tiang asked.

'You can probably guess as you can hear the same Radio Malaya news as I can. There is much talk about an amnesty and I am sure you want to know what *gwai lo* thinking is on the matter.'

Yes, they all wanted to know what was 'in the air'.

'I want your permission to make a journey down to Kuala Lumpur and visit the person you sent me to see last time.' – it was wrong to say 'Chan Man Yee' – 'who is in such a wonderful position that I can learn whatever is being talked about the amnesty and associated matters.'

'Comrade, yes, that is a good idea. A direct face-to-face talk is necessary. You must not, ever, use the telephone about any meeting.'

'Comrade, that would be a grave breach of security,' said Ah Fat, solemnly.

'You know where the person lives. You will go to the house in your normal manner making sure you are not observed. I know your trade craft is superb. I'll ask our members if they agree.'

'How will you go?' asked one of them. 'By road or air?'

'I'll go into Malaya by road and fly from Penang down to

KL.'

Votes were taken. Unanimous approval. 'Don't be away too long. Your editorship is what is needed here. We have just decided that, come the 1st of May, we will send the British Government of Malaya a letter under the name of Ng Heng, Representative of the Malayan Races Liberation Army, offering peace talks.'

'I fully understand the sanctity of that and, as the vote is unanimous and I am ready to move forthwith, I will leave tomorrow,' he said as he left for his own part of the camp. He sensed morale was low without any amnesty.

'We're off first thing tomorrow,' he said to the Bear and Ah Chong.

Ah Fat did not know that camp sentries were now briefed as to who was allowed to leave the camp because too many of the lower-ranked comrades had become so frustrated that they had tried to escape. This had to be stopped. Any unnamed person seen leaving was to be shot, not challenged first. The sentries were told that two named people would be leaving the camp early next morning, not three. The three men moved off but neither Ah Fat nor his Bear noticed that Ah Chong had bent down to tie his boot lace that had become undone.

'Only two,' said the sentry, 'whom we know. This third must be stopped.' He aimed from about twenty yards and blew Ah Chong's head off.

Ah Fat and the Bear continued as though nothing had happened as it was too risky to do anything else.

No one could recognise the corpse that was buried according to routine in an unmarked grave before *rigor mortis* set in.

6

Early April 1955, Kuala Lumpur: Back in KL, Ah Fat and the Bear were determined to put their dangerous job behind them, if only for a short time, and relax with their family. Wives and children hated seeing so little of them. They had no idea what their real job was but the money paid into their bank accounts did mean that they considered the job must be worthwhile.

After delivering his children to school in Jalan Petaling that first morning, a wonderful treat for them, Ah Fat went to the restaurant-cum-bar owned by his old friend, Ah Hong. Because of other customers being in earshot, he merely ordered a coffee and went to sit in a vacant corner. Ah Hong plonked it down on the table with no word spoken – trade craft – and Ah Fat slowly sipped it until the place was almost empty.

Ah Hong then sidled over, cocked an inquisitive eye at his friend and quietly asked if all was well. 'Yes, well enough, thank you,' Ah Fat, rubbing his hands together, answered with a grin before nodding in the directing of Chan Man Yee's dwelling. 'Have you noticed any changes in her circumstances?'

'No, nor am I aware of any,' Ah Hong answered slowly. 'I have not been asked to by the type of person I used to work for and appearing too inquisitive can be unhealthy.'

'Don't I know it!' countered his friend. 'That's why I am still alive.'

'From time to time people who come in here do talk about her, softly and by inference. I am a dab hand at appearing not to listen and what I gather is that most of them are the start of a chain of couriers. Which way they go, to the MCP HQ or to the guerrillas in the jungle, I don't know.'

That made Ah Fat ponder: people in Ha La had not given any hint of a KL courier link and even if Chan Man Yee was the start of a pro-MCP propaganda chain, Ha La would not know about it. 'One of them left an unusual newspaper behind, by mistake or on purpose I can't say, but it might be of interest to you. I've kept it to show you. I'll go and fetch it.' Off he went and returned with a copy of *Red Tidings*. 'One of the men who hinted that he had been talking to Chan Man Yee left it,' he said as he handed it over.

From the look on his friend's face there was no need to ask if he knew about it. What did surprise him was when Ah Fat, turning away from the few customers and facing a light on the wall, opened it and, taking a page at random, squinted at it.

'I'd like to ask you what you're looking for and whether you found it or not but it is better I don't. Instead, let me bring you another coffee, or perhaps something stronger?'

'Kind of you but no thank you. I'm on leave for a week and I could easily come again and have a chat. Do you ever show this newspaper to anyone else?'

'No. Do you want it?'

He had seen the government watermark and that, really, was all that interested him because it meant that there was a courier system that the Politburo had kept secret from him. *Disturbing!* 'Yes, I'll take it, it might come in useful. Can I use your phone, please, not the one at the bar but the one in your office for a local call?'

'Of course, any time.'

Ah Fat rang the unlisted number in C C Too's office. His voice was recognised and he was brusquely told to 'Come to my place this evening. Bring your wife and the two girls can have *ha king, ha king* as we natter.'

Ah Fat grinned at *ha king, ha king* as it aptly described chickens pecking at the dirt for something to eat and C C Too was referring to the two women, heads bobbing up and down, as, with lowered voices, they exchanged gossip, scandal and tittle-tattle that was only suitable for women's ears.

That evening, when the women were talking in another room, Ah Fat said, 'I have an important piece of news for you. The MCP Politburo has just decided that, come the 1st of May they will send a letter to the High Commissioner under the name of Ng Heng, Representative of the Malayan Races Liberation Army, offering peace talks.'

His host sat bolt upright in his chair at that, a look of satisfaction on his face. 'You're completely sure of this, aren't you?'

'Couldn't be surer. I was told by Chin Peng himself that the Politburo had passed the motion almost that very minute.'

'Great, great. The boys in Bluff Road and at HQ Malaya Command will also be overjoyed at learning that so early on.

What else have you for me?'

'Nothing till I have rung Chan Man Yee. I'll hold the phone away from my ear so you can hear what she says.'

He dialled the number and, after six or seven rings, the phone was picked up and, in Cantonese, she asked who was speaking. He introduced himself as he had done the first time, no names but saying that he was back in town from the north and that her friends, apart from sending their fraternal greetings, wanted him to meet her to find out what was happening about any peace talks, amnesty or ceasefire.

'I know quite a lot that maybe has not reached where you come from and I can tell you what I know when we meet.'

'Yes. I need to be fully briefed. When is it suitable to meet you where you are?'

There was no immediate answer. *She's wondering how she can arrange her contacts, I suppose,* Ah Fat thought. 'Can you come the day after tomorrow?'

'Yes. Time?'

'Nine thirty in the evening.'

It was Ah Fat's turn not to answer immediately. *Play her up. Make her a tiny bit anxious.* 'Yes.'

'Anything more before I ring off?'

'How did you get copies of *Red Tidings* and how do you like the watermark?'

Both listeners heard her sudden intake of breath. As if without thinking she asked 'how did you know I was getting any copies? I thought that line was secret.' A whimpering sound came over the line and a mumbled 'I only told him when he made love to me.'

In as stern a voice as he could muster, Ah Fat gruffly answered, 'didn't I tell you last time I know more than you think I know?' and rang off without an answer.

It was time to bring C C Too up to date. He reached into the inside pocket of his light-weight jacket, brought out the copy of *Red Tidings* that Ah Hong had given him and handed it over, saying, 'what is so interesting about this is that it has a government watermark on the pages, not an MCP one. That means it was one of those I either took or sent across to MCP HQ, not the ones I sent down into Malaya.' Mr Too nodded assent. 'What it also means is that the Politburo is sending copies of the newspaper down by a courier in its own set-up, something new to me. I don't know if that is serious or not. We both heard Chan Man Yee snivelling at the end as though "favours given" were not reciprocated in some way or other...'

Mr Too broke in with 'that means when you go and meet her, get her to tell you his name, either accidently or as an act of revenge.'

This time it was Ah Fat who nodded before saying 'I have some more of the MCP watermarked copies for you but they are locked up in my cupboard at home.'

'I'd like them. What I have in mind is, once the rumoured amnesty with its ceasefire and leaflets dropped with the surrender passes is under way, I can get my staff to produce more copies either to drop from the air or for my 'Q' Teams to place around known CT camps.'

Before they broke up Ah Fat gave C C Too Ah Hong's phone number. 'This is the number of the phone in the bar from where

Chan Nan Yee's place can be seen. I'll be there from about 8 p.m. onwards. That is ninety minutes before our meeting. What I would like is for your phone monitors to listen in from dusk onwards. I can only see what happens outside and won't be able to recognise anyone who leaves her place before I get there. My target might have a visitor who, one way or the other, might make a difference to how I broach any conversation with her. If you do have anything to tell me of, ring the bar number and ask for me. I'll then get the call transferred to the office.'

'Yes, of course I'll see to that. It might pay dividends. We'll listen in to you, also.' He grinned then, seriously, 'just suppose anything untoward were to happen to you, we might have to arrange a rescue.'

Ah Fat's wife came into their room at that moment, in high spirits, having had a great chat. 'You men say we women gossip. Yes, we do and we learnt how to from you,' and told him it was time to go home. On the way she giggled and said 'did you know that the woman he calls Wong is not his wife but only a girl friend?'

'No I didn't but, on balance, does it matter?'

No. PS 150, Restaurant-cum-bar, 150 Jalan Petaling, Kuala Lumpur: At half past eight the phone rang at the bar and Jason was called over. 'News,' was the curt message.

'I'll have this transferred. Wait a moment,' and Ah Fat asked Ah Hong to put the call through to his office. 'No listening in, please,' Ah Fat said, 'you know the rules.'

In the office, Ah Fat lifted the phone and said, 'Listening.

Send.'

'Apparently an hour ago a man came into Chan Man Yee's room and was told to go away, saying "I don't want to see you anymore."

'"Why not?" was answered by "you brought me a newspaper and I was so happy I wanted to show my appreciation in the only way I can, especially when I'm lonely. You started playing then, all of a sudden, you broke off and left me. I am so furious I don't want anything to do with you ever again."

'We heard quite a hard slap, palm of the hand on a cheek probably, then sobbing but not loud enough to shut out the sound of a door being slammed. We have heard the same voice before, in connection with his giving her some sort of newspaper.'

'Thank you for that useful news. Gives me something to work on,' and Ah Fat rang off. *She may want me to carry on but as a Politburo man, to say nothing of my not wanting her, that won't do. What can I give her instead?* He racked his brains. *Got it!* Back in the bar he asked Ah Hong if there was a lingerie shop open nearby. Yes, and he was told where.

He quickly found it and, trying to keep a straight face, asked the young woman assistant if there were any red silk knickers suitable for a woman of 'a certain age'. The assistant gulped, put her hand over her mouth and brought out a selection. 'I'll take three of the large size,' Ah Fat said, looking at his watch, 'can you make me another pair with yellow, red, blue and white stripes here and now?'

The assistant looked at him in wonder, then admiration. 'The tailor is still here but he'll charge you.'

'Please ask him. If he can make a pair, the same size as these in half an hour, I'll give him two hundred ringgit extra.'

She went into the back to ask the tailor, thinking that the customer was either over-sexed, a masochist or merely had a strange sense of humour.

Half an hour later, with his four pairs of knickers, Ah Fat went to the front door of Chan Man Yee's place and rang her bell. She came and let him in, reluctantly it seemed to him. He glanced at her face and, yes, there was a mark of her having been hit. 'I'll take you upstairs and make you some tea. I don't have anything stronger,' she said, in a low tone of voice.

Once settled with a glass of tea each, Ah Fat asked her for news. She told him what she knew then started weeping. He let her give way to her obvious sorrows then asked her if he could help.

She sniffed and snivelled but said nothing.

Sternly, 'What would the Politburo say to this, comrade?'

That brought her to her senses. 'I...I don't know. You won't tell them, will you?'

Time to be kind. 'I am a family man and I know when a woman has been hurt. I won't ask how you have been hurt so to make amends I have brought you a present.' She was too overwrought to wonder how he had managed to foretell her gloom. The multi-coloured knickers were separate so the package he gave her only contained the three red pairs.

She opened her present and, with a gasp of pleasure when she saw what was in it, took out the knickers, held them up to the light and fondled them appreciatively. 'How kind, how kind,' was all she could say.

When they had finished their tea, she asked him how she could repay him. He made as though to think of the answer. 'Tell you what. Of course I won't mention anything to the Politburo but please tell me the name of the man who made your cheek red.'

'How, how did you know that?' she queried anxiously, rubbing her cheek with her hand.

'I've seen it before. There's not much in this evil world that is new.'

She sat still, turning over something in her mind. 'All right, between us his name is Xi Zhan Yang and he is a Politburo courier, a senior one who knows what goes on, has to as courier, doesn't he?' Without waiting for an answer, she went on, 'We had a row last time. He led me on...' A sob. 'He led me on and then, when I was ready for him, oh comrade, after such a long time alone, he left me. It made me so angry it almost made me change my mind about all I've been doing.'

My cue! 'Chan Man Yee, if that really is the case, here is another pair of knickers.' He took them out of his pocket and showed them to her. 'Oooh,' she squeaked, 'why those colours?'

'They are the colours of the flag of Malaya. In a few months the colonial power will have gone. Maybe I will have gone to China' – *maybe not* – 'as the MCP is finished and if you want to revert to a life that most people want, wear these coloured knickers,' and he handed them over.

'And you?'

'Don't worry. I won't look to see which pair you are wearing!'

She burst into laughter. 'Can you come back in two or three

days when I've had a good think about this?'

When C C Too heard the tape, he almost collapsed with laughter. Another idea struck him... *It's not often that I put our prize stallion onto a job but this is one I will. He can charm the legs off a clothes horse.*

The next night Chan Man Yee's bell rang and, suspiciously and reluctantly, she opened the door. There was a Chinese man whose face was vaguely familiar but whom she could not properly place. In fact he had stood next to one of the policemen who had searched her bag and found the sheets of paper. 'What do you want?' she asked tentatively.

'I am a friend of the man who so upset you, Xi Zhan Yang. He boasted that...' She interrupted him. 'I don't want to hear his name. Go away.'

'Not so fast, please. He asked me to apologise to you so, if you could let me come in and talk to you privately, rather than on your doorstep, it could do you no harm.'

Unenthusiastically she allowed him to come in and upstairs they went. Once seated, he took a bottle of brandy out of his pocket and put it on the small table between them. 'You have been worrying. I know, from what Xi Zhan Yang told me, that you never drink. Regard this as medicine. Just a little drop will do you good and cheer you, and me, up,' and he smiled at her tenderly.

She hesitated. He leant forward and saying, 'he told me he had hit you in the face', gently stroked her cheek. Instead of jerking away, on a sudden impulse she took hold of his hand as she felt her 'down below' starting to throb. He sensed that he was winning her over. 'I can offer you three things,' he said softly. 'The first is...' and he stood up and going to the kitchen found two glasses, washed them out and brought them back. Saying nothing he poured a small amount of brandy into both of them and handed her a glass. She took it and he made sure their fingers brushed.

'This is the first?' she asked.

'Yes, this is the first.'

'And the second?'

'Wait until you are really ready for it. I'll tell you when I think you are.'

He lifted his glass and toasted formally, with the obligatory toast of *yam seng* – drink to victory – he downed the contents in one. Almost without thought so did she, nor did she refuse a refill, slightly more than the first lot. Her face mellowed and they talked casually for a while, then she asked, 'what is the second?'

He rose and, one hand under her rump and the other on her breasts, lifted her onto her bed and lay beside her. 'I'll give you the choice of the second or the third.'

'I'm ready for you,' she said softly and his answer was, 'shall I'll show you the third?'

'No, let's have the second one now, now, now,' and she started to undress him while he did the same for her.

An hour later, exhausted, he rose, dressed and went into the kitchen to make some tea. When he got back she was dressed once more. 'And the third? It can't be better than the second,' she added almost wolfishly.

He took an envelope out of his pocket. 'Open it and say if you want what it allows.'

She took it gingerly and, with a gasp so deep it made her cough, there was a permit for her to emigrate to mainland China. She read it through once, twice and then, after the third time, said, 'Yes, I accept that but only if you can come with me.'

'No, I can't do that, but I can visit you until you leave, either with the name on the permit or, if you were to prefer it, another name.'

'No, I'll go under my own name' and, unexpectedly, burst into tears.

Before Ah Fat and his Bear went back to Ha La, by way of Betong, he had another long session with C C Too, this time before he went to his office. After discussing Chan Man Yee he was told that Xi Zhan Yang had been picked up and would not be returning to MCP HQ.

'As I am not expected to know anything about him I am sure I won't be involved in any questions. But I have an idea what to do when any peace talks take place. Once the negotiators have gone into Malaya I may well be able to appropriate any of the documents that I know do exist about how the Chinese Communist Party sees what the MCP needs or can do. As you well know, there has been an MCP representative in Beijing for a long time and the radio in Betong is constantly used for messages between him and the Politburo. Anything I steal must be given to someone who without fail can bring to you. The area is sure to be heavily guarded and one of the conditions of a ceasefire talk will be that numbers involved will be kept to a minimum and extraneous movement restricted. Who can I give my findings to?'

C C Too put his head in his hands. 'A bell is ringing in my mind. Let me think.' *Yes!* 'The Director of Operations feels that your friend Jason Rance can somehow find his way up there. Quite how we've not even thought about. But if we can get him there, couldn't that be an answer?'

'It is a mighty big "if"...' and his voice trailed off. 'Yes, he is the only one I trust without endangering my own people.'

C C Too picked up his telephone and dialled the number of the Director of Operation's Military Assistant and merely said, 'I'm the Chinese who was sent for by the Director about Ten Foot Long.'

'Yes, I know who you are. How can I help you?'

'I have a man with me who must return north in a day or so. I think the Director would like to see him because quote "you have sown a tiny seed in my mind" unquote.'

'I'm with it. Hold on while I go and ask.'

The answer was, 'The General can squeeze you in between 1400 and 1420 this afternoon. Will that be enough time?'

'It will have to be. See you then,' and C C Too rang off and said to Ah Fat, 'I'll pick you up at your house at half past one.'

The two Chinese were ushered into the General's office and C C Too introduced Ah Fat, adding, 'Sir, apart from Mr Ah Fat being a childhood friend of and like a brother to Captain Rance, he has been our most active mole all through the Emergency years and is a non-voting member of the MCP Politburo. Normally I talk to him in the privacy of my house but meeting you in your office there'll be no one to recognise him so here is not risky for his safety.'

The General held out his hand and shook Ah Fat's warmly. 'Now, meeting you is something I really do appreciate and thank you for coming.'

'Sir, it's my pleasure also.'

'Sit down and I'll order up some coffee.' It was quickly brought in and the General glanced at his watch. *Shall I delay my next meeting? I'll see what C C Too has to say first.*

'Mr Too, bring me up to date. What is the actual reason for bringing Mr Ah Fat to see me at such short notice?'

'Sir, will you let Mr Ah Fat answer your question?'

'Yes, of course.' The General turned slightly in his chair and said, 'over to you.'

'Sir, as a non-voting member of the Politburo I can get my hands on stuff very few others can. A lot of encouragement comes over our radio from the MCP representative in Beijing who passes on what the Chinese Communist Party advises the MCP to do. Records are made of conversations. When any peace talks start and the Chairman is out of the way I have a good chance to get the paperwork and bring it out.' He looked up and saw the General staring at him, eyes button bright. 'The snag is that, in such an environment at that time, the only man I can trust to give the paperwork to without any rumours spreading of what would be seen as my duplicity, is my friend Captain Jason Rance, now serving with 1/12 GR.' He let that sink in before adding, 'and were my colleagues to learn about that, my life would be in even greater jeopardy.' He had another thought. 'I can't be easily contacted where I work, nor dare I come back here again so, if possible, I'd like to know your reaction before I leave.'

The General called in his MA. 'Charles, a very fast ball. Please apologise to my next caller, ask him to come and see me at...' and, biting his lower lip, '1530. Instead, give the Director of Intelligence a call and say I want him here now.'

The MA nodded and went to his own office and made the telephone calls.

The General then said to Ah Fat 'Yes, I see your point. You have asked for something that is not an everyday type of request. It will have to be thought through most carefully. But before my Director of Intelligence, Colonel James Mason, comes I must ask you this. Are you sure Captain Rance will agree to undertake what could be a scary job and without doubt against regulations?'

'Don't worry, sir, I know it. He has already saved my life once when he himself could easily have been killed and, if necessary, I am sure he'd do it again.' CC Too added, 'Sir, not now but any time you want to know details of what has just been said, I can tell you.'

'Yes, I'll be interested. But for now let me think of the implications before Colonel Mason gets here. You two, if you want, discuss anything you may have on your minds.'

The General took a cigarette case out of his pocket and offered one to his guests. Both declined and, lighting one for himself, sat back, frowning. *A chance I never expected,* he mused. *Will I still be here then and, if not, will anything we decide today crumble...*

His thoughts were interrupted by a knock on the door and the Director of Intelligence was ushered in. He first saluted his superior and looked around. The two Chinese saw a tall, imposing man with an air of innate authority not always noticeable in army officers. The General stood up. 'James, you know Mr Too but not our other guest, Mr Ah Fat.'

Hands were shaken. 'Take a pew James, and listen to this...' and he explained the reason for the sudden call. Apart from being given a précis of Ah Fat's and Captain Rance's backgrounds, he was briefed on what had been offered and the difficulties of seeing so far ahead for any planning.

'Yes, I can see the urgency in this, a most unusual and unprecedented situation. I'd like to ask Mr Ah Fat how is it that he has have been able to come to KL now?'

Ah Fat glanced at C C Too who gave him a nod. 'I was given the name of a mole in Bluff Road by the Secretary General of the MCP who told me to visit her to see what she had picked up during her work. I was tasked by the Politburo to edit a newspaper, *Red Tidings*, and the Politburo's plan was to print it on Government watermarked paper. It was thought that the only way to procure the paper was to get the mole to bring it from Bluff Road. I visited her as a member of the Politburo only after reporting to Mr Too and action was taken. Mr Too's men managed to put a bug on her phone...'

'Very successfully, too, if I am allowed to interrupt.'

'...that gave me the idea of having two lots of watermarked paper, Government watermarked for the MCP and MCP marked for the guerrillas. I so to manipulate the text in the copies for the comrades in Malaya that they would lose heart.'

'Neat, very neat,' muttered Colonel Mason.

'The Politburo sent me back to KL to see the mole to find out about any political future. It was later, when Mr Too and I were talking, after another visit to the mole, that I mentioned I could put my hands on material that would be kept quiet, so unknown, at any peace talks.'

The General, who had a soft spot for some types of eccentricity, butted in. 'James, this is where Captain Rance comes into the picture. He is the only person Mr Ah Fat trusts to give the paperwork kept secretly by the Politburo. Mr Too has no other safe method of retrieving such material. Have you? How does all that fit in with any of your Intelligence plans and how do you see us actually putting it into action?'

The Colonel considered his answer for quite a while. 'It is so vague, General, isn't it? I don't mean Mr Ah Fat's plan but the whens and wheres of any peace talks. We have yet to have any intimation...'

C C Too interrupted. 'Excuse me Colonel. I should have told you that my friend here has told me that the MCP Politburo have decided that they will send the High Commissioner, on the 1st of May, a letter under the name of Ng Heng, Representative of the Malayan Races Liberation Army, offering peace talks.'

'Now that certainly is interesting. Thank you for telling me. I think it is most important that we do get anything Mr Ah Fat can bring us but using a British army officer when I expect only a policeman in charge of any defence arrangements will be allowed anywhere near the area, is probably going to be too tricky.'

A quietness descended as the realisation of putting the scheme into action was considered.

Ah Fat said, 'I have a suggestion.'

'Let's hear it,' both officers said at the same time.

'Make Captain Rance's visit unattributable.'

That suggestion brought consternation to all three listeners. Ah Fat continued, 'This is off the top of my head so please hear me out. Some of my key men are willing to serve him. I doubt I'll be able to come back here for quite some time but my close escort, Wang Ming, known as *Hung Lo*, the Bear, has pledged to serve Captain Rance unconditionally, can meet up with him, maybe in KL around the time that the ceasefire talks take place, then take him to meet me, somewhere in the jungle of course, with the secret material at a pre-arranged secret place near the Thai border on the Malaya side.'

'He'll be court-martialled if he is found out,' said Colonel Mason.

'And my head will be on the chopping block if that happens,' added the General.

'Not necessarily,' broke in C C Too. 'Suppose he is asked to go north, say to Sungei Patani to give the Gurkha recruits or even a Police Jungle Squad somewhere around there a lecture on some particular aspects of guerrilla warfare and asks for a week's leave afterwards and then, in plain clothes, meets up with Ah Fat's Bear who will guide him to the chosen area.'

'Who will arrange the Bear's meeting up with Captain Rance? That is the tricky part, isn't it?' That was the General's question.

'Not really, sir,' said Ah Fat. 'The Bear can visit C C Too with the details of when and where in enough time and detail for a meet up to be possible. He is my deputy and we live in a different part of the camp from the others. His absence will not be noticed.'

'To make sure about your friend, have you thought of trying to ring him while you are here in KL?' the Intelligence Colonel asked.

'No sir, but I'd like to. My worry is that phones are insecure and I don't know where he is.'

'Then when we have finished with the General, I'll take you both to my office. Not only can I easily find out where your friend is but I also have a military phone that is more secure than any civilian one.'

A broad smile appeared on Ah Fat's face. 'That sounds just what I want. Thank you for the suggestion.'

The General looked at his watch and said, 'I've only got a short time with you so I'll say that we all have to take risks sometimes and the stakes are high so I'll stick my head out and say "yes" in outline. There is, however, a proviso: the politicians will all be elected Malayans by the time the terms of an amnesty are agreed on, likewise if and when any peace talks are arranged, military activity in that area will indubitably be vetoed. That rather sadly means I mustn't know any more about what we've being discussing. For now only we four in this room will know about it, other than Captain Rance, of course.

'General,' said the Colonel, 'excuse me but there is one more person I believe should know about what I might call the "cover plan" and that is, surely, the CO of Rance's battalion. You can override any doubts he may have. It won't be the present man as he's due for replacement at the end of July.'

'Good point. Thank you, James. If nothing happens there's no need to tell him. And as for you, Mr Ah Fat, you have my total support for all your magnificent hard work. You are one in a million. It's a great pity there aren't more like you and Mr Too.'

Both Chinese acknowledged the compliment. The meeting broke up and the Colonel Mason said, 'Come along with me,' and led them to his office, which was wired off from the others. Once inside he called for a Major subordinate and told him to look up details of 1/12 GR, find out where the rifle companies were deployed and which one was commanded by a Captain Jason Rance. 'I have details of every unit in the country,' the Colonel said, 'so it won't take long to find out.'

Indeed within a few minutes the Major reported that Captain Rance commanded A Company which was in Rompin and gave the telephone number. The Colonel dialled and, after a few rings, the answer came, 'OC A Company, Captain Rance here.'

The Colonel gave the phone to Ah Fat who, in Chinese, said '*Wei*, Shandong Cannon, it's Flat Ears here; sorry I can't talk to you face-to-face but only by fighting with the electric speech.'

Jason's roar of approval was heard by the others who grinned delightedly at Rance's obvious joy at hearing his old friend's voice.'

'Jason, listen,' still in Chinese, 'don't interrupt till I've finished...' and succinctly passed on his plan, warning him of possible come-backs if anything went wrong or he was discovered.

'Flat Ears, I'm with you all the way. Just tell me who to contact for details where and when.'

'I'll hand you over to *Sinsaang* Too. He'll be the link man. Good bye, Jason. See you later,' and he handed over the phone. 'Very briefly, I'll make contact with you as and when I can. Do you want a code word?' asked C C Too.

'Let's go for *Red Tidings Mark II*.'

The Colonel made a sign for Too to break off for a mo. 'I also must be in on this. Give me the phone, please. Captain Rance, this is Colonel Mason, Director of Intelligence in HQ Malaya Command. Are you willing to help this way?'

'Yes, sir, I am.'

'Excellent. All this is topper than top secret and apart from Mr C C Too and Mr Ah Fat, only the Director of Operations and I know about it. Only we five. It will be my responsibility to alert your CO about a cover plan for you to move north. In outline we feel it best for you to disappear on local leave after, say, giving a lecture for the Gurkha recruits in the Training Depot or to a Police Jungle Squad or whatever skulduggery will be needed for you to disappear is up to us, unless you have a better idea. Understood?'

'Fully, sir. It will be a change from Framework Operations and during any amnesty could be the best time possible.'

'Good, I'll hand you back to Mr C C Too,' who thanked Jason and rang off.

Before the two Chinese left, the Colonel wrote a number of a bit of paper and gave it to C C Too. 'This is my unlisted number. Give me yours.' The exchange was made. 'When either of us has anything to tell each other, both of us will feel free to call the other, using veiled speech, of course.'

'Of course. Colonel, I don't know how much you heard of

Captain Rance's Chinese but anyone who didn't know he wasn't a Chinese wouldn't believe otherwise.'

'If anyone is needed for a job like this, he is our man.'

They parted and the two Chinese went to the car park and drove off.

There may have been no one to recognise Ah Fat in the Director of Operations' office but there was one who saw him being driven out of the HQ Malaya Command camp. *That must be comrade Ah Fat. I know him too well. Playing a double game is he? A treacherous yanshu.* Not knowing the English for mole he gave it its Chinese name.

On the way back in his car, C C Too said, 'I have an idea that could help you. Let me give you some "bait", paperwork we give out when we don't want to give actual details. Have that with you when you go to get the Politburo's secret mail and if you are caught, your excuse will be that because of what you had filched when you went to KL is so secret, this was the only way you felt you could deliver it.'

'That's a great idea. Please get it to me within the next couple of days before I return. I'll keep it safe until I need it.'

It turned out to be a most lucky forethought.

Same day, Rompin, Negri Sembilan: Jason sat back in his office still stunned at hearing his boyhood friend's voice so unexpectedly. *Almost can't believe it. He's a plucky one, that's for sure.* He gazed out of the window with a 'thousand yard' stare, seeing nothing. A goose ran over his grave. *I've saved his life before but I had a squad of my men with me then. This time it will be the Bear and* *me alone...*

In the other office the corporal clerk had listened to his OC's burst of fluent Chinese with amazement, admiration and wonder. *A girlfriend? Another unusual operation? Or what?*

End of April 1955, south Thailand: Ah Fat and Wang Ming got back to Betong without any trouble. Both had felt rejuvenated by being away from the monotony and forced camaraderie there and seeing their family. Ah Fat was happy that Chan Man Yee would soon be in China and that arrangements for purloining the secret material had been talked about at such a high level. His sorrow was that he had not met up with his old friend. It was just as well for his peace of mind that he was ignorant about having been recognised.

Mid-May 1955, High Commissioner's office, Kuala Lumpur: Sir Donald MacGillivray's Personal Assistant knocked on the door of his master's office, was called in and went to the large table where the Great Man sat busy reading some papers. 'Excuse me, sir, for interrupting you but we have received a letter with a Thai stamp on it, addressed to you but rather curiously. The person who addressed the envelope obviously did not know the correct protocol. I nearly threw it away, feeling it might be one of those spoof letters we get from time to time, but curiosity got the better of me and I feel I must hand it to you without delay.'

'Micky,' Sir Donald said with a smile. 'Just give it me without being so long-winded.'

The PA handed it over and Sir Donald was galvanised by

what he read. Dated 1 May 1955, sent from South Thailand and signed by a Ng Heng, Representative of the Malayan Races Liberation Army, offering peace talks with the British Government of Malaya. *Can this be true?* He read it again. *I'll find out.*

'Micky, ten to one it's genuine. However, there's only one man who can verify if that is so and can recognise the name.'

'Sir, I know who you mean, Mr C C Too in Bluff Road. I'll give him a call and have it transferred to you.'

'Straightaway, please.'

The phone in C C Too's office rang. *Does this ever stop ringing so I can settle down to some work?* 'Too here. Can I help you?'

'Mr Too, it is the High Commissioner's PA here. Sir Donald would like to speak to you. May I put you through to him?'

'But of course,' and he heard the click as the call was transferred. 'Sir, Mr Too is on the line.'

'Mr Too, a quickie. I have just received a letter signed by a man whose name is given as Ng, N G, Heng, H E N G, apparently a representative of the Malayan Races Liberation Army, offering peace talks with the Government of Malaya. Can you elucidate for me, please?'

'Sir Donald, in one: Ng Heng is Chin Peng's secret code word. With that on the letter it has to be true.'

'Are you one hundred percent sure?'

'No, sir, two hundred percent,' and the High Commissioner smiled as he heard the chuckle at the other end on the line.

'Why now do you think, Mr Too?'

'Because he realises the collapse of the MCP's armed struggle. The CPM is acknowledging that the backbone of its guerrilla forces has been so badly broken that it would have to disband them and adopt the underground or subversion method of struggle if a political settlement, on their terms, is not achieved.'

'It's really as crucial as that, is it?'

'Yes, sir, it is. Is there anything else you want to ask me?'

'No. Many thanks indeed. Good day,' and, mind racing, put the phone back on its cradle.

From then on until an amnesty was declared on the 9th of September, the political machine went into high gear.

31 July1955, Seremban: Since April there had been no contacts, despite much weary, dreary patrolling. The Queen's Birthday Honours had seen an MC and two MMs for people in B and D Companies but there was nothing for anyone in A and C Companies. Apart from congratulating the recipients, nothing was said about those whose work was expected to be awarded, as nothing ever is. What was of interest was what was the new CO going to be like?

He was Lieutenant Colonel Eustace Vaughan who had served in 3/12 GR during the war before being seconded to the Gilgit Scouts. He was one of many Indian Army British officers transferred to the Royal Artillery after Partition before making his escape to command 1/12 GR, so he knew nobody. When his name appeared in Part I Orders, the Gurkhas, who have no 'v' sound and find 'gh' in names especially difficult, immediately knew him as 'Bhagwan' saheb: with a name like that, he had to be good!

He was a small, barrel-chested, bouncy man, round-faced,

bushy-browed and clean-shaven, with a deep voice. He had represented the Indian Army Rugger XV as scrum-half in the last pre-war competition. He handled Gurkhas well but his handling of British officers was apt to be clumsy.

Before the old CO was dined out and the new one dined in, on the same night as operations were still in force, they had a week's hand- and take-over. The out-going man had written the all-important annual confidential reports for the officers, brought forward because of the change in command. Captain Rance was graded 'C', average. Henry Gibson knew that with a 'C' grading no officer could expect to rise above the rank of major.

Remarks on Rance's operational ability were cattily clouded because of the fiasco during Operation *Dover*. 'Yes, he can be good but I advise you to watch him. He would not have been commissioned pre-war.'

9 September 1955, Kuala Lumpur: On 9 September an amnesty, during which surrendering CT's would not be prosecuted and given the option to be repatriated to China, was declared by the newly elected Alliance Government which felt the need to take some new initiative over ending the Emergency. The thought was that, with the British no longer part of the political scene for much longer, Malaya's own politicians would be able to solve the remaining problems politically now that militarily no major threat was posed. The Security Forces felt that the conditions the Government granted were too lenient; virtually a free pardon to all CTs who had committed offences before that date or in ignorance of the amnesty declaration. Many millions of surrender leaflets were dropped over the jungle, their texts exploiting human weaknesses by playing on the lures of monetary rewards for surrendering, for inducing fellow CT's to surrender and weapons handed in, medical help and a better life. The leaflets also exploited homesickness and grievances against superiors, some of these seeking to create internal disharmony.

At ground level, however, the conditions were seen as futile being lenient, too lenient, and having a touch of ingenuousness and complacency about them.

Voice aircraft also played a large part in promulgating the news. Certain 'surrender areas' were declared in which there would be a ceasefire and no troops were to be sent to the jungle until further notice. They would have been withdrawn from those areas two days earlier.

Rules were that in other areas patrolling could continue but fire was bit to be opened by the Security Forces without first challenging any CT met and if they did not open fire, the Security Forces were forbidden to. Sure enough the Communists, with an eye for the main chance, utterly ignored the Government's initiative and took the situation as being a golden opportunity to build up their supplies and in many places to increase their own offensive.

Mid-October 1955, central Malaya: Comrade Yeong Kwoh was the second most senior comrade in the Politburo and still operated as hitherto. On hearing the broadcast about the amnesty and the conditions pertaining to it, he sent small groups of the quite large force he commanded to the other commanders in the general area to tell them to foregather for an important meeting. It was to take place somewhere in the high jungle-covered mountains to the east of the same area in the west of which the CO of 1/12 GR had been killed. They took much less time than normal, relying on any soldiers they met not firing on them with their not opening fire in the first place. The orders each sub-commander received were plain: they themselves with their escorts to attend the meeting whilst their deputies arranged for food to be scavenged, it being much easier to get than before.

After seven years of operations, the more recent ones being more of an exercise in not being discovered and keeping alive, the standard of every man's fieldcraft was such a high calibre that they were almost impossible to track. Their eventual destination was about two days' walk from the Bahau-Simpang Pertang road, hidden in some caves up a mountain side.

Once all participants had arrived and appropriate fraternal greetings given, Yeong Kwoh officially welcomed them. In his speech he stressed that although the density and duration of operations were less than they had been and that he had had no communication with the Secretary General for more than a year – 'and I don't even know where he is' – the armed struggle would continue, taking advantage of the amnesty to collect stores and making reconnaissances of danger spots they normally were unable to reach. 'I have no news of any ceasefire or peace talks other than details given over Radio Malaya. Before we start our discussions you'll be pleased to learn that no one knows we are here.'

But he was wrong and Special Branch had found out that,

somewhere in the thick jungle to the west of the Bahau-Simpang Pertang axis, a large-scale meeting was due to take place, safe in the knowledge that the amnesty protected the guerrillas from any Security Force action. However, by that time the new Government realised it was not achieving the results it had so naïvely expected as surrenders were far fewer than had been anticipated and rumours of the CT stocking up were found out to be true. Orders were therefore given to find out where this meeting was taking place but to take no action against it, in accordance with amnesty rules that the Government itself had devised, until an official warning had been given over the radio that action was forthcoming if the CT were not going to surrender. The military planners were told to set up a large scale operation to scour the jungle to pinpoint them. 1/12 GR was only one of the many Gurkha battalions involved.

So secret was it deemed to be that the only order – sent by hand – from Battalion HQ to 'out' companies was to motor to a given RV area 'when operational orders will be given. You will only tell the local Police that you must leave at night and warn them to have the village gates unlocked at your given time. You must not be late,' Jason read. He personally went to tell the Police who faithfully acknowledged the order yet, at the appointed time, the gates were not open but heavily locked and there was no policeman present to open them. In retrospect wrongly, he wasted twenty minutes waiting for someone to come with the key to open the gate before, in frustration, he told his driver to smash the lock with a heavy wrench from the vehicle's tool box. Away they went, got to the RV late so were in the wrong place in the long line of vehicles and the new CO was bitterly furious at Jason's obvious inefficiency. Jason learnt later that nearly two thousand troops were being deployed so no traffic snarl-up was ever more unpopular.

'You are late. Why can't you obey simple orders,' snarled the CO, coming up and shining his torch in Jason's face. 'You have jeopardised the Brigade Order of March and now the battalion is late. You will hear about this. Get ready to move now,' and he stomped off in a towering temper.

At the debussing area A Company was given a large area of mountainous jungle to search. For two weeks they plodded their way through 44-map miles of jungle, painstakingly searching everywhere. Much evidence of fresh and stale guerrilla movement was found but no contacts were made. On the fourteenth day Jason was called to the set and told to move to a point no more than a mere quarter of a mile from the main Bahau-Simpang Pertang road. *We could have motored here in half an hour and saved ourselves a long walk* more than one soldier concluded.

After re-rationing and getting new kit they were sent on another ten days of 'more of the same' until all troops were called to assemble at Bahau where they were given fresh orders and, at long last, told why the operation had been mounted.

After three weeks searching for the suspected guerrillas and finding nothing, Radio Malaya broadcast a message to Yeong Kwoh: 'Come out and surrender or you will be bombed in three days' time.'

There was an 'O' Group before the bombing and company commanders were given orders to ambush swathes of jungle considered likely as approach axes prior to the CT crossing the main road to escape east, the 'inner ring'. At the same time the main road was to be swamped with searchlights and armoured cars watching known or likely crossing places, the 'outer ring'. Artillery and mortars were also to be used in areas the troops could not cover. To the planners it was foolproof.

'Comrades, our survival is of the highest importance. We will leave this place in two groups, both of which will make their own efforts to cross the Bahau-Simpang Pertang road and go east' and Yeong Kwoh told them where to aim for. 'I recommend both groups try during the small hours by first sending over a couple of men to test any enemy reaction. My view is that the *gwai lo* will be so bored by that time of night many will be dozing so our escape will be easy.'

The night they planned to cross the road they saw the silhouette of a British soldier standing in the cupola of his scout car. They watched him for some time and thought he might be asleep. So they sent a few men across the road to see what would happen. Nothing did. The soldier was asleep and the rest of the group with all the high-ranking Communists thereby got away. This emerged when one of the guerrillas, the vice chief propaganda, gave himself up soon afterwards.

For three nights and two days the RAF employed 'maximum effort' to eradicate all the baddies thought stupid enough to have stayed in the area. A Company, 1/12 GR, was sent to search where the bombs had been dropped. It was really tiring work, climbing over or under the fallen trees, poking around looking for corpses. After intense searching three dead monkeys and a dead pig were the only casualties found – and three mangled copies of *Red Tidings*.

'Saheb,' head tilting to one side, 'what sort of war is this?' a Gurkha soldier asked Jason. 'Did they bomb empty jungle because they wanted to get rid of their old bombs or do they want to give new pilots live training? Otherwise what was the point of bombing?' The question was not meant to be sarcastic and many asked it.

The company returned to Rompin and had a few days to relax in after such a long, tedious and fruitless time. Catching up on the office work the Adjutant phoned. 'Jason, the Brigadier has been invited by the Air Officer Commanding, an Air Vice Marshal, to go to KL to discuss the Smash-Hit procedure. He has only been AOC for a mere six weeks but is mustard keen on using his bombers. The Brigadier considers you have had the most experience of the process and method on the ground. He has told the CO that the AVM is not expecting you as such but, even so, believes you can add to the discussion. He has gone so far as to give the impression that as you are a convert to bombing's efficacy...'

Jason broke in. 'Peter, don't make me laugh.'

'Jason, I know you are a hard one to please,' the Adjutant countered, 'be at Brigade HQ by noon tomorrow. You will fly up to KL and back by Auster with the Brigadier.'

'Peter, orders is orders so "Wilco, out".'

Jason presented himself at Brigade HQ and, for the short ride to the airstrip, the Brigadier chose to drive, telling the Gurkha driver to sit in the back. His Land Rover had a star, back and front, and a flag in front. Jason sat next to the Brigadier. They passed a group of Chinese who were laughing. With ill-judged levity Jason said, 'Sir, do you know why those Chinese are laughing?'

A 'no' was grunted back, then, 'tell me.'

Unwisely Jason answered, 'Because they think I'm the Brigadier and you are my driver.'

Silence.

The air-conditioned office of the impeccably dressed AVM had the walls covered in trophies of one sort or another. The airman stood up as the Brigadier and Captain Rance were ushered in by the PA. The AVM shook hands with the Brigadier but before Jason was introduced the phone rang and, reaching forward in a hurry, his arm moved a photo that had been facing him and now faced the visitors. Jason saw it was a wedding of...he dare not stare at it...his one-time fiancée and a swarthy looking almost dwarf of a man. Behind the couple stood the AVM and a woman, presumably his wife, both faultlessly attired. Almost pole-axed with surprise, Jason tried not to show he'd seen it as the once-dead resentment welled up inside him, making him catch his breath, with thoughts pounding in his head.

The AVM put the receiver down, glanced at his watch and without any more ado, stood up and said, 'Let's move out to the Conference Room' where an Air Commodore and a few Squadron Leaders, all equally impeccably dressed and looking most serious, were already waiting. The RAF contingent sat facing the two Army officers.

To exorcise his rekindled marital snub Jason had physically tired himself out by hard days in the jungle as the best tonic and so had made the jungle almost the realm of the recluse. In the air-conditioned Conference Room all the 'near misses' and frustrations came whelmingly to the forefront of his mind. Subconsciously acknowledging that the 'kill-to-contact' ratio was not impressive, knowing that the 'Smash-Hit' theory was also less than all that efficient, he felt his gorge rise inexorably as the AVM started to castigate the infantry generally and Gurkhas in particular, lambasting British officers' inability to explain matters to their men. Jason's normally buoyant spirit deflated like a pricked balloon: the comparison between where he was now and in the jungle crushed him – the very nature of primary jungle, its close-horizoned, all-pervading, never-ending green of trees, vines, creepers and undergrowth that prevented the eyes from seeing as far as the ears can hear, so voices have to be kept low and noise kept to a minimum. It is a litany of sounds and a living lexicon of lore for those who understand it. It is a state of permanent semi-twilight, gloomy even when sunshine does dapple the jungle floor with shadows, and dark in creeks and narrow valleys at noon. It is a state of permanent dampness, rain or sweat, of stifling, windless heat, of dirty clothes, of smelly bodies, of heavy loads, of loaded and cocked weapons, of tensed reflexes, of inaccurate maps, of constant vigilance, of tired limbs, of sore shoulders where equipment straps have bitten in, of a chafed crutch, of the craving for a cigarette and a cold beer for some and a brew of tea for others. At night it is darkness, when fireflies prick the gloom with flickering lights and rotting leaves shine eerily. It is a state of mind that has to be stronger than mere physical robustness. It is a challenge. It can never be taken for granted. It is hated by hundreds. And yet, for those who have the jungle as their first love, no other type of terrain can ever measure up to it for its infinite variety and the subtle beauty of its primordial nature. The comparison with there and here...

His thoughts were brought to the here and now when, to his unmitigated horror, he heard the Brigadier say, 'I have brought my most recalcitrant company commander to meet you, sir, as I have converted him to accepting Smash-Hit as the answer to killing the CT...haven't I?' as he turned to Jason sitting beside him.

Still dazed by his mixed emotions, Jason fixed his eyes on the AVM – *the blighter's looking into me not at me* – and, decidedly, defiantly and deadpan, said, 'No, sir. The first time I had to ask for Smash-Hit was where we had found a CT camp. I personally surrounded it without their knowing, discovering sentry posts and the water point. I was forbidden to attack it and one of the five Lincoln bombers dropped one of its bombs unfused on the by-then empty camp. As for the two nights and three days of bombing after Radio Malaya's warning the guerrillas they were doomed if they didn't surrender, I was told to search for corpses. My company searched the bombed area for three days, a most difficult task, moving under and climbing over fallen trees. We found three dead monkeys and a dead pig.' The atmosphere turned more frigid than the air-conditioning and Jason, still fixing the AVM with the stare of a basilisk, said, 'In my view, sir, that was a waste of taxpayers' money.' Had he known the dictum 'stand up and be counted' this was the one time in his life he truly, truly obeyed it.

There was a deathly hush before the AVM rose, looked at Jason and the Brigadier as though they were too reprehensible to carry on a conversation with and, wordless, swept out of the room. His underlings did likewise, a silent chorus without a hero.

Also in silence the Brigadier stood up and left the room, Jason perforce following him. Still wordless they went to the car the Brigadier had been given and in silence were driven to the airfield where the Auster was waiting to fly them back. They got out of the car and at last the Brigadier spoke. 'I am not taking you back. The car will take you to the station and you will go back by the night train,' the first words spoken since the Land Rover drive.

There were no sleeping berths vacant so Jason sat in his chair until he arrived at Rompin station at 0200 hours. It was cold and he had to wait on the platform for four hours until dawn when the curfew was lifted and the village gates opened. Sitting, staring into the dark, only seeing 'that' face in 'that' picture, the bile of bitterness unslaked....until, with a glorious smile nobody could see, he said to himself *with a father-in-law like that I'm now glad she left me*.

The mile walk to his camp warmed him up and sitting in his room drinking a large mug of tea, he sadly told himself that talking like he had to such senior RAF officers was indeed a black mark – *but those people have no idea what it's like on the ground* – and he 'kicked himself' for forgetting his military manners. He shrugged and grinned, *but I've got it, including her, off my chest*.

As the AVM and his wife sat over dinner he gave her his views of the unsuccessful meeting he had set so much store on. 'The young officer who so blatantly disregarded my ideas is a hard case. I wonder if our daughter ever met him when she came to Malaya. Even if she did, he's not the sort of man she could ever fall in love with, that's for sure. I was so angry with him I never bothered to ask what the blighter's name was.'

'Although I don't know him, darling, I am quite sure you are right. You so wonderfully always are,' his wife consolingly cooed.

The Brigadier told the new CO that Captain Rance was obviously in need of a rest and that some local leave when it was suitable was an answer. Lieutenant Colonel Vaughan agreed and waited a few days before going to visit A Company in Rompin. He had a wander around with the Company Commander, met and chatted with the men. He saw their reactions were smarter and happier than in the other companies. He said to Jason, 'let's go inside and have a talk in your office.'

Seated, he said, 'oh, by the way, I've brought some mail for you,' and gave Jason a letter. He took a note book out of his pocket. 'You can read it after our talk. First, why were you late that first night? You threw out the most carefully laid plans for the Order of March. Did you forget to tell the police about the gate or something?'

Jason told his CO about what had happened 'and when I got back I went to see the Officer in Charge of the Police District who heartily apologised and told me that the Chinese policeman detailed to open the gate disappeared earlier on that night and has not been seen since.'

'Then I'll forgive you this once. Just as well you didn't try to excuse yourself when you at last met up' and he clenched his teeth in vexation as he remembered how frustrated he had been at the time. 'And the Brigadier has told me how embarrassed he was when you blew your top with the boys who wear crab-fat grey. Right?'

So that's why they are called 'Crabs'! 'I was in the wrong, sir, and I apologise to you but the AVM was derogatory about our Gurkhas which upset me' and he explained what had previously happened with a Smash-Hit venture.

Chakrabahadur Rai brought in two steaming mugs of tea. 'Read your letter,' said the CO.

It was from his mother. A close friend had had so vivid a dream of seeing Jason's impending death when he was at the top of a tree sitting at the end of a branch, moving about dangerously 'when a Chinese your age appeared at the bottom of the tree and said "don't worry I'll look after him",' and, to the dreamer's great relief, 'you did not fall off.' So real was the dream that the friend had rung the next morning. Jason looked at the date of the letter and thought back. *That's the date of when the CT fired on me from four yards' range.* He worked out the time difference and the dream and the CT firing on him were almost simultaneous.

He broke into a sweat and mopped his brow. The CO watched him narrowly. 'All right?' he asked.

'Yes, sir, thank you. Just some strange news from home.'

'Which always makes you break out into a sweat?' the CO asked pointedly.

Jason gave no answer

'I think you need a bit of a rest. When you are ready, let me know and you can go on some local leave.'

Ah Fat's suggestion came to his mind but he decided not to mention it lest questions were asked.

'Drink your tea before it gets cold.'

Soon after that the CO drove back to Seremban, convinced that Captain Rance was, basically, fit but just a bit overwrought. *I'm glad I 'had it out' with him.* The bit that he had not 'had out' with him was that the Brigadier vowed that any recommendation for promotion or a bravery award were both O U T as far as he was concerned so no battalion citation for either need be forwarded.

7

18-23 November 1955, south Thailand: The Secretary General of the MCP was feeling both optimistic and frustrated. He was hopeful for a favourable Peace Talk summit as there had already been two preliminary meetings, both in Malaya, at Klian Intan, a tin-mining village near the Thai border. He had sent his chief confidant, Chien Tiang, to the first one on 17 October and the outcome had satisfactorily led to a second, exactly a month later at the same place. Again, progress had been made. His frustration was caused not only because since March his radio that had direct contact with Beijing had broken down but also by not having heard from Yeong Kwoh, his Deputy in Malaya, for more than a year.

One morning an unexpected visitor arrived saying he had come all the way from China with an important message. So unusual was this that the sentry told him to wait while he went to ask one of the Politburo before letting him in. 'Can you believe me, Comrade?' he asked, 'he says he's come from China and it has taken many months to get here. Can that be true?'

Chien Tiang went to see who it was, and indeed the man was a messenger from the Chinese Communist Party as well as being trained to mend the broken radio set. 'Red Salute, Comrade, you don't know how welcome you are. Come along in, meet the Secretary General, have some refreshment and, after a wash and rest, tell us what you have for us.'

The first priority was to mend the radio and later on that same day communications were restored. Chin Peng was delighted and said, 'Comrade, now it is time to give us your message. Come to my office.'

Once seated the courier said 'My message for you is about any peace talks you will be involved in and what both the propaganda people of the Soviet and the Chinese Communist Parties want you to do and say and bargain for is so secret that I was not allowed to bring it written down so had to learn it by heart instead. Ten pages of a closely written directive and it's taken me so many months to reach here I've forgotten the four major points,' and he looked dolefully at the ground as he spoke, full of embarrassment.

'Now we have our radio repaired that's no worry, is it?'

'Let me see if they come back to me as I tell you what I do remember' so the courier recited as much as he could of his secret message until he reached the four major points but once again he drew a blank. 'It is no good, they've gone from my mind,' he admitted.

'That's no worry comrade. With our radio now operative, we will ask our representative in Beijing to find out what the four points are.' They were devastated when told that nothing would be forthcoming.

When Ah Fat heard that he made a mental note. *C C Too will be interested when he learns how far spread is the interest about the peace talks and that now, even with radio contact, Beijing won't say.*

Another unexpected arrival was a courier who wanted a direct meeting with the Secretary General and asked to see him more forcibly than normal protocol permitted.

'Comrade Chin Peng is busy. What do you want with him?' was the gruff reply. 'You can't just barge in as though you were his equal.'

'I was told to deliver this letter personally and immediately on arrival' and he took an envelope out of his pocket. Unexpectedly it had the logo of the Royal Thai Embassy in KL on it. *Could be important!*

'Come with me. I'll see if the Comrade Secretary General can spare you a few minutes.'

When Chin Peng saw the envelope he knew he had to give the messenger priority: he tore the envelope open and there was a message from one of his prize sleepers he had not heard from for a long time. The gist of it was that on 20 April he had seen comrade Ah Fat leaving HQ of Malaya Command in a police vehicle with another Chinese he had not recognised. Intrigued he had gone to the HQ entrance and, for a small sum, had learnt that the other man was a Mr C C Too, a senior government propaganda official, and they had visited the Director of Operations.

The Secretary General, clenching his teeth, knew this was something he could well have done without. He wrote a short letter for the courier to take back: 'Thank you for your valiant efforts. After we have won our political agreement, great will be your reward.'

The courier gave the Red Salute and retired.

Seven months! Yet nothing has exploded. It could be a bold attempt to find out something for me. But he has never mentioned it. We'll watch him very carefully from now on but won't take any positive action yet.

23 November 1955, onwards, south Thailand and Malaya: With the repair of the radio and receipt of most of the courier's message, a Politburo meeting was held. Ah Fat, not realising that he was an object of suspicion, attended as usual. The main point of discussion was the tentative date of the Peace Talks, 28 December, at a largish village named Baling, west of Klian Intan. Once he had heard that Ah Fat let his mind wander: how best to put what Jason had termed 'Operation *Red Tidings Mark II* into action? After the meeting he went to his own part of the camp and asked Wang Ming, his ever-faithful Bear, to come to his room for a serious talk.

Seated in a couple of easy chairs, Ah Fat said, '*Hung Lo*, I have arranged with C C Too that *Shandung P'aau* and I, aided by you, both as innocent civilians, must meet, over the border, just before the peace talks take place on 28 December in Baling. We don't know if there will be any troops in the area but, even if there are, we won't be with them. The way you can help is to leave here and, bribing your way over the border as we have done in the past...'

'I can use my Thai passport.'

'Yes, of course you can. You will phone C C Too and say, "Operation *Red Tidings Mark II* now" before going on to KL.

Too will arrange to alert *Shandung P'aau* who will meet up with you where it can best be arranged. The reason is I want to give him some documents that are held in the secret box in the Secretary General's office and I daren't go too far from the border myself. With me so far?'

Yes, the Bear was.

'C C Too may arrange your meeting in KL or in Sungei Patani. I expect *Shandung P'aau* will have a Gurkha with him and he's sure to want you to stay with him all the time, except when he is in the Gurkha camp. After that, quite how I don't yet know, but C C Too will have told you, I want you all to move to the Gunong Lang area east of Kampong Lalang to meet me. I will have one of our men with me. Our meeting point will be the old hut above the tin mine. You know the one we pass when we move out that way?'

'Yes, I know where you mean. It will be good to meet up with *Shandung P'aau* again.

'Yes, take a couple of men to the border, change into plain clothes and give them your guerrilla clothes to bring back to me. I'll bring them back with me for the meeting.'

The Bear sat quietly, envisaging any snags. 'I won't be armed, will I?'

'No. Sorry about that but you've brought up a good point. Tell C C Too to tell *Shandung P'aau* to carry a pistol, even though he, too, will be wearing plain clothes once you have started coming my way.'

27 November 1955, Kuala Lumpur and Seremban: The unlisted phone in C C Too's office rang and Wang Ming introduced himself when asked who was calling. 'I have been told that Operation *Red Tidings Mark II* is ready to launch and so *Shandung P'aau* has to be alerted.'

'Where are you?' C C Too looked at his watch and noted 1029 hours.

'Just this side of the border. Are you in a hurry to see me?'

'No desperate hurry but make it as soon as you can. Use this number when get here. Best to stay at home until I call you. Everything okay?'

'So far we are all healthy and,' unusual for the Bear to add any superfluous commentary, 'long may that remain. Details later but there's great excitement and heads are nodding,'

Can't get vaguer or more veiled than that, can one? Too grinned and then rang Colonel Mason's unlisted number and introduced himself. 'We have a date for when the operation Captain Rance named *Red Tidings Mark II* must be launched. Is this line safe or shall we have a face-to-face meeting?'

'Can you come round right away? I'll alert the gate sentry to allow you in.'

'Yes, I'll come round now. The sooner we meet the better.'

In Colonel Mason's office C C Too told him that he had had a phone call from Ah Fat's deputy, from the border, and 'I told him to come to KL. He hinted that there was a lot of activity in the MCP HQ but only once he's here will I get details so you and I will have to meet again. Our first priority must be getting Captain Rance out of the battalion unostentatiously to meet up with us here before leaving for the meeting with Ah Fat. We have some time as the proposed date is 28 December.'

'Yes, that agrees with what we've heard here. Let me think.' The Director of Intelligence had heard how Rance had reacted with the RAF and how 'feathers had flown'. The thought was that he had been overtaxing himself and so needed a few days local leave. 'The General has blown hot and cold about bringing Rance into it but bring him into it we must. It will seem unusual to his CO for me to ask him but I'll word it somehow so as not to sound suspicious. I will suggest that he is being asked to lecture to the Gurkha recruits on jungle warfare before they disperse in mid-December after the Passing Out Parade, which, I have heard, is to be inspected by the High Commissioner, but which may be too early for when Ah Fat wants to move. And after that he takes some local leave up north, say in or near Penang' – *a bit of casuistry?*

'That will be phase 1 and I'll only come active in phase 2.'

The Colonel nodded. 'That's how best to play it. Keep in touch and thanks for coming round.'

Colonel Mason was a friend of the Colonel of the Gurkha Training Depot so he was the first person he rang. 'John, it's James from KL. How's it going?'

'James, good to hear from you. How's the family?'

'Fine. The wife's with me and the kids are back in England in college. I've something to put to you.'

'I knew it, let's have it.'

'Would you like your recruits to have a lecture on jungle warfare before they pass out?'

'They have been doing jungle training so this might be a bit of icing to put on the cake. Who have you in mind?'

'Captain Rance of 1/12 GR. His prowess in the jungle on ops is unsurpassed.'

'Yes, I've heard the name but have yet to meet him. Let me look at my programme. We're pretty busy practising for the Passing-Out Parade...' his voice trailed away and it sounded as if pages of a book were being turned over. 'I can only fix him an hour on the afternoon of Friday the 16th.'

'That's too early for us our end. A pity but there it is.' Pleasantries were exchanged before they rang off.

'CO 1/12 GR speaking!'

'Eustace, it's James Mason from KL here. I've heard about young Rance and the RAF and the idea that he needs local leave. Correct?'

'And how!' *But why should you worry?*

'When do you think you'll let him go on local leave?' *Again why? I'll hear him out before asking him.*

'Let me look at my diary.' He put the phone on the table and Mason heard sounds of a book being opened. 'Not before Monday, 19th of December.'

'The Director of Operations had some idea that Rance lectured the recruits before they pass out but the date, Friday the 16th of December, is the last possible date given, so that has to be dropped. However, from an Int point of view, I'd like to have a word with him. Do you know where he'll go on leave?'

'No idea' *and no interest.*

'Can you get him to ring me just in case he goes to or through KL? I'd like to hear just what is the matter with Smash-Hit?'

'Have you got a number you'd like him to ring?

'Yes, please take this down and give it to him.'

After a few more words, the conversation ended. The CO sat silently, staring at the far wall. *There must be more to this than meets the eye. And if there is, should I be worried?* He called out to the Adjutant, 'Get Captain Rance to come and see me after lunch.'

'What do you know about going to the Gurkha Training Depot to lecture the recruits?' the CO asked Jason, standing to attention in front of him.

'Who are you referring to, sir?' he replied in puzzlement. After being told the CO wanted to see him, all he could think of was his bad standing with the Brigadier and the RAF. Lecturing Gurkha recruits was a new one.

'To you,' answered the CO, more hesitantly than he had expected to. 'Have you been told anything about it?'

'No, sir. This is entirely new.' His obvious ignorance of anything previously planned was plain.

'No matter, it had been mooted by the Director of Operations, though why I can't imagine. The Training Depot staff is more than capable of giving lectures on jungle warfare.'

Jason said nothing and kept his features rigid.

'I have been rung up from HQ Malaya Command and asked where you are going on local leave.' Here he hesitated, 'it was inferred that you were overwrought after all that time in the jungle' – 'as was shown when you spoke to the RAF' he did not say – 'a few days local leave, possibly in Penang, would let you relax. What are you views on that?'

Jason remembered Flat Ears talking to him in Rompin. So that's how they're playing it! 'Sir, I'll go if you think I ought to. A couple of weeks away would do me no harm. I could go to KL where I was born and visit friends if they are still there. I don't have to decide here and now, do I?'

'No, and I don't care where you go, so long as it's not back to the AVM's office.'

The look of disgust that Jason gave him, followed by an expectant gleam that, as the CO said to himself later, looked like a hunter who has found some spoor after a long search, made him think that were Jason to have given a lecture to the recruits he might have started talking about surrounding camps as opposed to bombing them. He saw that he had gone too far. 'You can go on leave for two weeks, leaving here on Monday the 19th of December.'

'Is that all, sir?'

'No, as a matter of fact it isn't. The Director of Intelligence, Colonel Mason, wants to talk to you about the Intelligence aspect of Smash-Hit.'

The CO rang him up. 'James, it's Eustace. I have Captain Rance with me and he has mentioned KL as a place to go on local leave. I have therefore got him here to talk to you. Ready?'

'Yes.' The CO gave Jason the phone. 'Captain Rance, sir.'

'Colonel Mason this end. Thank you for ringing. Hold the phone tightly to your ear. Bring a Gurkha orderly and two pistols and at least twelve rounds of ammunition for each. When will you be coming to KL?'

'Monday the 19th of December, sir, by the day train.'

'When you get to KL, a senior Police officer, Mr C C Too, will arrange your accommodation. Got something to write with?' Yes, Jason had. 'Then ring this number,' which the Colonel gave him. 'I may not see you myself, despite what you may have been told. Once you get to KL you'll find out why,' and he rang off. Jason asked the Adjutant if he could get the Chief Clerk to give him and his batman a warrant to KL for the 19th and back two weeks later.'

'Yeah, go and fix it. And, Jason, remember, we junior officers are all on your side.'

15-20 December, 1955, Kuala Lumpur: On Monday afternoon Jason and Chakré, pistols and ammo in their hand luggage, got out of the train at KL station. 'Chakré, come with me to find a telephone'. He dialled Colonel Mason's number, introduced himself and said he was still at the station. 'Take this number down.'

Jason repeated it then, turning to Chakré, said it in Nepali. Gurkhas have a marvellous power of memory. By that time the phone was dead. *He doesn't waste time!*

'Chakré, what was that number?' and, given it again, he dialled it and was answered by a woman's voice. 'Excuse me, Madam, I am Captain Rance and am looking for Mr C C Too. Is that his house? Are you Mrs Too?'

A dulcet-toned voice answered. 'No, it is not his house and

he is not married. This is the house of his girlfriend, Miss Wong. I have been told to expect you. His house is at Federal Hill, not all that far from the Lake Gardens. Don't go there but ask a taxi to bring you to this address,' and she gave a house number in Ampang Road. He heard her speak, as though over her shoulder, in Chinese, and calling out what sounded like Wang Ming.

Not my old friend, Hung Lo, *the Bear, surely? There are more pieces in this jigsaw puzzle than seemed likely at first count: Ah Fat on the phone, lecture, pistol, Director of Intelligence, C C Too and the Bear!* 'Chakré, Providence has something for us. Let's go and find out what it is.'

Wang Ming opened the front door before there was time to ring any bell and he and Jason almost fell into each other's arms, so long was it since their last meeting. A young lady came to the door and ushered them inside. Jason introduced himself and Chakré whose English wasn't up to much and his Chinese was nil so Jason kept him abreast of the conversation as they sat in the front room with tea and a noodles snack. 'Mr Too will be here shortly,' she was saying as C C Too himself arrived.

He greeted Jason warmly. 'We haven't met since September 1952, if my brain doesn't let me down.'

'Correct, sir. That was at the tail end of Operation *Janus*. The time certainly flies.' He introduced Chakrabahdur.

'You have been asked for because your childhood friend Ah Fat has told me you are the only person who can ensure the success of his plans. More later. First of all, household arrangements: at the back are two spare rooms: I can put Chakrabahadur in with you or with the Bear, whichever you prefer.'

Jason said, 'We'll doss down together.'

Too looked at his watch. 'Go and clean up. Be comfortable, wear what you like. We'll have a meal in half an hour and then I'll tell you what our plans are.'

Before they had a chance to settle down and talk, a taxi drove up and stopped outside the house. Doors slammed and in came Wang Ming's wife and 15-year-old son, Wang Liang, the mirror image of his father. She breathlessly explained that her son had somehow heard that *Shandung P'aau* was with his father and had begged her to let him come and see him.

Wang Ming said that he had often spoken about how Jason had initially won them over and it would be a great kindness if *Shandung P'aau* could show his son his tricks. Jason, realising a happy companion on a dangerous mission was always better than an unhappy one, adroitly played up. He held Wang Liang spellbound as he made his hands 'talk' to each other, took the top off his thumb and put it back again, wobbled his eyebrows then his knees and by the time he'd put his finger up his nose the lad was in stitches of laughter. Jason had a friend for life. Wang Ming dismissed them with a smile and back home they went.

After their meal Jason was told why he had been inveigled into coming to KL. 'With no lecture to the recruits makes it much easier for us. As I hinted earlier, your childhood friend Ah Fat is helping us from the "inside", very bravely, and you, on the "outside", are a vital link in his efforts to get us secret news from the MCP at the time of any peace talks. He wants to give you and no one else any documents he can secretly get for us here in KL. It has been quite a struggle one way and another to get you here as the change in political leadership has meant that the Director of Operations no longer has the final say in anything of this nature. In the heart of his heart he would dearly like to speak to you, as would Colonel Mason. Both have had you in mind for quite a time. I managed to get Ah Fat to meet him and that was when he phoned you.' He looked at Jason conspiratorially.

'Yes, it was a great shock to hear him call me and I was sorry we could not talk for longer.'

'So delicate is your being involved, especially now the Malays not the British are "calling the shots" that the top military brass do not want to know you are involved. You are therefore unattributable. Ah Fat cannot get far from where he is, even going over the border into Malaya is a risk. Were it known that you suddenly left your battalion for no apparent reason, it would be "embarrassment squared". A lecture to the recruits would have been cover from any unusual activity on your part so that followed by some local leave was planned to get you from Rompin to the north with no suspicion.' He looked at Jason with a glint of devilment in his eyes. 'In the event I don't think there'll be any damage done but, what do you British say? "Belt and braces"?'

'Correct,' said Jason, grinning, and told Chakré what had been said so far. 'So that's why we have pistols, saheb,' he answered.

'From now on you three will be together,' continued C C Too. 'For your journey north you will go in one of my unmarked vehicles, an old one that no one will remember, which the police use for odd purposes. The driver happens to be one of those you first met when the Bear and others decided you were a better bet than the MCP.

'Ah Fat and the Bear have already arranged their RV, the Gunong Lang area from east of Kampong Lalang. You have to pass through a Malay population not a Chinese one to reach it. You'll be remembered if only by your height, which we don't want.'

Jason contemplated his best way to manage. 'I could be a reputable European were I a herbicide officer or a bee keeper but I could sustain neither role were I to be asked any pertinent question, so I think a disguise is the best answer. At the start of the Emergency there was a mad scheme to make me look like an Indian before going to recce a village. It never happened but I was stripped down to my underpants and a make-up artist, a woman, wearing gloves, dabbed on a layer of paint from a bottle marked mid-coconut. Why she only didn't pain my face I don't know. "That's the bottom layer," she said. While it was drying she did my face. I can remember her saying "Shut your eyes and raise your eyebrows. If your eyelids are left unvarnished, they'll give you away" and very carefully she painted my skin with a small brush. That quickly dried. She then covered me for the second coating, waterproof, same colour. "It will last for several months," she told me.'

Jason shook his head. 'Then she said "Sorry about that but there's nothing quicker and we dare not have you fall into a river or rained on so look like an out-of-season zebra. I will give you a bottle of remover to take with you. It may be indispensible. You will be able to clean up there and then if you have to. It stings a bit when applied."'

C C Too said, 'You have a wonderful memory for detail. I

can arrange for something like that tomorrow.' The local filming company's 'shooting' team was in his debt. 'Tell your Gurkha what you have told us.'

'Saheb, let me try and paint you if the Chinese saheb can get the stuff,' Chakré said after Jason had told him the outlines of how to put it on. 'You could have got someone else to do it here but going to Sungei Patani like that you'd be taken as the Dashera joker,' and he roared with laughter.

Jason repeated the joke and everybody laughed.

'I expect my arms and face will be all that I need to paint,' said Jason 'but we must have the stuff that gets it off before we get back to the battalion.'

'What clothes have you besides your uniform and what you're wearing now?' C C Too asked.

'None,' Jason replied.

'Oh! They won't do.' He looked at the two men as if measuring their sizes for clothes. 'That Indian tailor who sells second-hand clothes. You know him, don't you?' he asked Miss Wong. 'Take my car and go and buy two sets, sizes of Jason and his man, of Malay peasant's clothing and two conical hats to keep out the rain.' He felt in his pocket and produced some money. 'This should be enough,' he told her.

'I've something else for you,' said C C Too, getting up and leaving the room. He came back with a small attaché case. 'Take this with you. It has a false bottom. Put the papers Ah Fat gives you into it.'

Jason looked at it. 'Yes, it's small enough to carry in our kit otherwise it will seem strange to be seen walking with it.'

It was midnight before they were finished.

18 December 1955, south Thailand: Ah Fat was worried. There was nothing he could put his finger on as such but there was a 'something' unusual in the air. When he met members of the Politburo they were not quite as open with him as they had been. He wondered if news of Chan Man Yee's defection to China had somehow leaked back. *Hardly likely.* He had not gone to the Police HQ: *was I seen with C C Too leaving or going to HQ Malaya Command? Could have been but it's too late to worry about it now.*

He worked out how best to rob the main secret box in the Secretary General's office. He had seen the place where its key was hidden. He had always felt that Chin Peng's unmilitary mind lacked any type of trade craft: so certain was he of absolute and fervent dedication to the Party, he merely kept it on a piece of cord hanging on a nail at the back of the box. For sure, the box was almost flush with the wall but, even so...!

It was planned for the delegation to the peace talks at Baling would leave the MCP camp to get to the jungle edge before being escorted onwards on the Tuesday, the 20th. The three-man team would go with their plans all worked out – hadn't they been rehearsing for days now? – and take no paperwork with them. Once he had seen them leave and as soon as it was dark, he'd go to the office, open the safe and clear it out. As a cover plan he would have the paperwork C C Too had given him, and which he had kept sedulously hidden among his clothes in his room, not having a small attaché case with a false bottom in it – far too sophisticated! – to put in the secret box were he interrupted and he'd say he'd forgotten to hand them over before. He'd have one of his own men with him, one of those who had surrendered to Jason that time in 1952, who would be glad to be doing something positive.

20 December 1955, south Thailand: Shortly before dusk Ah Fat, with his man discreetly placed watching him, briskly walked over to the main office. In his hands he carried his 'bait' paperwork. *Move purposely as though you had something to do. People don't bother with a busy man. Don't saunter, it looks suspicious.* There was no one about. He tried the main door but it was locked. He rattled it and, from the back, came the Duty Watchman. 'Comrade, open the door. I have some paperwork to deliver.'

The duty watchman took the key out of his pocket and opened the door. He noticed Ah Fat's bodyguard nonchalantly shuffling his feet in the middle distance and asked what that comrade was doing. 'He's my bodyguard.'

'Comrade Ah Fat, may I ask why you need a bodyguard, especially one with a haversack? You don't normally have one.'

'Comrade Duty Watchman. You know that the Comrade Secretary General and two others are due to go to Baling. Just suppose the *gwai lo* try some trickery while they are away. What does a man like me do without a bodyguard?' He made no comment about the haversack.

'Comrade Ah Fat also knows that this place is out of bounds after work. The comrade knows it is a golden rule.'

'When you are a non-voting member of the Politburo like I

am, you can talk about golden rules if you want. Understand?'

Miffed by being censured, the Duty Watchman said nothing but, not unmindful of how the full members of the Politburo had been behaving towards this comrade for the past few days, he became more suspicious.

Ah Fat moved into the inner office, switched on the light, groped around for the key and opened the secret box. He'd planned to give his bodyguard the stuff he took out and until then he'd hide the papers under his shirt. He put the 'bait' documents on a table beside him.

Inside the safe he recognised the paperwork that was prepared after the Chinese courier's visit and removed it, stuffing it inside his shirt. It could be chilly in the evening so he had put on a pullover as well as a cape because it had started to rain when he left his quarter. As he pulled down his shirt and arranged the cape, he heard the Duty Watchman call out, 'Comrade Lee An Tung, come here will you?'

Ah Fat cursed. Lee An Tung was bad news. Hearing footsteps outside he picked up the 'bait' papers from the table and turned to meet Comrade Lee as he came into the room, the look on whose face boded no good. 'Comrade, I'm surprised to see you here. Lost anything?' he asked with malicious innocence.

'Comrade Lee An Tung. No, I have found something,' Ah Fat answered, lying with the plausibility of a skilled politician and the inflated optimism of a house agent. 'But I have to admit that I do have a guilty conscious. I am getting absent minded. Look at these papers,' and he showed him what was in his hands. 'Take them and read them and I'll explain them when you have done so.'

Almost greedily the Head of the Central Propaganda Department took them under the light and scanned them. 'Where did you get these from and why only now are you putting them in the secret box?' Ah Fat noticed his tone was less distrustful.

'I managed to get them from Chan Man Yee when the Comrade Secretary General sent me down to meet her, when was it now?' and he put his hand on his forehead as though trying to think when, not realising that he had used the so-far secret name of the agent.

'I don't know who you mean by Chan Man Yee and I won't ask but why so long after you've come back are you only now putting them in the secret box in a most shifty manner? Can you explain yourself?'

Ah Fat, ever the consummate actor, groaned melodramatically. 'Believe it or not, on my way back I put them in such a secret place, a new suitcase I'd bought with a secret compartment that I was not used to,' adlibbing furiously and dangerously, 'that it entirely slipped my mind. It suddenly came to me that I had still got them and, so ashamed was I of myself, I thought I'd slip them into the secret box before anyone knew I'd forgotten them.' *Will be buy it?*

Lee An Tung laughed. 'Yes, comrade, it happens. A pity you remembered after our delegate departed but, no worry. So put them in and close the secret box and that'll be all about it.'

They parted amicably yet the worm of suspicion in Lee An Tung's gut was not fully stilled. *Could be true but it is unusual for that Ah Fat to be so forgetful. How to make sure?*

Ah Fat and his bodyguard met up between the office and the

wire surrounding the camp. 'All ready?' Ah Fat asked him quietly, looking round as he did.

'Follow me to where I have loosened the perimeter wire. Once we have crawled through it I'll tighten it so it won't look as if we've left camp.'

'Good thinking, indeed,' said Ah Fat, 'let's get going.' Once over a small mound that shielded them from the camp, the bodyguard switched on a torch, found the track which they walked along for four hours until it was time for a long rest.

I'll call on Ah Fat after I've had a meal on the excuse that I'd like to hear more of what Chan Man Yee has done for our cause. I may pick up something either to allay my distrust or ... and the Head of the Central Propaganda Department shuddered at any alternative. After his supper he went to Ah Fat's quarter which was, surprisingly, empty. He called out, wondering if his quest was in the bathroom. No answer. He went inside and knew, just knew, that his quarry had gone somewhere. An idea struck him. *I'll search for his suitcase with a secret compartment.* He searched diligently but did not find one.

He went over to the quarters of the Security Section and ordered a search of the camp for comrade Ah Fat, 'and especially look and see if the wire has been cut.' There were fewer men available than normal as many had gone with the Secretary General's team. Lee An Tung was not popular and, after a hard day's work, the men were not anxious to go prowling about the camp at this late hour, especially as it was raining, so they were unusually slow in answering, as if they showed resentment at the order. Lee An Tung was 'jumpy' and, in no uncertain terms, rebuked them harshly. The men made a cursory walk round the camp, cursing at getting wet, saw nothing untoward, and liking Ah Fat more than Lee An Tung, the senior man told him a bare-faced lie about his still being in camp when he made his report. *Not often you can give these people a taste of their own medicine* he thought vindictively.

22-23 December 1955, Gunong Lang area, north Malaya: A shabby vehicle had left Miss Wong's house late on the 20th and driven the three men up the main highway, stopping after six hours. There was nowhere else to sleep but in the vehicle. They moved off at dawn, having had a bite to eat at a roadside place and branched off east along Route 67, towards Baling. After about twenty miles they turned north along a minor road and at the first junction they doubled back south to slightly north of Kampong Lalang, ten miles to the north of Baling, early in the afternoon. From there they could see east to Gunong Lang rising to a height of 3756 feet. The map distance to their destination was not quite ten miles, on foot it would be considerably farther.

By then they felt cramped so got out of the car and eased their limbs. Clouds full of rain loomed menacingly. Jason spoke to the driver: 'You have done us well and thank you. What I want you to do now is to drive on to the village where there is bound to be a shop. Look for three plastic sheets and buy them. I can't see us being able to cook for the next forty-eight hours so look out for anything tinned, fish will do, not forgetting to buy or borrow a tin opener, as well as some biscuits.'

'I have a bottle with me. If I clean it out shall I bring some tea back with me?'

'Yes, that's a fine idea.' He groped in his pocket and gave the driver some money. 'Be as quick as you can.'

Away went the driver and in half an hour returned with all that had been asked for. He was only just in time as it started to rain and the plastic sheets were immediately draped over their shoulders. They swigged the tea by turns, feeling the better for it. 'You'll be all right on your own, will you?' Jason asked the driver.

'Yes. When will you want me back here?'

'Tomorrow, late afternoon.'

The driver drove off and the three men moved along a path towards the jungle, hoping to find a shack used for the night when people stay out in the fields to watch the paddy.

At dusk they espied a lean-to hut. 'We'll doss down here,' said Jason. 'I expect it will be full of fleas.' And it was.

Ah Fat had hoped that, if lucky, he and his bodyguard could reach the RV above the old mining quarry on the west side of Gunong Lang before their absence, especially his, was noticed. At worst they had at least twelve hours' start on any follow-up group, probably even longer if the rain had obliterated their foot prints. He had told his bodyguard to fill a haversack, unobtrusively, with enough 'hard tack' provisions to last the pair of them for forty-eight hours.

Jason, Chakré and Wang Ming had a restless night, bitten by fleas and a wind off Gunong Lang making it colder than usual. 'Tell you what, let's make a fire and heat up a tin of fish before we start off. Get us warm and give us a bit of strength.'

Chakré went to search for kindling and Jason asked the Bear what time they should reach the RV if they moved quickly and had no interference. 'Along this track it shouldn't take us more than four hours so easily before midday.'

'Exactly where is the RV?' Jason enquired, so many other thoughts having crowded into his mind he had forgotten to ask, not that he had needed to know till now.

'It's at the top of an old mining quarry. Ah Fat told me to bring you to an old hut that's almost falling to bits as it has not been used since the start of the Emergency. "Give us something to aim for" he had said.'

The part of Security Section that had gone with the delegates split once it reached the border, some men guarding the route to Baling, others patrolling into Malaya, both to east and northwest of Baling, 'just in case', as the man in charge delicately put it. A couple due to patrol in Malaya said to their leader, 'Comrade, we have not been outside for a long time. We are armed. Will you allow us to go to the Gunong Lang area and see if we can't shoot a deer? Our rations have not had much meat in them for some time.'

'You're the one who can make the noise of a deer so like the real animal that the deer would more often than not come up to you, aren't you?'

'Yes,' and he gave a most realistic demonstration and the others smiled gleefully, thinking of a full belly of deer meat.

'Yes, you'll do. I don't see why not. There will be no Security Forces in the area as Protocol has forbidden any except in and near Baling. Yes, go ahead and come back either this evening or tomorrow morning early.' A thought struck him. 'How will you bring a dead deer back?'

The man grinned. 'Depends what size it is. Small and we'll hang it from a pole: large, we'll come back for reinforcements.'

And with that off they went.

At twenty past 11, as Jason's trio were climbing up the side of the quarry, they heard a shout from above them. Looking up they saw Ah Fat waving at them, grinning broadly. All three waved back and, climbing up the last few yards, joyfully met, embracing one another, Ah Fat complimenting Jason on his disguise. 'Let's have one hour together then we two must go back,' he said, 'and first of all I must hand over those papers.' He called over his bodyguard but, as he opened the haversack to take them out, a deer belling not far away surprised them. Ah Fat's bodyguard cocked an ear. 'Strange, it's not the right time of day for a deer to call. Nor have we seen any droppings.'

Ah Fat sensed danger. He did not give over the papers. *Don't tell me they're searching for us and keeping distance by belling. Perhaps not, but I don't like it.* 'Jason, can you bell like a deer?'

'Yes, but I haven't done so for quite a while.'

Another belling was heard. 'Answer it.'

Jason put his head back and called loudly. An answer was returned from quite near. 'That's no deer,' said the bodyguard. 'That's a man.'

'Sure?' Ah Fat and Jason asked simultaneously.

'I tell you, it's a man,' the bodyguard insisted.

'Hide, just up the slope behind that clump of bushes. Jason, keep on answering and let them come.' Ah Fat was clearly in charge. 'Are you armed?'

'Yes, we are. We have pistols.'

'Get them ready loaded and if I say shoot whoever comes, shoot. It'll be the only way we'll save our lives.'

More belling, this time from quite near. Jason answered. From about twenty yards away two men broke cover. Ah Fat recognised them as part of the Security Section. *Hide or show my face?* 'If they try to kill me, shoot them,' he called softly to Jason and Chakré as he stood up and shouted out, 'What do you think you're doing here? On whose orders are you so far from camp?'

Plainly startled, they snarled back. 'Comrade Ah Fat. We have to ask you the same question. We have heard rumours about you. And we have caught you out here – and the other two.' By then the Bear and the bodyguard had joined Ah Fat who answered haughtily. 'Comrade, you will be severely punished for such intolerant indiscipline,' but as he said it he knew he could not let them go back to the camp. 'Jason, be ready to shoot to kill,' he called out of the side of his mouth in English.

'Proof, proof,' almost screamed both of them, advancing with rifles already cocked. Jason saw it was time to move. *The curse!* 'Bring them nearer, Flat Ears,' he said just loudly enough for Ah Fat to hear.

'Come here and let's talk this over,' Ah Fat called out in a conciliatory fashion, rubbing his hands together as was his wont.

As the two men came up to him, as if from nowhere, 'Ch'uan Jia Chan,' – May your entire family be wiped out.

Startled, they stopped in their tracks and looked around. Jason and Chakré, looking like two Malay peasants, came out from behind the bushes. Jason spoke to them in Malay, asking them why they were being so aggressive.

'Nothing to do with you,' one answered roughly.

Jason turned his head slightly and once again muttered the curse, this time pitching his voice as though it came from the feet of the man who had last spoken. The man jumped back. 'Ghost, ghost,' he cried out, appalled. He turned his attention to Ah Fat and said, 'you're responsible. You deserve to be killed' and both men brought their rifle to their shoulder, into the aiming position.

Just as they were about to squeeze their trigger, Jason and Chakré fired several .38 bullets into both men's head, killing them. The two deer hunters had managed to loose off a round each as they fell, firing high, so missed hitting anyone.

'Search them, one never knows what one might find.' said Ah Fat, thoroughly shaken at the near miss.

There was nothing worth keeping except their identification papers.

'Undress them and tip their corpses into the quarry. If no one comes this way for a day or two, their bones will be picked dry and so won't smell.'

'Yes, this is the only way to get out of that nasty, unexpected interference,' observed Jason, 'it would have put the kibosh on everything if they had stopped you giving me the papers.'

Ah Fat said, 'Jason, all that has made me forget to give them to you.' He told his bodyguard to get them out of his haversack and Jason told Chakré to get the case out of his. On seeing the case, Ah Fat precipitously asked, 'why bring that?'

'Because it has a false bottom.'

It was almost second sight, he explained to himself later, that made him ask whose it was and, on learning it belonged to C C Too, said, '*Shandung P'aau*, let me have it, will you? Something tells me I'll need it. Too won't mind, I'm sure.'

'I know you, *P'ing Yee*, well enough not to argue. I'll tell C C Too it was your price for bringing out the papers. Now we really must move but I just must mention the most unlikely coincidence of your newspaper having the same name, *Red Tidings*, as the operational codeword used after my CO was killed for the follow-up.'

'Is that really so?' exclaimed his friend. 'That means Lady Luck intended both of us to be successful.'

Before they parted on their separate ways, after more embraces, Jason thanked the Bear for all his help. 'It was good working with you once more. Will we meet again?'

'*Sinsaang*, I am sure we will. See what I have kept as my lucky mascot,' and he took out of his pocket the mast head of a copy of *Red Tidings* wrapped in a piece of plastic.

23-25 December 1955, Kuala Lumpur: As Jason and Chakré moved downhill with the papers safely in Chakré's haversack, Jason said, 'the car should be waiting for us at the side of the road where we left it. We'll ask the driver to take us to somewhere people won't bother about us, have a wash, a meal and before a good night's sleep.'

'Saheb, that's a good idea. By the time we get back to the road it will be too late to start back anyway. The driver won't mind either, I'm sure.'

As they crossed the dry paddy fields they saw, to their happiness, that the car was waiting for them. Approaching, they waved to the driver who waved back. As they reached the car, he wrinkled his nose and said, '*Sinsaang*, you and your friend need a good wash. I have fixed up a place for us three for the night,' and, with the panache of a good conjuror, produced a thermos and two cups. 'I am sure a drink of hot tea is what could be just what you want here and now,' he said.

To show his gratitude at the man's forethought, Jason sang the first two lines of the popular Chinese pop song, *Green Plumb and a Bamboo Horse,* in a shrill falsetto, 'My heart is full of hope and I wish we could do more than just talk as a couple. It would be a chance to open our hearts together and maybe go to see a film.'[9]

The driver bent double in laughter, unable to join in although he knew the words.

They started off for KL just before dawn, having paid their bill before they turned in for the night. Christmas Day, a public holiday, meant less traffic on the road than normal and they

9 The poem *Trip To Changgan* (長干行, Nanking's old name) is the base of the pop song *Green Plum and Bamboo Horse* (Li Bo 701-767). A young man and a young woman, intimate childhood friends, grow up together. He used to play with a piece of bamboo and pretend to ride on it as if it was a horse, and holding a green plum. Now in love and the time has come for them to marry, they look back to their childhood days with fond memories.

reached Kuala Lumpur in daylight. Jason suddenly remembered the date, which he had entirely forgotten, and wondered if Miss Wong would be having a family party. He told the driver to stop at a café where he could telephone and ask her.

She answered the phone and seemed delighted when she recognised Jason's voice. 'Oh yes, come to my place. Mr C C Too is also here, and here he is, wanting to talk to you. I'll hand the phone to him.'

'Jason, all okay? Just yes or no, no details.'

'Yes, but, and I'll tell you the but when we meet.'

'Nothing serious?'

'Not to us. All later.'

They sat down to a Christmas dinner at 9 p.m., Jason first giving C C Too the secret papers before being 'wiped clean' by Chakré, followed by a glorious shower and putting on their own clothes. Mr Too was rabidly curious about what had happened and it was only after the last mince pie did Miss Wong excuse herself and leave the men. Missing nothing out as Jason told his story, also mentioning how Ah Fat had some sort of premonition about the attaché case and begged it.

'He's more than welcome to it. And, I may have something for you. How many bullets did you fire?'

Jason told him. 'I will give you the same number of live bullets before you leave us.'

A frown crossed Jason's brow but before he could ask why, he was told 'if you don't have the same amount of rounds as when you left when you hand back the pistols, you will have to explain yourselves,' and he chuckled, showing he 'knew all about it'.

'Thank you, it hadn't occurred to me. You have saved me having to answer some awkward questions.'

C C Too fully examined the papers and seeing that the Soviet Union and China were both heavily interested in what was happening to the MCP and that 'the fight must be continued' he briefed the relevant people. The Alliance government, not having been given their provenance, was not sure how accurate that news was and as the origin of the information was not forthcoming, disregarded it thereby wasting valuable 'ammunition'.

24 December 1955, South Thailand: During the morning Lee An Tung saw Ah Fat going into his quarters and thought now was the time to make an arrest. Calling one of the patrol guards to him, he said, 'Comrade, I want you as witness when I make a serious arrest. Come with me.'

The guard, trying not to show any surprise, merely trailed after Lee An Tung who surged forward. On reaching Ah Fat's abode, he opened the door without any preliminary knocking and strode inside. Ah Fat, sitting on a chair, got up. 'What can I do for you, comrade?' he asked in his normal voice.

'I have come to arrest you for stating a falsehood and being a traitor to the cause.'

Ah Fat looked at the speaker, a perplexed expression on his face. 'Pray elucidate, comrade.'

'For stating you had a suitcase with a false bottom when you do not have such an item in your possession. I've had my suspicions ever since learning you had been to see the Director of Operations in Kuala Lumpur with a C C Too: we were all suspicious so, as most of the Politburo are not here, I took the liberty of searching your room when you were in another part of the camp. I found no such item, hence my action here and now.' He turned to his guard. 'Seize him.'

'Not so fast, comrade, not so fast. Just have a look on that table in the corner will you before you do anything really stupid?'

His complacent manner did not deflate Lee An Tung, who merely thought traitor Ah Fat was trying to delay the moment of truth. 'See that the comrade does not try to escape,' he said over his shoulder as he bounced towards the table. He saw nothing like a suitcase with a false drawer. 'What is it you want to show me?' he demanded peremptorily? 'I see nothing here.'

Ah Fat slowly went over to the table and lifted a pile of papers, thus disclosing a small black suitcase. Saying nothing, he picked it up, opened it and, pressing a button in its side, showed the by-now perplexed Lee An Tung how the bottom had opened on a hinge and showed its secret compartment.

Lee An Tung staggered backwards in acute embarrassment.

Suavely and chuckling inside himself, Ah Fat, in as cold a voice as possible, said 'dismiss the escort.' With gimlet eyes looking at his adversary, 'Do you arrest me for telling you an untruth or do I arrest you for stating two deliberate falsehoods in front of a mere nobody, to my acute detriment?'

Realising he had put himself firmly in the wrong, Lee An Tung abjectly apologised, asking fraternal forgiveness for being wrongly over-zealous.

Ah Fat, inside mightily relieved, paused before answering. 'Comrade, if you are sincere, let us shake hands on your mistake, neither of us ever mentioning your abysmal error ever again.'

It was accepted. They shook hands and Lee An Tung almost slunk out of the room.

25 December 1955, Baling: When the two men who had gone hunting did not come back the Security Section chief put it down to defection so nothing said was the easiest way of dealing with the situation.

31 December 1955, Seremban: Jason and Chakré got back to the battalion at the end of the year and life carried on as usual.

31 December 1955, south Thailand: The Politburo, with its non-voting member, met and passed a resolution that the Secretary General would go to China and, until the MRLA was ready for Phase 2 of its military struggle to be launched, only activity in the border area would continue. In any case many states were declared 'white', full peacetime conditions prevailing as remaining guerrillas were eliminated. It was also decided that there was now no advantage in continuing the production of *Red Tidings*, issues of which had lapsed over the excitement of the peace talks.

POSTSCRIPT

June 1970, Jungle Warfare School, south Johor, Peninsular Malaysia: In the fifteen years since Operation *Red Tidings* and its similarly named newspaper had become history, much had happened. Officers with sufficient jungle expertise and seniority to command the British army's Jungle Warfare School were a diminishing breed, almost an endangered species, in that the path to promotion now lay in Western Europe. The Military Secretary, a most senior officer, was wondering who could fill the recent vacancy for the job during the last couple of years of its existence before the British Government's 'East of Suez' policy of only keeping troops in Hong Kong and Brunei because Hong Kong and Brunei were paying for them. He called for a list of possible starters and his eye fell on the name of Major Rance, 1/12 GR. He asked for his file and read it. *He is not as well staff-trained as a lieutenant colonel should be but he has earned 'staff qualified' for a job he did in Bangkok, he has much jungle experience and a prodigious linguistic ability.* Let him be promoted to do the job, the Military Secretary decided. Thus it was that Jason Rance found himself a lieutenant colonel, the last ever incumbent of the Jungle Warfare School in July 1968.

June 1970 saw the start of the very last course for British

troops before the School closed, although there were rumours that a final, final course would be run for students of the South Vietnam and Thai armies even later. In his office, Jason read the names of the students and saw a Lieutenant Theodore Ridings, 1/12 GR. A faint bell rung: *can it be the son of the CO whose death played such a part for me in A Company in 1954 and 1955? I'll find out when the students come.*

And, yes, Theodore, Ted for short, Ridings was the son of the late Edward, Ted for short, Ridings, Jason's one-time CO.

Jason called the young man into his office. 'I am sure you have the potential of your late father,' he said, seeing his son as the commander of the last long exercise. 'You'll be interested to learn that the Gurkha Captain in charge of the 12 GR Demonstration Company is Kulbahadur Limbu, with a DCM he won in Borneo. He was the ace tracker in the battalion, first as a rifleman then as a corporal. When you meet him, talk to him and you will learn a lot about tracking and much that is not in the jungle warfare syllabus.'

'Oh, sir, I certainly will. Thank you for telling me. My mother sends you her regards and has asked if it possible I can have some leave at the end of the course to go to Seremban to visit my father's grave. My mother would like me to take a photograph of it.'

'I am sure that can be arranged,' was the answer and the young man went off to join his student platoon.

It was the last exercise of the course, the one that lasted ten days. When Jason took over command he had told the staff that it would be known as Exercise *Red Tidings*. He gave no reason but somehow it pleased him. On the second phase, the company dug in at the bottom of a steep hill, Panti by name, before an uphill attack against an 'enemy' camp at the top, in dug-in and well prepared positions, manned by Gurkhas. Jason went to watch how Lieutenant Ridings was managing and was satisfied with what he saw.

After the attack was over and the Gurkha 'enemy' had disappeared to take up more positions for the company to proceed against, comments on the attack were made by the British Directing Staff and the Commandant added his few words of praise.

Then, on the spur of the moment, he decided to walk back down the hill to view the students' overnight camp which he had yet to see. It took twenty minutes to get there and, on hearing voices, he peered round a tree and saw a dozen Chinese youths closely examining the lay-out.[10] Watching them was an older man, in his early thirties. He somehow seemed familiar.

Jason walked out and as soon as the youths saw him they ran away. The older man stayed put then, raising his right fist and with a big grin on his face, called out '*Shandung P'aau*, it's Wang Liang, your Bear *Hung Lo*'s son. I remember you from when I was a schoolboy and you made me laugh by making your hands talk to each other and so many more lovely tricks one night in Kuala Lumpur.'

---

10 Your author found Chinese youths inspecting a students' overnight camp and measuring its defensive weapon pits on one similar final exercise in 1971. The Malaysian police verified that they were a batch of recruit guerrillas on their way north to join the MRLA.

Jason, momentarily taken by surprise, stared at the man in disbelief and yet, and yet... 'Wang Liang, is it really you?'

'Yes, really me and I never thought I'd get such a good chance to let you know what I was doing.'

'I nearly came across you when your enemies tried to kill you when the Police asked you to go and visit the Temiar to find out what was happening as they know you were the only person they would speak to. They named it *Operation Blowpipe*, didn't they?'[11]

'Yes, it just so happened that I had two weeks before taking over this job and the Police took advantage of it. It all happened so quickly. Yes, I was lucky that time, wasn't I?'

He came over and they embraced. '*Shandung P'aau*, before he died *P'ing Yee* told me my father was horribly killed on the Thai border and you got your revenge, for which I thank you.' [12] So moved was I that I am now a *yanshu* – a mole – working against them.

The lads who ran away are new recruits for the second "Emergency" and it is my secret job to watch over them. We were warned by the secret papers that *P'ing Yee* gave you that time at Gunong Lang.'

Jason shook his head in surprise and wonder. *So long ago!*

'How have you managed to stay alive all this time?'

Wang Liang, putting his hand into a top pocket, said 'I have kept my father's mascot that he showed you so many years ago,' and he brought out an old, tattered piece of paper, still wrapped in its piece of plastic and showed it to Jason, 紅色消息, *Hung Sik Siu Sik,* Red Tidings.

---

11 See *Operation Blow Pipe*.
12 See *Operation Blind Spot*.

JP CROSS
OPERATION
BLACK ROSE

گل   تور

'CROSS SPINS HIS TALE WITH THE EYE
OF INCOMPARABLE EXPERIENCE'
JOHN LE CARRÉ, ON OPERATION JANUS

JP CROSS
OPERATION
JANUS

NOBODY IS BETTER QUALIFIED TO
TELL THIS STORY OF THE GURKHAS' DEADLY
JUNGLE BATTLES AGAINST COMMUNIST
INSURGENCY IN 1950S MALAYA'
JOHN LE CARRÉ

JP CROSS
OPERATION
RED TIDINGS

'NOBODY IS BETTER QUALIFIED
TO TELL THE STORY OF THE GURKHAS'
DEADLY JUNGLE BATTLES AGAINST COMMUNIST
INSURGENCY IN 1950S MALAYA'
JOHN LE CARRÉ

JP CROSS
OPERATION
BLIND SPOT

'CROSS SPINS HIS TALE WITH THE EYE OF
INCOMPARABLE EXPERIENCE'
JOHN LE CARRÉ, ON OPERATION JANUS

JP CROSS
OPERATION
STEALTH

ຂັງ

'CROSS SPINS HIS TALE WITH THE EYE
OF INCOMPARABLE EXPERIENCE'
JOHN LE CARRÉ, ON OPERATION JANUS

JP CROSS
OPERATION
FOUR RINGS

ຂັງ   ຂັງ

'CROSS SPINS HIS TALE WITH THE EYE
OF INCOMPARABLE EXPERIENCE'
JOHN LE CARRÉ, ON OPERATION JANUS